Max Damage

Book 9 in the Hal Spacejock series

Stay in touch!

Author's newsletter:
spacejock.com.au/ML.html

facebook.com/halspacejock
twitter.com/spacejock

Works by Simon Haynes

All of Simon's novels* are self-contained, with a beginning, a middle and a proper ending. They're not sequels, they don't end on a cliffhanger, and you can start or end your journey with any book in the series.
Robot vs Dragons series excepted!

The Hal Spacejock series for teens/adults

Set in the distant future, where humanity spans the galaxy and robots are second-class citizens. Includes a large dose of humour!

Hal Spacejock 1: A robot named Clunk
Hal Spacejock 2: Second Course
Hal Spacejock 3: Just Desserts
Hal Spacejock 4: No Free Lunch
Hal Spacejock 5: Baker's Dough
Hal Spacejock 6: Safe Art
Hal Spacejock 7: Big Bang
Hal Spacejock 8: Double Trouble
Hal Spacejock 9: Max Damage
Hal Spacejock 10: Cold Boots (2019)

Also available:
Omnibus One, containing Hal books 1-3
Omnibus Two, containing Hal books 4-6
Omnibus Three, containing Hal books 7-9
Hal Spacejock: Visit, a short story
Hal Spacejock: Framed, a short story
Hal Spacejock: Albion, a novella

The Robot vs Dragons Trilogy.
High fantasy meets low humour!
Each set of three books should be read in order.

1. A Portion of Dragon and Chips
2. A Butt of Heads
3. A Pair of Nuts on the Throne
4. TBA (2019)

The Harriet Walsh series.

Set in the same universe as Hal Spacejock. Good clean fun, written with wry humour. No cliffhangers between novels!

Harriet Walsh 1: Peace Force
Harriet Walsh 2: Alpha Minor
Harriet Walsh 3: Sierra Bravo
Harriet Walsh 4: Storm Force (2019)
Also Available:
Omnibus One, containing books 1-3

The Hal Junior series

Written for all ages, these books are set aboard a space station in the Hal Spacejock universe, only ten years later.

1. Hal Junior: The Secret Signal
2. Hal Junior: The Missing Case
3. Hal Junior: The Gyris Mission
4. Hal Junior: The Comet Caper

Also Available:
Omnibus One, containing books 1-3

The Secret War series.
Gritty space opera for adult readers.

1. Raiders (2019)
2. Frontier (2019)
3. Deadlock (2019)

Collect One-Two - a collection of shorts by Simon Haynes

All titles available in ebook and paperback. Visit spacejock.com.au for details.

A Hal Spacejock novel

SIMON HAYNES

Bowman Press

v 1.2

This novel, like the author, employs British spelling.

Published 2018 by Bowman Press

Text © Simon Haynes 2018
Jacket design © Bowman Press 2018

ISBN 978-1-877034-37-4 (Paperback)

'Warning. Breathable atmosphere at nine percent and falling.'

'Don't tell me, I know this one.' Hal Spacejock scanned the flight console, trying to locate the right button. There were about nine hundred to choose from, but he was convinced one of them would have a picture of fresh air on it. The problem was, he had no idea what such an icon might look like.

'Getting warm,' said the ship's computer, as Hal's finger approached an instrument cluster.

Hal made up his mind, and he pressed a small orange button with a swirly pattern.

'Hyperdrive modulator enabled.'

'What's a hyperdrive modulator?'

'Don't worry about it,' said the Navcom, in a neutral female voice. 'It's way beyond your skill level.'

Hal pressed the button again.

'Hyperdrive modulator disabled. Atmosphere now at five percent and falling.'

The viewscreen flickered, and Hal eyed the large blue and green planet displayed in the centre. They were on a cargo run to planet Dolor, and it was their first proper job since his previous ship, the *Volante,* had been destroyed some months earlier. So far, things were going smoothly. Well, apart from the Navcom's practice drills, which always seemed to end in disaster. 'All right, I have no idea where the button is. Give us a clue.'

'You need to identify the area of the ship with the leak, seal the bulkheads, then activate the emergency repair systems. After that, you should trigger the distress beacon and call for a rescue ship.'

Hal pursed his lips. The button would have to be the size of his hand to contain all those icons, and there was nothing remotely big enough. 'Okay, so where's the control that does all that?'

'There *is* no control to do all that,' said the Navcom calmly. 'You have to perform the actions in sequence, using a selection of buttons. Incidentally, your breathable air is now at one percent and you will be dead in five minutes.'

Hal sat back in his chair. Years ago, when he decided to become a space pilot, he imagined gripping the control stick, pushing the thrust to max and belting around the galaxy on an endless, exciting joyride. Instead, flying a ship was about as interesting as programming a computer, or doing his own taxes... and he'd never had the slightest interest in either. 'All right, end the simulation.'

'What simulation?' said the computer calmly.

'The emergency simulation you've been testing me with. I failed, we ran out of air and I'm dead, so you might as well end it now.' It was at this point that Hal noticed it was getting a little hard to breathe, and so he wasn't a hundred percent shocked at the Navcom's next words.

'It's not a simulation,' said the computer calmly. 'We have an atmospheric leak in the third passenger cabin, and you've already lost ninety-nine percent of your breathable air.'

'I'm going to *die?*' Hal felt an icy rush in the pit of his stomach, and he started frantically pushing buttons all over the console, with little regard for the icons. As they blooped and bleeped, and various indicators flashed and scrolled, he kept up an angry diatribe. 'One of these damn things will sort it out, I know it will. Unless the button's a dud as well! They sold me a damned lemon, that's what they did. Brand new ship, my left elbow. It's a total crock!' Then he remembered how he got the ship in the first place. 'This is Clunk's fault!' he cried. 'He was supposed to buy me a brand new ship, but instead he's fobbed me off with a cut-price deathtrap.'

'The *Albion* is a brand new ship,' said the Navcom. 'Unfortunately, we're experiencing a few teething problems, but they're covered under warranty.'

'Teething problems? *Warranty?*' By now Hal was finding it really hard to breathe. 'I'm going to die out here, in the vast loneliness of space, but you reckon that's just fine because I won't have to pay for the repairs?' He pressed a couple more buttons, then gave up. 'All right, you win. Call Clunk to the flight deck.' Hal didn't like asking the robot for help, not when the help came with a superior, knowing attitude and a whole lot of condescension. On the other hand the alternative was his own imminent death, so he decided to live with it.

'I cannot call Clunk.'

'What?'

'He powered down. It helps him charge his batteries a little quicker.'

'So power him up again!'

'Unable to comply. There is a fault in the internal communications system.'

Now Hal understood the full gravity of the situation. His faithful co-pilot, Clunk, was off with the pixel fairies, while he,

3

Hal, was running out of air. 'Okay, fire up the distress beacon. Let's get someone here to help.'

'Unable to comply. Distress beacon is not functioning.'

Hal closed his eyes. 'That's it then. I'm going to suffocate to death and there's nothing I can do about it.'

'Not necessarily,' said the Navcom.

'You mean there's still a chance?' said Hal hopefully.

'Indeed. There's a chance you'll do something monumentally stupid, like activating the self-destruct sequence, or severing the fuel lines whilst trying to open the cargo hold. If that happens, I guarantee you won't die of asphyxiation.'

Hal didn't know whether to shout and scream, put the fire axe through the console, or get up and run about the flight deck waving his arms over his head. In the end he did none of the above, because he heard a whoosh as the lift arrived. With a rush of relief, Hal realised Clunk must have woken up, recognised the danger, and come to the flight deck to save him.

But, instead of the lift doors opening, they remained firmly closed. Then, Hal heard a polite knocking. He got up and ran to the lift, and on the way he noticed he was getting light-headed. 'Clunk? Clunk, is that you?'

'Yes, Mr Spacejock,' said the robot, his voice muffled.

At that moment Hal could have hugged him, cold metal skin and all, but the lift doors were still closed and he couldn't reach. That, and he wasn't saved yet. 'The Navcom says the air is leaking. Can you fix it?'

'Indeed I can–'

'Great!'

'–once I get the elevator doors open.'

'What?'

'The elevator has malfunctioned, and it seems the doors are stuck.'

'Are you *kidding* me?' Hal would have said more, but there was very little air left and he didn't want to waste it shouting. 'What the hell am I supposed to do now?'

'Go to the airlock, Mr Spacejock. Close the inner door, and–'

'If I do that I'll suffocate even quicker. Is that your brilliant idea?'

'No, the airlock has an emergency supply. Lock yourself in, and it will keep you alive while I calculate a solution.'

Hal didn't delay. He ran to the airlock, opened the inner door and darted inside, sealing the door behind himself by spinning the big, spoked wheel. 'Now what?' he called, but of course Clunk couldn't hear him. Hal had already let most of the air out when he opened the door, so he reckoned he had seconds to live... unless he managed to pressurise the airlock. Fortunately, there weren't many controls. One panel was marked 'inner door', and it had two buttons. The other was marked 'outer door' and that had two more. Alas, neither of them had a handy button marked 'Save Hal from asphyxiation'.

Hal had no intention of touching the outer door panel, so he reached for the inner one. The upper button was green, the lower one red, and he decided to press the green one.

There was a buzz, and an electronic voice spoke from concealed speakers. It was thin in the sparse atmosphere, but Hal heard it clearly enough.

'Please stand by. Opening outer airlock door.'

Shocked, Hal stared at the panel. It was fixed to the bulkhead right next the inner door, and it clearly said 'inner door' on the panel, so of *course* it was going to open the outer door. Hal pressed the button again, then hit the red one as well, just in case.

'*Closing inner door,*' said the voice. There was a buzz. '*Unable to close inner door.*'

'Of course you can't,' growled Hal. 'It's already closed!'

'*Opening outer door,*' said the voice calmly.

'Stop opening doors!' shouted Hal, who was now so light-headed he could barely stand up. 'Just give me some air!'

It was no use, though. The voice belonged to a simple automated system, not some hyper-intelligent AI which could tend to his every need whilst beating him at chess and ordering fresh supplies of coffee. Seconds later the last of the air ran out, and Hal slumped against the wall before sliding to the deck. As his eyes closed, his last conscious thought was that Clunk would have been better off spending half as much on a decent second-hand ship.

❦

'Urgh. My *head!*'

'You're alive, Mr Spacejock. Isn't that good news?'

Hal opened one eye and saw Clunk looking down at him. The robot's squashy, furrowed face showed a mix of concern and relief, and his yellow eyes gleamed in the darkness. 'Half alive,' croaked Hal. 'How did you rescue me?'

'I got out of the lift, pumped the airlock full of oxygen, sealed the leak in the third cabin and turned the atmospheric generators to maximum.'

'Good job. And thanks.' Hal realised he was still in the airlock, and with Clunk's help he got to his feet. His head was pounding, but at least he was still breathing. 'Do you know what the Navcom called this deadly disaster?' he grumbled. 'A teething problem!'

'These things happen, Mr Spacejock,' said Clunk, in an even male tone. 'The *Albion* is brand new, and I'm sure we'll find many such problems during our initial voyages.'

'Wonderful,' muttered Hal. 'I bet this thing was built by robots.'

'Actually, industrial workplace laws state that spaceship construction must be supervised by humans. If it were left to robots–'

'There wouldn't be any seats, and the toilet would only flush once a year,' finished Hal. 'Efficiency above all, that's your motto. Even when it comes to basic human comforts.'

They left the airlock, and Hal felt something crunch under his boots. He looked down, then turned to stare at the lift. The nice new doors, the ones which usually slid back and forth with a pleasant humming noise, were little more than twisted wreckage. Bits and pieces of plastic littered the deck, and thanks to the missing doors he could see right into the lift interior. 'When you said you got out of the lift...' he began.

'The doors wouldn't open, and time was of the essence.' Clunk used his foot to push aside a broken plastic panel. 'We'll order some new doors after we land.'

'Oh no,' said Hal firmly. 'We're not going anywhere near a planet until you've checked every circuit on this ship. Twice.'

'But Mr Spacejock, that could take days!'

'Do we have a tight deadline for the cargo delivery?'

'Eight hours and thirty minutes. But if I have to–'

'Tested and checked twice, Clunk. And no skimping. I don't want another one of those teething problems when we're plunging through the atmosphere at a million miles an hour.'

Clunk opened his mouth to object, then changed his mind and nodded. 'Very well. I will perform a full inspection.'

'Inside and out?'

'Everywhere. You have my word as a robot.'

Satisfied, Hal swept bits and pieces of plastic door panel off his big comfy pilot's chair, and sat down. 'Navcom, show me a news bulletin.'

'Unable to comply.'

'Let me guess. That's broken too.'

'Negative. There is no service because you neglected to pay the bill.'

'All right, so pay the bill.'

'Unable to comply. Our automated bill-paying service has malfunctioned.'

'Of course it has.' There was a beep from the console, and Hal scanned the displays. They were all showing something, although he had no idea what those somethings were. 'What was that sound, Navcom?'

'A distress beacon.'

'It can't be. You said it's busted.'

'Ours is, but that was someone else's.'

There was another beep.

'You mean someone's in trouble out here?' demanded Hal.

'That's generally what a distress beacon indicates. Otherwise it would simply be called a beacon.'

Hal frowned. His ship was fragile, and more things could go wrong at any moment. On the other hand, someone might be in even worse trouble than he was. 'Can we communicate with them, or is that broken too?'

'Attempting to contact the vessel.'

There was a pause.

'Putting them on main,' said the Navcom.

The big viewscreen cleared, and a dark, fuzzy picture appeared. It kept rolling, there was interference, and the scene appeared to be full of smoke. Then there was a flash, and the light illuminated a woman, her face close to the camera. She was wearing a flight helmet, visor up, and she had a cut across her forehead. As Hal stared at her, she coughed and waved at the smoke. Then she squinted at the camera, moving her face close, and he realised she was about his age. Good looking too, he thought subconsciously, with short dark hair and high cheekbones. 'Is everything okay?' he called, before realising that was a pretty daft question. Clearly everything was far from okay.

There was another electrical flash, brighter this time, and Hal saw the woman was wearing a dark green flightsuit with insignia at her shoulders. With a shock, he realised it was a military uniform. He also noticed the woman was sitting in a cramped cockpit, the space barely bigger than she was, and the flight consoles on either side of her were emitting smoke and showers of sparks.

Then the woman spoke, gesturing around the damaged cockpit. Hal saw her mouth moving, but there was no sound. 'Navcom, turn up the volume!' he said urgently.

'Unable to comply.'

'Don't tell me it's failed.'

'Negative. The other ship is not transmitting.'

'So *her* mic is broken?' Hal shook his head in disbelief. No doubt it had been assembled by the same idiots who'd screwed the *Albion* together.

Meanwhile, the woman was still trying to talk to him, and he couldn't help noticing there was an urgency to her movements. He could see her ship was on fire, and he guessed her air was running out. After his own close escape, he knew exactly what

9

that felt like. 'It's okay,' he said, speaking slowly and clearly. 'Sit tight. Help is on the way.'

The woman raised a hand towards the camera, reaching for him, her face desperate. Then, without warning, the screen went dark.

Hal turned to the console, all business. 'Navcom, set course for the distress signal.'

'I would advise against it. There's a–'

'Don't argue, just do it. That woman needs us.'

'But the ship is–'

'Navcom, if something goes wrong on the way, Clunk will fix it. Now set course and fire up the engines.'

'Complying.'

The engines came on, and there was a smooth burst of power as they turned away from their destination and rocketed deeper into the system. Hal gripped the armrests as the ship tore through space, and a fierce grin appeared on his face despite the danger. This was more like it! Proper space travel!

He turned as the lift arrived, and he was surprised to hear the hum of the doors opening... even though they no longer existed. 'How did they make the noise?' he asked Clunk, who was just stepping out of the lift.

'What noise?'

'The humming sound.'

'Oh. That's a recording. The doors themselves are silent.' Clunk gestured impatiently. 'But I'm not here to talk about sound effects. I couldn't help noticing the engines are running.'

Hal nodded. 'We're on a rescue mission. There's a fighter pilot out there with a damaged ship.'

'Military?'

'No,' said Hal. 'She just got up one day, decided to buy

herself a combat ship, then put on a uniform and started shooting at things.'

'Could you raise your left hand when you're being sarcastic? Only you're so convincing I can never tell.'

'For real?'

Clunk raised his left hand, then lowered it again. 'But tell me, is this person in real trouble?'

Hal remembered the smoke, and the sparks, and the desperate look in the pilot's eyes. 'Yeah, you could say that.' He turned to the console. 'Navcom, show Clunk the recording.'

'What recording?'

'You know, the distress call.'

'I don't have room to record any calls,' said the Navcom. 'With the pitiful storage aboard this ship, I barely have room to record the time of day.'

Hal glanced at Clunk, who shrugged. 'It was an optional extra,' said the robot. 'The price seemed a little high, so I didn't tick the box.'

'Did you leave off anything else?'

'There's no hot water system, and the onboard library doesn't have any books.'

'That's disgraceful!'

'You wanted books?' said Clunk, surprised.

'No, of course not. But I certainly need hot showers.'

The console speakers crackled. 'Approaching target area,' said the Navcom.

Hal looked up at the screen. 'Put it on main.'

A vast, empty vista appeared, sprinkled with stars, but completely devoid of ships in distress, burning or otherwise. 'Where is she?' asked Hal.

'Directly ahead.'

Hal squinted at the screen. 'You mean that tiny little dot?'

'No, that's the asteroid field. The damaged ship is inside it.'

Hal and Clunk exchanged a worried look. They'd navigated asteroid fields before, and it was a slow, tortuous process. Little chunks of stone would bounce harmlessly off the ship's armoured hull, but larger rocks... well, they could tear great big holes right through the toughest armour.

'Is that why we're parked all the way out here?' demanded Hal.

'Correct. From this point on, we might encounter stray asteroids.' The Navcom hesitated. 'I did try to warn you, but you insisted on answering the distress call.'

'I had no choice,' said Hal firmly. 'That woman's in trouble, and as a fellow space pilot it's my duty to help her.'

'That's very noble of you,' said Clunk. Then he gave Hal a shrewd look. 'This pilot. Was she attractive?'

'Like you wouldn't believe,' confessed Hal.

'Aha.'

'Don't aha me. I'd still be going out there if it was a big, hairy plumber called Albert.' He gave Clunk an aggrieved look. 'As long as he promised to fix me up with some hot water, of course.'

'Then we'd better get the rescue operation under way,' said Clunk. 'Unfortunately, it sounds like there's no time for a slow approach.'

'You're not wrong. When she called it looked like the cockpit was on fire. Smoke everywhere.'

Clunk nodded. 'Therefore, I'm going to activate a special display mode which should help us navigate the asteroid field with the minimum of fuss and drama.'

'I wouldn't bother,' remarked Hal. 'It's probably broken.'

Clunk ignored him and took the pilot's seat, leaving Hal

the spare. The robot's hands flew over the controls as he programmed the display, and soon there was a lattice overlaid on the main screen, dividing it up into hundreds of equal squares. Each little square contained a scrolling text window, all of them moving individually and displaying reams of data.

'Are you tracking all the rocks with those stats?' asked Hal, impressed.

Clunk glanced up at the screen. 'No, that's just to cover up the live image. If you can't see the asteroids hurtling past, it'll reduce the fuss and drama considerably.' With that he gripped the control stick and pushed the throttles to max, and the *Albion* charged towards the asteroid field like a raging bull.

2

Elsewhere in the same system, Cylen Murtay was nervous as he met the president's chief of staff. He needn't have worried, though, because the woman was genial and friendly. She kept him engaged in light conversation as she escorted him to the president's inner sanctum, known colloquially as the Square Office.

The chief knocked at the big double doors, and they swung open to reveal a large, round room with a crackling fire in a grate, comfortable furniture and a big lacquered desk. Sitting behind the desk was President Oakworthy, a small, grey-haired man who was busy reading a sheaf of papers. He was wearing old-fashioned glasses and a knitted cardigan which looked like it had lined a dog's basket for most of its life, before being put back into service.

There was no sign of a terminal, or a commset, or any electronics whatsoever, which Murtay found surprising. Still, it wasn't his place to question the most powerful man in the Dolorian system.

'Mr President,' said the chief of staff. 'Your three o'clock is here. This is Cylen Murtay, the aide from Foreign Affairs.'

The president lowered his papers and looked at them over the top of his glasses. Then he glanced at his ancient gold wristwatch. 'You're early. It's only two-thirty.'

'It's just gone three,' said the chief. 'Shall I send your watch off to be fixed again?'

The president gestured. 'Later. First I want to hear what this young man has to say for himself.'

Murtay swallowed nervously. 'I'm afraid it's private, Mr President. Your ears only.'

'Chief? Would you mind?'

The chief nodded and left, and once the doors were closed the president got up and came around the desk. He was dressed in bell-bottom corduroy trousers, which went with his cardigan about as well as raw eggs went with ice cream, and he was also wearing a pair of brown suede shoes.

Murtay suddenly realised why it was called the Square Office, and he struggled not to grin. Also, the news he was about to give the president was dire, and it would send mixed signals if he was cracking up while trying to give his report.

'Take a seat, son.'

They took to the comfortable armchairs either side of the blazing fire, and the president looked at the aide expectantly. 'All right. What's up?'

'Sir, we've had a communique from the Mayestrans.'

The president winced. 'This can't be good.'

The aide knew exactly what he meant. Half a dozen nearby systems had been at war for close to a decade now, and more kept getting dragged into the conflict. 'It's not good at all, sir. They claim we're harbouring rebels.'

The president groaned. 'That's the first step, isn't it?'

'Yes sir. Next they'll want to send a fleet, and after that it'll be military bases.'

'And before we know it, we'll be embroiled in their senseless war.' The president got up, went over to the fire and spread

15

his hands towards the flames. 'What about the other lot, the Henerians? Have they said anything yet?'

'Nothing sir. We're expecting a communique from them next.'

'Damn both of them,' growled the president. 'The Galaxy would be better off if they took each other out and left the rest of us in Peace.'

'Yes sir.'

The president glanced at him. 'Don't repeat that. It's not our official position.'

'I understand.'

There was a pause as the president warmed his hands. 'I won't allow it, you know,' he said at last. 'I won't allow my people to be bullied and intimidated. I certainly won't allow them to be shot at and bombed.'

'Yes, Mr President.'

'Send them both a message. Tell them we're neutral, and we're not interested in their conflict. Tell them we've never seen a military ship from either side in our system, and if one shows up we'll toss it right back out again. Tell them...' The president gestured. 'Oh hell, you know what to tell them. Strongly worded, mind. I don't want any doubt.'

'Yes sir.'

'Good lad. Off you go, then.'

Murtay got up and left. On the way out he met the chief of staff, who spared him the briefest of glances before dashing into the Square Office... no doubt to confer with the president.

Moments later Murtay was outside, hurrying towards his government-issue car. As he got in, he wondered whether to call his mother, who lived by herself on the city outskirts, right here on planet Dolor. If war was coming to the system, he should move her to the country.

Then again, if Dolor was bombarded from orbit, how would the countryside be any safer than the city?

—

In one sense, Clunk's screen hider worked well, because Hal couldn't see any of the huge asteroids whipping past the ship from all directions. However, it was a total failure when it came to preventing fuss and drama, because Hal was creating plenty of the former and experiencing a ton of the latter.

'Slow down, Clunk!' he shouted, gripping the console with both hands. 'This is madness! We're going to hit something!' Hal would have grabbed for the controls, but he was pretty sure that would turn the likelihood of hitting an asteroid into a stone cold certainty. He knew time was of the essence, but what good was a rescue mission if they scattered themselves all over space in the process?

Meanwhile, Clunk was unperturbed. His eyes were closed and his expression was set as he directed the ship this way and that, taking them deeper into the asteroid field. So far, he'd managed to avoid running into anything, but Hal knew a huge rock could strike them from any direction, taking them out in an instant.

'Target dead ahead, range three kilometres,' said the Navcom calmly.

Hal felt a flash of irritation at the flight computer's unhurried tone. The other two were taking everything in their stride, but their lives weren't on the line like his was. Clunk and the Navcom could both be rebuilt, their minds restored from backups, so it was no wonder they were so relaxed. But what about him? One decent hit and it was goodbye and good night.

However, as time passed and Hal failed to die unexpectedly, his nerves became a little less frayed. He began to think of the woman in the fighter, instead of himself, and he wondered whether she was still alive. They hadn't wasted a second since receiving her distress call, and he knew they were doing everything they could to reach her in time. Hal just wasn't sure it would be enough, and he'd carry a crushing weight of guilt if she died before they could save her.

He wanted to ask Clunk how the rescue operation was going to work, but he could see the robot was straining every processor to get them to the damaged ship. So, he kept quiet and tried to see where they were going through the scrolling text boxes covering the main screen.

'One kilometre,' said the Navcom.

Hal heard the engines throttling back, and in the ensuing silence he heard the patter of small stones on the hull. It sounded like hail on a tin roof, and he hoped none of the pieces were big enough to punch a hole right through.

'Five hundred metres.'

The forward thrusters came on, higher-pitched than the main engines, and Hal felt himself slipping towards the console as Clunk slowed the *Albion's* urgent, headlong rush. The sound grew louder, and Hal gripped the armrests as he was almost thrown out of his chair. The ship's artificial gravity was still working, but Clunk was really pushing it to the limit as he struggled to reach the damaged fighter in time.

Then the thrusters cut out, and everything was silent.

'Are we there yet?' asked Hal.

Clunk opened his eyes and nodded. 'Any closer, and our thrusters might prove dangerous to the pilot.'

18

Hal got up. 'Come on, then. Let's go save her.'

'Not so fast, Mr Spacejock.' Clunk still had his hands on the controls, and when he moved them, Hal felt the ship dart sideways, before stopping once more. 'I must remain here, keeping the *Albion* out of the path of oncoming asteroids.'

'But that means...' Hal stared. 'Are you saying...?'

'Yes, Mr Spacejock.' Clunk looked at him, his expression a mask of concern. 'You must rescue the pilot by yourself. It's the only way.'

Instead of fear and apprehension, Hal felt a sudden thrill at the idea. Sure, he'd have to don a spacesuit and leave the safety of the *Albion*, but he'd be a genuine hero if he saved the pilot from her stricken ship. 'Okay, so what's the plan?'

Clunk deleted the text boxes from the main screen, giving them an unobstructed view of the asteroid field. There was an endless vista of tumbling rocks, large and small, and they were all bathed in harsh light from the local star. The shadows were inky black, and Hal knew they concealed even more rocks. And there, right next to a huge, slow-moving asteroid, was the nimble little fighter. The hull was scarred with battle damage, the paintwork scorched all the way down one side, and the left wing had been torn off, leaving a jagged hole. Fortunately, the canopy looked intact.

As for the cockpit... that was in total darkness, with no signs of life.

'It will be incredibly dangerous out there,' said Clunk. 'A micro-meteorite could go right through you. Radiation exposure will be a factor, unless you hurry back. The fighter's power core might go critical, blowing both of you up. And finally, the ship's electrical systems could be live, so you'll need a pair of rubber gloves.'

'Yes, yes, I know all that. But how am I supposed to get over there?'

Moments later, with Clunk's instructions committed to memory, Hal hurried towards the cargo hold, where he pulled open a locker and started dressing himself in the bulky space suit stored within. Fortunately, Clunk had trained him on the procedure in the past, although Hal still managed to put the pants on backwards, and on his first try he connected his oxygen line to the waste recycling system.

In his defence, he was going as fast as he could.

Once dressed, Hal donned the helmet with its mirror-finish visor. After it was firmly snapped in place, he activated the air tanks and felt cool air wafting on his face. 'Ready,' he said.

There was no reply.

Hal thumped a gloved first on the side of his helmet, then tried again. 'Clunk? Do you read?'

Nothing.

Then Hal remembered the *Albion's* dodgy comms system, and he realised he would have to conduct the entire rescue mission on his own, with no help from the robot at all. He paused for a second, but there was no time to worry about it. He'd just have to do his best.

Taking a second suit from the locker, he stuffed it into a carry-bag and placed a spare helmet on top. It was meant to be a backup for the pilot, but the fighter didn't have an airlock, so he had no idea how he was going to pass the thing to her. Still, Clunk had insisted he take it along, and he didn't want to come all the way back again for the spare, so he obeyed.

There was a small door near the back of the hold, and Hal

pulled it open to reveal the *Albion's* emergency jetbike. He'd ridden one before, so he expected a long, powerful bike with triple jet thrusters, a big fuel tank, a huge headlight and almost as much power as a rocketship.

Not even close.

This thing looked like a child's tricycle crossed with a clothes airing rack. Skinny metal struts held the frame together, there was an engine the size of a teapot, and it sported a single exhaust no thicker than his thumb. To make things worse, there was enough room in the launch tube for a midsized car, and the tiny, under-powered little bike looked even more like a toy sitting in that huge, empty space.

Thoroughly disappointed, Hal realised Clunk had skimped on the options... again. Still, there was nothing for it. He'd just have to make do.

Climbing into the tube, ducking his head to avoid cracking the helmet on the ceiling, Hal closed the hatch behind himself and approached the extremely unimpressive little jet-trike. He swung his leg over the saddle and sat down, and he discovered the thing was so small his knees almost met his chin. In fact, there was barely enough room to jam the spare spacesuit on his lap. He frowned as he pictured himself pootling towards the damaged fighter, hunched over the handlebars as he tried to extract more speed from the miniature clown bike.

If the pilot wasn't dead already, she'd probably laugh herself sick at the sight of him.

Clunk had warned him about going too fast, but as he inspected the instruments, Hal decided the robot had been having a laugh. In fact, he almost got off again, because he was convinced he'd reach the fighter quicker if he jumped out of the hold and flapped his arms... despite the vacuum of space.

Sighing under his breath, Hal found the red starter button

and pressed it. There was a gentle pop, and he felt the machine vibrating gently. Then, with a resigned look on his face, he activated the hatch at the far end of the launch tube.

The air in the tube thinned and cleared, and Hal twisted the throttle to max. Some small part of him still hoped the weedy looking vehicle concealed a powerful heart, but it most certainly didn't. The vibrations increased slightly, and the jet-trike proceeded down the launch tube at walking pace.

'Call this a launch?' muttered Hal, thoroughly disappointed. 'I can crawl quicker than this.'

No wonder Clunk hadn't been too worried about sending him into space alone. His only danger now was dying of boredom.

Slowly, the trike made its way out of the tube, and Hal emerged into the deep yellow glare of the Dolorian system's primary star. His visor darkened automatically, turning day into night, but Hal wasn't bothered, even though he could barely see where he was going. At this speed, he'd have time to get off and push the trike out of the way of any asteroids he might encounter.

He tried twisting the throttle some more, in case it was stuck on one-quarter, but it wouldn't budge. So, he scanned the way ahead for the fighter jet.

There it was, slightly to his left. He'd spotted an intense flash as electricity arced between damaged components, and he eased the trike around until he was heading straight for it.

Slowly, he got closer, until the flashes and sparks were just ahead. He relaxed his hand on the throttle, cutting the engine, then realised it wasn't going to slow him down. Desperately, he looked for a reverse thruster, but there didn't appear to be one. So, he twisted the handlebars, and the bike swung round, flames jetting as it obeyed his input.

Now he was travelling backwards, going faster than he expected, and heading straight for the fighter. Hal opened the throttle, and as the miniature engine poured thrust from the skinny little exhaust, he twisted in his seat to stare at the combat ship. He seemed to be heading directly for the canopy, and he willed the little trike to a halt. Some rescue this would turn out to be, if he smashed the canopy and let the pilot's remaining air out.

As he got closer he saw blobs of liquid around the fighter, and he guessed it was fuel leaking from the ruptured tanks. He wasn't sure whether his thrust would ignite it, there being no oxygen, but he hoped not. Break the canopy *and* fry the pilot? He wouldn't be a hero, he'd be a wanted criminal.

Hal made it, just. The bike struck the canopy with a gentle bump, and as it came to a halt, he cut the thrust and peered down into the cockpit. There was a series of electrical flashes inside, and he saw the pilot looking up at him, her face pale and strained. Slowly, Hal turned the jet bike until the weak little headlamp was pointing directly into the cockpit, and then he smiled and gave the pilot a thumbs-up.

She studied him for a moment, then reached up and closed her visor, concealing her face. He noticed she was now wearing a silvery space suit, much less bulky than his own, and he guessed it was for emergency use only. Then, as he watched her, she reached for a T-shaped control and gave it a firm pull.

Nothing happened.

She pulled it once more, and again nothing happened.

Hal's face fell. The pilot couldn't open the canopy, which meant she was trapped inside. Then he saw her moving in her seat, shifting lower and raising both feet until the soles of her boots were touching the canopy. She drew her legs back and kicked upwards, hard. When that didn't work she did it again and again, until she finally gave up.

Meanwhile, Hal was looking around for inspiration, and he found it nearby. There was a rock roughly the size of his head, and he reckoned it would bust the canopy like an eggshell if he got a decent run-up.

So, he rode over and gathered it up, then drove to a point a hundred metres away. He turned on the spot, held the rock under one arm, and opened the throttle.

It was all he could do to aim at the ship, because every instinct told him to pull up and avoid the impact. Instead, he held his course as long as he dared, before releasing the boulder and turning the trike sharply away from the fighter. He passed so close the exhaust played across the canopy, leaving scorch marks, and then the big chunk of rock hit the perspex dead-on.

There was a puff of air as the canopy blew out, with most fragments whirling away into space. Several lanced straight into the cockpit, where the pilot was sitting. Hal was already on his way back, and before he was halfway there, the pilot pushed off, launching herself out of the cockpit and into space. It was a gutsy move, Hal realised, because if he missed her in the semi-darkness, she could drift off between the asteroids, never to be seen again.

She was holding her left arm, and Hal realised she'd been injured by the flying perspex. There was no time to worry about that now, though. He had to collect her and get her to the *Albion*.

Coming to a halt, Hal reached out and took hold of her flight suit, pulling her towards him. This also moved him and the trike towards her, but more slowly, and once she was close enough, she managed to sit behind him, wrapping one arm around his chest. He looked down and saw a tear in the silver fabric, and then she put her other arm around him, clamping her hand over the tear to try and seal it.

As he turned towards the ship, she leaned closer, pressing the front of her helmet to the back of his. 'Please hurry,' he heard her saying, her voice barely audible. 'The air's pouring out.'

He had a spare sitting in his lap, but there was no way for her to put it on. So, Hal opened the throttle and willed the under-powered little trike home, knowing every second was going to count.

3

Hal was only halfway to the *Albion* when a powerful searchlight came on, the intense beam probing the shadows and illuminating the huge rocks all around him. The odd thing was that this light came from *behind* the jetbike, which meant there was someone else in the asteroid field.

Hal guessed they'd answered the same distress call, in which case they were out of luck. He'd already performed the heroic rescue, and he had no intention of sharing the credit.

The female pilot sitting behind him noticed the searchlight as well, because Hal felt something pressing into his back. The woman leaned her helmet against his, and when she spoke he felt a chill up his spine. 'Hide from them. Hide right now, or I'll shoot.'

'Relax,' he said quickly. 'I'm on your side.'

'Just...hide. Quickly.'

In order to point the gun at him, she'd released the rip in her suit, and Hal could see the edges flapping as the air poured out. He reached down and held it firmly with his left hand, then looked around for a good hiding spot.

He could see the *Albion* ahead, through the dense asteroid field, but it would take fifteen or twenty minutes to get there. He needed somewhere closer, and, luckily, he was surrounded by large rocks. He angled the handlebars, one-handed, and the little trike performed a slow, lazy turn until they were concealed behind a huge boulder.

Meanwhile, Hal glanced over his shoulder, trying to see who was after them. There was a spaceship all right, but it wasn't what he expected. Nosing between the asteroids, coming from the opposite direction to the *Albion*, was a chunky spaceship with a cab up front and a flat tray on the back. A big red crane sprouted from the rear, and Hal could just make out a sign painted across the nose:

Albert Herry towing services.

Insurance Aproved.

Hal rolled his eyes at the spelling, but he had bigger things to worry about. Another of the odd-looking towships had just appeared to his left, threading its way towards the wreckage with its own spotlight illuminating rocks. This one had a big chrome bull bar, a row of spotlights and more springy aerials than a dodgem car ride. Then a third towship turned up as well, but after one look at the first two it turned and flew off.

Typical, thought Hal.   One little crash, and you're surrounded by the things.   Fortunately, none of them had spotted the *Albion*.

By now, his trike was slipping behind the asteroid, and Hal spun it around and applied the throttle, bringing them to a halt. Then, very slowly, he fired the lower thrusters. Someone watching from the other side of the rock would have seen empty space, then the top of his helmet, and then Hal's face appearing from behind, like a slow-motion jack-in-the-box.

When Hal was satisfied with the view, he cancelled their upwards motion. By now, the towships had spotted each other, and they were illuminating one another with million-candlepower searchlights. He was eager to see what happened next, but then he remembered the pilot sitting behind him. With the rip in her sleeve, she must be almost out of air by now. 'We need to fix your suit,' he said.

There was no reply, and Hal noticed the gun wasn't pressing into him any more. He wondered if the woman was losing consciousness, and he hoped she didn't wake suddenly, twitching her finger and pulling the trigger before she knew what she was doing. He thought about reaching round to take the gun, then decided against it.

Hal felt in his own suit until he encountered the Space Suit Repair Kit... also known as Quaktape. Taking the roll, he released the pilot's ripped sleeve and turned the tape over in his thick gloves, until he located a big, easy-to-use flap. He tore off a generous strip and wrapped it round and round the pilot's damaged suit until he was satisfied it wasn't leaking. Then, making sure their helmets were touching, he spoke to her. 'I've taped you up, and we're hiding from the towships. They're not after you, they're just looking for work.'

There was no reply.

'Can you put the gun away?' asked Hal.

Nothing.

Hal gave up trying to communicate, and turned his attention to the towships. By now they'd found the stricken fighter, and the two towships were facing each other, about ten metres apart and another twenty from the damaged fighter. Hal saw hatches opening in the side of the towships, and then a bulky figure emerged from each vessel. The towship operators were wearing old-fashioned spacesuits, much-repaired, and they began to move towards each other using nifty little jetpacks. One, from the ship marked Albert Herry, was wearing an orange suit with black oil streaks all over it, while the other was wearing an off-white ensemble with a silver flash across his chest.

When Hal first spotted the towships, he assumed they were working together, but now he noticed something aggressive in the men's stance. From the look of it, the two of them were about to have a dust-up in space.

They met, and the man in the orange suit drew his arm back and threw a punch at the other. His fist connected, but instead of sending the second man flying, half the force of the blow was transmitted back up the first man's arm, and he immediately started spinning on the spot. Meanwhile, the second man aimed a kick at him, and when it connected they both flew apart, back towards their ships.

'Lunatics,' muttered Hal.

The men were certainly persistent. Firing their jetpacks, they charged each other, arms outstretched. They collided with a thump that Hal could feel, if not hear, and bounced off each other, spinning away into the asteroid field.

The man in the white spacesuit recovered first, and he flew over to Herry's ship and started wrenching on the spotlight, trying to rip it off the vehicle. Unfortunately, he couldn't get purchase, and he was still trying to pull it off when the second man took out a remote control and yanked on the joystick. The searchlight moved instantly, pointing downwards and trapping the second man's fingers between the metal case and the roof of the towship. He was stuck there, waving his spare arm in agony, as Herry went over to *his* ship and tried to kick the door panels in.

By now, Hal was getting worried about his *own* air supply. The towship operators didn't look like leaving any time soon, and Hal couldn't stay there indefinitely... even though he wanted to see the outcome.

Fortunately, the fight was almost over. Herry gave up trying to kick the reinforced hull in, and instead took out his remote control again. This time he used it to extend the big red crane on the back of his ship, and when it was stretched out as far as it would go, he swung it round in a full circle. The second man was still trapped by the searchlight, and now, as he struggled to free his hand, he was swatted by the crane. He went flying, spinning end over end, but before he'd gone twenty metres he'd corrected his spin and was heading back towards his own ship.

'Surely that's it,' thought Hal.

Nope.

While the second man was on his way to his ship, Herry reached into his towship and came out with a big metal crowbar. He held it in one hand, slapping the end in his gloved palm, then fired his jetpack, charging the man in the white suit. His opponent saw him coming and reached into his own ship, pulling out a crowbar twice as long, twice as thick, and plated with chrome from end to end.

That was it for Herry. He turned around and fled back to his own ship, darting inside and closing the hatch behind himself. Then, after a neat little U-turn, he rocketed away to safety.

The man in the white spacesuit gestured after him, then returned to his ship. He clambered in and approached the fighter, reversing towards it at speed.

The whole fight had only taken three or four minutes, and Hal wondered whether to make a break for it while the towship operator was busy. Alone, he would have done so, but he decided not to risk it with the armed pilot holding a gun to his back.

As the towship moved closer, Hal saw writing down the side:

Max Damage. You wreck it, we tow it.

Once the ship was close enough, the man Hal assumed to be Max Damage emerged, and he began busily attaching a cable and hooks to the stricken fighter. Idly, Hal wondered how much the fighter was worth in salvage, and he realised he might have towed it back to the *Albion* behind his jetbike. Then again, the township operators would have gone for *him* with the crowbar, and with an injured pilot on his hands there'd been no time for Hal to mess around with tow ropes.

Max had finished attaching hooks now, and he started winching the fighter towards his ship. As the smaller ship began to move, he fired the township's jets to maintain position, and that's when it happened. Weakened by the crash, a whole section of the fighter tore loose, ripping tubes and piping as it exposed the power core. There was a burst of flame followed by an intense flash of light, and Hal ducked as pieces of ship went flying out from the explosion, scattering amongst the asteroids, bouncing off them and ricocheting into space.

Slowly, he raised his head, and he saw the township spinning away from the explosion, her lights out and engines dead. As he watched, he saw Max knocked clear, just before the odd-looking ship crashed side-on into a large asteroid. The crash went on and on, the township scraping itself to pieces against the big rock, and then the remains broke apart with a muted explosion.

Hal stared in shock. He could see Max floating in the asteroid field, limp and immobile, either unconscious or dead. Hal half-expected to see the other townships coming back, then realised there'd been no time for a distress signal. That meant the rescue was down to him.

'Hold on,' Hal told the pilot sitting behind him. 'Looks like I've got another passenger.'

Hal's air was running out by the time he got back to his ship. It had taken longer than expected to collect Max, because with three of them onboard the little jetbike had no acceleration at all. After he collected the man, it took five whole minutes just to get up to speed, and Hal was forced to turn round and start braking again while he was still five minutes from the *Albion*.

Still, he made it safely, and after a bit of tricky work with the controls he managed to park the jetbike inside the *Albion's* launch tube. The outer door closed, atmospheric pressure returned, and with an intense feeling of relief, Hal took off his helmet and climbed down off the bike.

With Hal out of the way the female pilot slumped forward in the saddle, while Max was lying across the back of the jetbike like a sack of potatoes. He was a big man, much taller than Hal, and Hal hoped the guy didn't react badly when he discovered his ship had been destroyed. A fist-fight with a big, angry giant was the very last thing he needed right then.

Air was the first priority, so Hal found the emergency releases and took their helmets off. First he removed the pilot's, and he discovered she was in her mid-twenties, with short dark hair and high cheekbones. She seemed to be breathing, which was a good sign, but she was definitely unconscious.

Next, Hal turned to the man he'd thrown across the back of the trike. He took Max's helmet off, and that's when he got a huge surprise, because Max was a woman. She had long blonde hair tied up in a ponytail, and appeared to be about thirty years old.

Hal remembered the way Max had driven off the other towship operator, and he vowed not to get on her bad side.

For now, though, he wasn't even sure she was alive, and so he tried to check her pulse. It was impossible with his thick gloves on, and he pulled one off with his teeth then tried again. She was definitely alive, but as he was checking he suddenly remembered the gun, which was still clutched in the fighter pilot's hand.

The pilot who was slumped on the jetbike, right behind him.

Hal turned, and was reaching for the gun when the pilot came to, alerted by some sixth sense. She sat up groggily, raising the weapon to point right at Hal's chest. 'How many...how many on board?' she asked him, her voice low. She looked dazed but the gun was rock-steady in her hand, and Hal had no doubt she'd use it.

Slowly, Hal raised his hands. 'There's just the two of us.'

'You'd better be telling...the truth.'

'I am!'

The pilot closed her eyes, swaying in the seat. Then, with effort, she forced another question out. 'What's your...relationship...with Mayestra?'

'I just checked her pulse, I swear,' said Hal quickly. Then he frowned. 'I thought her name was Max?'

'Mayestra is a planet. Enemy...star system.'

Hal felt relieved. 'Never been there. At least, I don't think so.'

The woman looked at him, her eyes full of suspicion.

'Look, I'm just a freighter pilot,' Hal explained. 'I'm delivering cargo to...I don't know, some planet in this system. I got your distress call and altered course to pick you up.'

The woman said nothing, but at least she seemed to be listening. Either that, or she was about to pass out again.

'You're safe here, I swear, so will you please put the gun

away?' Hal gave her a smile. 'I promise we'll drop you off wherever you want to go. You have my word.'

The pilot glanced round at Max, who was lying across the saddle behind her. 'Is she your co-pilot?'

'No, she's a towship operator. A pair of them showed up to take your fighter away, then had a punch-up before one of them left. Then this woman tried to tow your ship and it exploded.'

'You said there were only two on board? Where is...where is...' The pilot said no more, because her eyes closed and she toppled sideways off the bike. The gun clattered on the floor, and Hal ran around the trike to snatch it up, shoving it into one of his spacesuit's many pockets. Then he crouched next to the woman to check her pulse. She was alive, but her pulse was weak and he knew he'd have to get help for her quickly. There was no doubt the crash, waiting for rescue in the smoke-filled cockpit, and the trip through space with a ripped suit had taken everything out of her. She had a nasty cut on her forehead, too.

Suddenly, a big hand grabbed him by the neck, and his head was tilted back until he was looking into the blonde woman's face. She'd recovered while he was tending to the fighter pilot, and now she had him at her mercy.

'Where the hell did you spring from?' she demanded, in a rough voice. 'If you think you're getting the salvage on that fighter, you can damn well think again.'

'Glglgl,' said Hal.

Max relaxed her death-like grip, just a touch.

'Rescue,' said Hal quickly. He drew a deep, shuddering breath. 'Saved you and her. Don't care about salvage.'

The big woman had piercing blue eyes and a scar down one side of her face, and she looked suspicious and angry.

However, Hal had no time for explanations or introductions. The pilot was slumped on the deck in her spacesuit, her eyes were closed, her face pale. 'Talk later,' said Hal urgently. 'She needs medical help.'

Max glanced down, then nodded. Moving gingerly, she climbed off the trike, towering over Hal by a head, and then she picked up the unconscious pilot with ease, putting her across her shoulders as though she weighed next to nothing.

Hal opened the hatch leading to the cargo hold, then went through and waited for Max to follow with the pilot. Hal half-expected to see Clunk there, to congratulate him on the successful rescue, but he remembered the robot was keeping station in the flight deck.

So, he hurried to the inner door, while Max strode along behind him with the pilot. The pilot was still wearing her lightweight silver suit, which crackled like tinfoil with every step Max took.

Hal operated the door, and he led Max along the passageway. Halfway along, a smaller passage led to the left and right, with three cabins on either side. Hal opened the nearest, and Max laid the pilot gently on the bunk before pulling a blanket up to her waist. 'First aid kit,' said Max. 'Quickly!'

Hal ran to fetch it, and when he came back the pilot's spacesuit was open, and Max was staring at the dark green uniform underneath. 'She's young for a wing commander,' she said in surprise. Then she shook her head and took the first aid kit, emptying it on the bed until she found a hypo. She checked the label, then pressed the device to the pilot's neck and activated the plunger. Next she took a bottle of antiseptic, poured some on a cloth and cleaned the wound on the pilot's forehead, gently moving aside a lock of dark hair to get at it.

'Can I leave you here a minute?' asked Hal.

Max waved him away impatiently, so he turned and ran for the lift, stumbling along in the bulky spacesuit. Hal clicked his fingers impatiently as the lift carried him upwards, and as soon as he reached the flight deck he called out to Clunk. 'All aboard. Let's get out of here!'

Clunk obeyed, turning the ship before powering the ship towards the edge of the asteroid field. 'How is she?' he asked, once he was satisfied with their course.

'How are the pair of them, you mean.'

'But that was a single-seater,' said Clunk, with a frown.

'Weren't you watching?' said Hal, gesturing at the screen. 'There was a fist fight, and an explosion, and then another explosion. I rescued pilots from two different ships, and after we got back one of the women stuck a gun in my face. I just managed to talk her out of shooting me when the other grabbed me by the neck. Now one of them's healing the other.'

'Is she badly hurt?'

'There's a cut on her forehead and she's unconscious.' Hal frowned. 'The fighter pilot had a gun, Clunk. She was asking me how many of us on board, and something about an enemy system, but then she fainted.'

'Where is the gun now?'

Hal dug around in his spacesuit, then handed the weapon over. Clunk took it and handled it expertly, sliding a small catch to remove the charge pack before stowing the pistol under the console. Then he put the power pack inside one of his chest compartments.

'By the way,' said Hal. 'That jetbike is an under-powered joke of a thing.'

'I know.'

'Why didn't you order a more powerful one? Something with a bigger engine?'

'Because I've seen you trying to control a more powerful one,' said Clunk, which was the end of that particular argument.

Hal looked down at himself. 'Right. I'm going to put the suit away. Set course for wherever this cargo is going, and do not stop for any distress calls.'

Clunk opened his mouth.

'I mean it!' said Hal. 'This system is swarming with towships. Let them deal with any more problems, or we're going to be stacking rescued pilots in the corridors.' And with that, he went to get changed.

4

Cylen Murtay looked around the office nervously, but if anyone was aware he'd taken half an hour to casually drop in on the president of Dolor, they weren't showing it. He took his seat, fired up his terminal, and wondered what the hell he was going to do next.

He'd gone to a lot of trouble to wangle a meeting with the president, and he still couldn't believe it had worked. He'd told the president's staff he had the full backing of his boss, had written himself several glowing letters of introduction, forging the signatures, and had basically lied through his teeth.

And it had worked. He'd gone over his boss's head and warned the president about the Mayestran threat. It was a threat he considered so important, he'd staked his career on it. Maybe even his liberty.

The problem was, the president had just ordered him to contact the Mayestrans and the Henerians with an ultimatum, and he had no authority to do so. In fact, he wasn't supposed to be concerned with either of them, since his real job was collating information on the cultural mores of nearby systems. His reports on social niceties went off to ambassadors and embassy staff in those systems, who used them to avoid diplomatic incidents and embarrassing faux pas.

Talk about overreaching his authority.

To give himself time to think, Murtay brought up a map of the local galactic sector on his terminal, idly panning across the vast expanse of stars until he reached his home system. He zoomed in on the primary, and three orbiting planets appeared, Dolor the second-furthest from the centre. Close to the central star there was a thick asteroid field, which was the source of most metals and minerals in the system.

He zoomed out again, and started scrolling outwards, along the spiral arm. Inhabited systems appeared in blue, and they stood out like welcoming beacons amongst the thousands of barren stars filling his screen. As he scrolled further, a red-bordered zone appeared. It encompassed half a dozen stars, all interconnected with fine white lines, and Mayestra sat in the middle like a fat round spider skulking in its web. Last time he checked, the red zone had only included five systems, and Murtay noted the new addition with a frown.

He'd been warning his boss about the Mayestrans for two years now, but his warnings had gone unheeded. He'd advised his superiors to beg for, borrow or build warships to counter the threat, and he lost count of the number of times he'd suggested deploying defences throughout the system.

There's no money, his superiors told him. *The war is a long way away. They won't bother us. Now tell us which sandwich fillings the Thrakians prefer when they sit down to afternoon tea.*

Well, now that a Mayestran force was on the way, maybe his superiors would sit up and take notice at last. Unfortunately, they'd left things far too late.

Murtay scrolled the map sideways, and soon encountered an area marked with dark green. The Henerians were just as busy adding neutral planets to their little fiefdom, even though they claimed they were only defending themselves.

He noticed they'd also annexed a new system, and he was about to add this to his notes when a movement to his right caught his eye. He glanced towards the far end of the big, open-plan office, and was surprised to recognise the Foreign Minister making a rare visit to her department. She was accompanied by Murtay's boss, several high-level bureaucrats and a gaggle of staffers.

And then Murtay noticed something troubling: they were all heading straight for his desk.

Clunk was piloting the *Albion* towards planet Dolor, blissfully unaware of the war between the Mayestrans and the Henerians. After all the excitement, he was relieved they were back on track, and he was looking forward to delivering the cargo... and getting paid.

He'd completed a quick inspection of the ship, as ordered by Mr Spacejock, but unfortunately the deadline on their delivery was getting close. So, instead of checking everything twice, he'd checked a few major things... once.

However, the ship was behaving herself, and as long as the thrusters didn't cut out during landing Clunk felt he could handle anything else. Truth is, he was embarrassed at the faults which kept showing up in the *Albion's* systems, and he was determined to sort everything out before they lifted off again.

He was just about to call ahead and book a service when he noticed a message light flashing. 'How long has that been going?' he asked the Navcom.

'Three minutes and five seconds.'

'Why didn't you sound the message tone?'

'I tried, but it's broken.'

Clunk frowned. 'Next time, tell me about the message yourself.'

'Unable to comply. The system is automated.'

'But the system isn't working.'

'Correct,' said the Navcom patiently. 'That is why the message tone didn't sound.'

Clunk shook his head in annoyance, then activated the message. 'Hello?'

'This is Space Port Delta ground control. Albion, *do you read? I repeat–'*

'Albion here,' said Clunk quickly. 'Reading you loud and clear.'

'About time,' grumbled the controller. *'I've been calling you over and over. Listen, there's a Mayestran fleet in the sector, and they're hunting rebels. Do not, I repeat, do* not *approach them.'*

'Thank you, ground. We'll keep our distance.'

'Just FYI, but they're landing troops at the spaceport,' said the controller confidentially. *'They're planning on searching every ship, so if you're carrying anything you shouldn't be, now's the time to ditch it.'*

Clunk smiled. 'Thank you, ground, but we have nothing to hide. We're engaged in a legitimate cargo job.'

'Fine, but if it were me, I'd turn round and get the hell out of here.'

'Are things that bad?' asked Clunk.

'Not yet, but I wouldn't want to be a Henerian right now.'

Clunk accessed his internal database. 'They're at war with each other. Why do they call the Henerians rebels?'

'Makes them sound like they're in the wrong, I guess. Anyway, I've cleared your landing slot. Take care, Albion.'

'Thank you, ground. You too.' Clunk cut the connection. It was lucky the pilot Mr Spacejock had rescued from the asteroid field was a Mayestran, he thought, or they'd be in real trouble. Imagine the fuss it would cause if they'd actually rescued one of the Henerian rebels!

Idly, he brought up a schematic of the ranks in the Mayestran Navy, with links to their insignia and uniforms. He scanned a few, and noticed they were predominantly red and black. Then he switched to the Henerians, who wore deep green. How like humans, he thought, to dress in distinctive colours and arrange themselves into teams, before launching themselves into futile combat.

Still, he and Mr Spacejock didn't have to get involved with such unpleasantness. They would hand the injured pilot back to her people after they landed, and that would be the end of that. Then, with any luck, they'd be able to fly to a system far, far away for their next cargo job.

Clunk decided to call the lower deck, introduce himself, and reassure the rescued fighter pilot that her people would be waiting for her. Ideally, he would have used the intercom, but it was still out of order. So, he decided to go in person. 'Navcom, please engage the autopilot.'

'Unable to comply. Autopilot non-functional.'

'Why?'

'Shoddy workmanship,' said the computer.

Clunk glanced towards the lift, debating whether to leave the controls and go below decks. He wouldn't be long, and it wasn't like there was anything for the ship to run into.

But no. A lifetime of caution told him to remain. Speaking with their guest wasn't that important, and he decided the fighter pilot would just have to learn about the Mayestrans after arrival. So, instead of leaving, he plugged into the console and started a suite of diagnostics, hoping to fix the intercom. And the autopilot. And anything else he encountered.

Murtay got up nervously, and as the Foreign Minister approached he bowed his head briefly. 'Good afternoon, ma'am.'

Foreign Minister Lobelia Harris was a portly woman with cropped black hair, and she wore a pair of gold hoop earrings that swung wildly as she came to a halt. 'Murray, is it?'

'Murtay.'

'I hear you just met the president.'

It wasn't a question, and Murtay could hear the menace in her voice. 'Yes ma'am.'

'How in god's name did you manage that? Someone like you should have been stopped at the main entrance, never mind actually being admitted to the Square Office.'

'A contact approached the president's chief of staff, and she felt my concerns were important enough to bring to the president's notice.'

'So that's how you did it.' Harris scowled at Murtay's boss. 'Your staff can't go running to the president with baseless rumours, Jim. You're getting a reprimand for this.'

'Y-yes, Minister.'

Murtay hid a smile. His boss was a balding, elderly man who was looking forward to retirement, and the man's job description could have been written as 'don't ruffle any feathers'. Well, in a properly-run department, Murtay wouldn't have needed to go over his head. Then the minister's words filtered through, and he frowned. 'I'm sorry, did you say...baseless rumours?'

'Of course I did!' snapped the minister. 'The Mayestrans are no threat to us. They're after a group of rebels who attacked an unarmed transport.' She glared at him. 'Anyway, you're supposed to be writing cultural reports. These matters don't concern you.'

'Minister, I've been doing my job for six years now. In that time, eight of the systems I was writing reports on have fallen to either the Mayestrans or the Henerians. Every case started with a request to hunt down so-called rebels fighting for the other side.'

'We have assurances.' The Minister gestured impatiently. 'Like I said, it's none of your concern. You were paid to do a certain job, not go around creating panic. I've a good mind to reassign you to some backwater, just to teach you a lesson.'

Murtay opened his mouth to object, but at that moment the map disappeared from his terminal and a warning notice appeared in heavy black writing:

Incoming broadcast. All stations.

'What is this?' demanded the minister. She turned to the others, but they all looked as surprised as she was.

Every screen in the office went blank, and then a still image appeared. Murtay wasn't an expert on the military, but he guessed it was coming from a Mayestran warship. The first clue was the bridge full of officers, resplendent in their red and black uniforms. The second clue was the seal of the Mayestran navy, which flashed up on the screen complete with crossed swords and guns. And the third clue came from the commanding officer, a tall, grey-haired woman with an impressive row of campaign medals. Because, once she spoke, she removed all doubt.

'Greetings, inhabitants of the Dolorian star system. I am Captain Liton Strake, commander of the Mayestran warship *Kestrel.*' The captain smiled, but it was more wolfish than welcoming. 'According to our intel, Henerian rebels have been using your system as a base from which to attack our fleet. Therefore, I arrive with a peacekeeping force to protect ourselves from these vicious, unwarranted attacks.'

And so it begins, thought Murtay.

'My cruisers will soon commence a scan of your entire system, and any rebel ships we detect will be hunted down and destroyed. A detachment of troops will land at the major spaceports on each of your three worlds, where they will be authorised to search all vessels. Departures from all regional spaceports are hereby prohibited.' Captain Strake stared into the camera, her expression severe. 'Anyone offering assistance to these rebels will be treated as enemy combatants, and they will be detained for interrogation. You will not resupply, repair the ships of, nor give medical treatment to any Henerian native. Instead, you will secure them and call on us to handle the matter.'

A bullet-point list now appeared on the screen, just in case anyone watching hadn't got the message.

'Thank you for your time, and I trust this contact between our peace-loving systems will grow into a strong and fruitful alliance. Captain Strake out!'

The screen faded, and then the Mayestran Navy seal appeared once more. Underneath was their somewhat ironic motto: We bring Peace and Harmony to All.

'And when that fails, we'll drop bombs on you,' muttered Murtay. He turned to look at the minister, his boss and the others, and he almost laughed out loud as he saw their stunned expressions.

'Did he say... troops?' said the minister faintly.

Murtay grabbed her arm. 'Minister, we have to talk. I can tell you what's coming next, and then you can put your staff to work on countermeasures.'

'We can't possibly fight them,' said the minister, her voice rising. 'They have warships, and troops, and... they're going to crush us!'

'Keep your voice down,' muttered Murtay, looking around the office. His fellow workers had all seen the message, but they didn't need to witness their minister throwing in the towel. 'All of you, come with me.'

'Where to?' The minister eyed him hopefully. 'Do you have an underground bunker?'

'No,' said Murtay. 'The conference room.'

Murtay led the group out of the main office, and they all took seats around the boardroom table. Everyone was dazed, and they didn't object when Murtay stood at the head of the table, activating the big screen on the wall behind him. A few swift strokes, and he had the local star map displayed for all to see.

'Unfortunately, there's nothing we can do about the warships. We only have a handful of customs vessels, but they're so old they can barely reach orbit. They're armed, in a fashion, but they'd be lucky to shoot out a Mayestran cruiser's tail lights before return fire blasted them from the skies.'

Murtay looked around the table, and he realised his frank summation of the situation wasn't helping. Then again, there was no time to coddle these people, and the sooner they realised they were being dragged into a war, the better.

'I've spent months studying the progress of the war in other neutral systems, and after the first contact there's usually a demand for permanent bases. Then the fleet moves in, and after that, factories in our system will be retooled to make uniforms, ammunition, and other war material. Food will be stockpiled and rationed. All private ships will be commandeered by the invaders, and will then be used as transports.' He paused for emphasis. 'Within a few short months, our system will be stripped clean, our economy in tatters. Once that happens, the Mayestrans will move on to another system like a swarm of interstellar locusts.'

A young woman put her hand up. 'How do we stop them?'

'It's too late for that. The time to start building defences and warships has long since passed.' For two years Murtay had been expecting the invasion, and now that it was actually happening, he had all the facts and figures at his fingertips. 'The lead time for building a star cruiser is three months. Destroyers one month. Battleships, up to a year.'

'Can't we...buy some?'

'Who would crew them?' Murtay glanced at his boss. 'Anyway, I've been told there's no money. Over and over again.'

'We could pay someone to defend us!'

'Every other system in this sector is trying to shore up their own defences. They're not going to send ships and personnel to protect us.'

'So how do we defend ourselves? Should we just leave? Go somewhere safer?'

'There are eighty million people in this system. It would take years to move them all, and where would you take them?' Murtay saw the minister looking thoughtful, and he guessed she was already planning her own escape. To twist the knife, he raised a point which may or may not have been true. 'In other systems, high-ranking officials who tried to flee were imprisoned, and many of them were executed. The Mayestrans and the Henerians prefer to keep our leaders right where they can see them. That's the real reason they're landing troops at our spaceports.'

The minister deflated like a balloon. 'Wh-what can we do? You have to tell us!'

Murtay hesitated. What he was about to suggest was madness, but he believed it was the one thing the Mayestrans wouldn't expect. So, he leaned forwards and started to explain his plan.

And, even though he was just a lowly staffer, whose job involved suggesting the appropriate aperitifs for cocktail parties at regional embassies, the high-ranking officials hung on his every word.

5

'Right now, there are over two hundred private vessels in the vicinity of Dolor.' Murtay turned to point at the big screen, which was displaying a dense list of ships sorted by size and capacity. 'Asteroid miners, cargo vessels, towships, the customs cutters I mentioned earlier... it's quite a list, as you can see for yourselves.'

'That's not enough to evacuate everyone,' the minister pointed out. 'You could barely fit all the sitting members of parliament in those ships, let alone members of the public.' Then she brightened. 'Of course, you could always move the government first, and come back for–'

'I already told you, evacuation is impossible.' Murtay eyed his audience. 'Instead, I suggest we put together an armada the likes of which has never been seen before. A collection of ships which will send the Mayestrans packing.'

There was dead silence.

'You know all those little ships are not armed, right?' said a young woman. 'They'll be shot down by the dozen. It'll be a slaughter.'

'Yes, of course. But first, we *are* going to arm these ships. And second–'

The minister snorted. 'We have no weapons. Nothing we

could fit to ships, at least. And even if we did, think how long it would take!'

'And second,' finished Murtay, ignoring her. 'They won't be going anywhere near the Mayestran fleet.' He looked around the assembled dignitaries, and he realised he had to explain quickly before he lost them all. 'It's an old trick, and it relies on the element of surprise. Secrecy is vital, and we have to coordinate everything down to the nearest second.'

'Yes, yes,' said the minister impatiently. 'But what *is* this miraculous trick?'

Murtay knew he had their interest, if nothing else. He displayed a system map on the screen, then zoomed in on the asteroid belt. 'Dozens of ships mine these rocks every day, hauling ores and minerals back to Dolor. What I'm proposing is that we send every ship we have to the belt.'

The young woman objected. 'But only a third of those ships you showed us are miners. What are the others supposed to do?'

'They're going to collect as many large rocks as they can. They can fit them in their cargo holds, lash them underneath... it doesn't matter how, they just have to carry them away from the asteroid belt. And then... well, see this animation for yourselves.' Murtay zoomed out, and the audience could see planet Dolor with the Mayestran fleet nearby, the latter marked with a red circle. The asteroid belt was closer to the primary star, and as he played the animation, a ragtag fleet of vessels left the asteroid field and slowly made its way towards Dolor. There was a whole stream of them, and they fanned out as they approached the planet, passing either side of the Mayestran fleet, keeping well clear of the warships. Then, one by one, they circled the planet and landed.

'What was that supposed to achieve?' demanded the

minister. 'Do you think you're going to scare them off with a flyby? Because I can tell you right now, these people–'

There was a flash, and then another, and one by one the Mayestran ships winked out with little explosive puffs. Soon only a few remained, and as they tried to run, they too exploded.

There was a long silence.

'What just happened?' asked the minister. 'Was it sabotage?'

'Let me replay a segment, but zoomed in this time.' Murtay rolled the animation back to the point where the flotilla of small vessels split up, just before they passed either side of the Mayestran ships. This time he focused on one or two small ships, and as they peeled off, dozens of tiny specks were released from their cargo holds. The camera followed these specks, thousands of them in total when all the ships were counted, all spreading out and moving at high speed. When the specks encountered the Mayestran fleet, they destroyed every last ship.

'Those little rocks are enough to blast a whole fleet?' said the minister, shocked.

'They're not that little, and at the speed they're travelling they'll go through anything.' Murtay zoomed in on the flagship, and they saw it shredded before their eyes. 'They won't see them coming, they won't be able to stop them, and they won't be able to get out of the way.'

'It won't work, you know,' said Murtay's boss. 'They have a cruiser, and it has shields.'

'I know. But they won't have their shields up.'

'How so?'

'They'll be lowering their shields to welcome our official party on board.'

'What official party?'

'We're going to ask them to assume control of Dolor, along with the rest of the system. It's–'

There was an uproar, drowning out the rest of his words. Murtay waited patiently, and as the cries finally died down, he continued. 'It's what they want, and we'll give it to them. A delegation led by President Oakworthy will personally take the paperwork to their commanding officer, and they'll have to lower their shields to get our officials on board. We just have to time it so the delegation arrives at the same time as our barrage.'

Everyone eyed the screen, which was littered with the spreading remains of the Mayestran flagship. 'Let me get this straight,' said the minister. 'You're proposing to send the president into space, and then you're going to put him aboard that ship just before you blow it up?'

'The president, and all our most senior ministers,' said Murtay. 'You can't send underlings, it has to look like a genuine offer to hand over our system.'

'Are you out of your mind? Anyone going aboard that vessel will be killed for sure! It's suicide!'

'They only have to think the officials are on board. In reality, we'll send a remote-controlled shuttle. By the time they find out it's empty, it'll be too late. They'll have lowered their shields.'

There was a lengthy silence.

'What about repercussions?' said the minister at last. 'Even if this works, they'll just send another fleet after the first.'

'All they'll know for certain is that one of their fleets has been destroyed. They won't know how, and that'll give them plenty of food for thought. They'll assume we have powerful defensive weapons, maybe Empire tech, and they'll never bother us again.'

'That's all very well, but what if one of their ships escapes?'

'They won't. The incoming rocks will be scattered enough to encompass the whole fleet.'

'And how will the pilots of our ships release the things?'

'Simple. Turn the ship in space, open the hold, fire the jets for a second or two, and the rocks will sail out the back on the original course.'

'It's madness,' muttered the minister. 'Complete lunacy.' She looked around the table. 'If anyone else has a better idea, now's the time to mention it.'

There was complete silence, and nobody met her eyes.

'Very well. I'll take this insanity to the Cabinet. You,' she said, pointing at Murtay. 'You're coming with me, and you can bring that infernal animation of yours, too. If they laugh your plan out of parliament, I'll be needing a scapegoat.'

Hal stowed his space suit in the locker, adding the spare suit in its carry bag, then threw in the two helmets Max and the fighter pilot had left in the launch tube. Finally, he secured the jetbike, sealing the tube's inner hatch before heading back to the passenger cabins.

Once he reached the cabin containing his guests, he raised his hand to knock on the door, then paused. Hal wasn't sure whether to disturb them, because they might still be in shock. He knew what it was like to lose a ship, since he'd lost two of his own, one of them recently. It was easy to describe the feeling, because it was just like watching your house full of belongings burning to the ground.

With a rare flash of empathy, he realised the two women would be feeling alienated and lost. He'd have to work hard to make them feel at home aboard his ship, extending the hand of friendship until they recovered from their ordeal and were able to move on.

So, vowing to tread lightly, he raised his hand and knocked. 'Just me,' he said. 'How's everything going?'

'Come in,' said a voice.

Hal entered, and the first thing he noticed was the fighter pilot, who was sitting up in bed with a bandage around her forehead. She looked pale and drawn, but she managed a wan smile. 'You're the one who answered my distress call. Thanks for that.'

Hal gestured. 'Don't mention it. It was nothing.'

'Hardly that. By the way, I'm Sam.' The pilot gestured at her green uniform jacket. 'Wing Commander Sam Willet, officially.'

She had a pleasant voice, and she looked so vulnerable that Hal could barely believe she shot at other people for a living. 'I'm Hal Spacejock, freighter pilot. Nice to meet you.'

'Max told me all about the rescue. You saved us both, Hal. You should be proud of yourself.'

Hal felt chuffed, but then he noticed a second pertinent fact: the towship pilot wasn't in the cabin. 'Speaking of Max, where is she?'

'Right behind you,' said a voice, making Hal jump.

He turned to see Max wearing his dark blue bathrobe, her long blonde hair still damp from the shower. She had a mug of coffee in each hand, and she pushed past Hal and handed one to Willet while keeping the other for herself. He couldn't help noticing Max had his favourite mug, while Willet had his second-favourite. He frowned at that, because he only had two mugs. What was he supposed to drink coffee out of... a space helmet?

But then he remembered his vow to make the women feel at home, and he shrugged off the petty annoyance.

'Good coffee,' said Willet, after taking a sip.

Max shook her head. 'It's the cheap stuff. Bought in bulk, and already stale.' She put her mug down, then glanced at Hal. 'The water in your shower is cold. You should get it fixed.'

'I know. My co-pilot forgot to tick an option.'

Max frowned at him. 'Say the word, and I will beat him for you.'

'Er, no, it's fine. I'll, er, deal with him myself.'

'A beating... it's the only way they learn,' said Max firmly, and she drove her fist into her open palm. 'You must show your underlings who's boss. There must be no doubt.'

'Don't worry, he knows,' said Hal quickly. The woman made him nervous, not just because of her height and willingness to use her fists at the drop of a hat. No, there was something in her manner, something that told him Max hadn't always driven a beaten-up township for a living. He guessed she'd been a cage fighter or a bounty hunter or a bouncer... definitely something involving lots of wanton violence.

'So, what is the plan?' Max asked him.

'We're dropping our cargo off at the nearest spaceport. You can make your own way from there, right?'

Max snorted. 'I cannot stay in this system. I will come with you when you leave.'

'You will?' Hal recalled his promise to make the two women feel at home. Yes, but not *give* them a home, he thought. The pilot, Sam, was no bother, but Max was trouble with a capital T, a capital E, and a capital everything else in between.

'Of course. You must take me somewhere better.' Max

55

gestured at the hallway. 'Also, you will get the hot water fixed, and you need coffee.' She brandished his best mug. 'Much better coffee than this.'

'Er...yes. Sure. Anything to help.' Hal turned to Sam, who'd been watching the exchange in some amusement.

Before he could ask about her demands, she gave him a reassuring smile. 'I'll be fine,' she said. 'Drop me off at the spaceport, and I'll get a shuttle back to the nearest Henerian fleet. Hopefully, the rest of my squadron will be waiting for me.' Then she frowned. 'Most of them, anyway. Some didn't make it.'

'What happened?' Hal asked her. 'Why were you flying through the asteroid field?'

She studied him thoughtfully, not sure how much to say. 'We ran into a Mayestran patrol, and they outnumbered us at least three to one. There was a bit of a dogfight, we got a couple of theirs, they got a couple of ours.' She shrugged. 'Their numbers started to tell, and we had to cut and run. I made it to this system, but I'd taken a few hits and my controls weren't a hundred percent. I meant to hide in the asteroid field while I took stock, but then the controls failed completely. I brushed one of the bigger rocks, and you saw the result.' She turned to Max. 'I'm sorry about your ship.'

'Don't be,' said Max. 'I was getting bored with the tow business. Too many operators, not enough wrecks.'

'You might want to rethink that,' said Sam. 'If the Mayestrans turn up with a battle fleet, there'll be wrecks all over the system.'

'I will not deal with Mayestrans,' said Max shortly. She looked into her empty mug, then headed towards the corridor. 'I'm getting another coffee. Excuse me.'

56

After she left, Hal turned to Sam. 'How long has this war been going on?'

'I signed on ten years ago, as a cadet. I was just a kid then, and it had already been going for years.' A shadow crossed Sam's face. 'It's a never-ending war, and the casualties keep piling up.'

'Well, look on the bright side,' said Hal. 'After we land, you might get a couple of days peace while you're waiting for a shuttle.'

She nodded, then looked up at him. 'Which way are you going? After you've unloaded, I mean.'

'Not into a warzone,' said Hal flatly. He saw her expression. 'I'm sorry, but they'd take my ship, and we only just got her. After my last ship was destroyed, I thought I was out of the cargo game for good. I won't get another chance.'

'Fair enough. Just asking.'

'Do you want to get back that badly? I thought you'd just want to...leave. Get away from the fighting.'

'Desert?' Sam shook her head. 'We're up against it right now, but there are millions of lives at stake. Every pilot makes a difference.'

Hal was pretty sure she'd be going back to face her own death, and it saddened him more than he could say. Then Max returned, carrying a brimming coffee mug. 'You should rest,' the woman told Sam. 'You look tired.'

'I will. And thanks, both of you.'

Hal left the cabin, and Max followed, closing the door.

'You can have this one,' said Hal, indicating the cabin alongside. 'No passengers on this run, so they're all empty.'

Max opened the door, and the light came on automatically. There was a neat bunk, made up, a desk with a chair fixed to the floor, and a terminal screen. 'Good enough,' she said.

Hal turned to leave, but she grabbed his shoulder. 'No. I need to speak with you. In here.'

He followed her into the cabin, and she turned and closed the door, standing with her back to it. She towered over him, and he felt trapped and apprehensive. 'If this is about the coffee...' he began.

'Screw the coffee. The coffee doesn't matter.' Max strode past him and sat on the bunk. She winced as she did so, and Hal remembered the way she'd dismounted gingerly from the jetbike.

He looked down and saw the bruised fingers on her right hand, from the crushing searchlight, and he also remembered the way the crane had swatted her off the towship. The blow had been hard enough to break bones, but she hadn't complained. 'Are you hurt?'

'Just bruising. It will pass.' Max looked up at him. 'I cannot land at the spaceport.'

'Okay.' Hal looked around the cabin. 'You can always stay in here. They don't bother searching, most times. They just approve the paperwork and move on.'

'You don't understand. I cannot land there, not at all. The risk is too great.'

'Why?'

'That is my business.'

Hal blinked. 'But we're delivering cargo. I can't just fly somewhere else. I mean, do you have any idea how much it costs to fill this thing? The first time I saw a fuel bill, I thought it was for the whole month.'

'If they find me on board, I will be arrested. You too, as an accomplice.'

'*Now* you tell me?'

'What would you have done, left me in space to die?'

'No, of course not. But–'

'There is a place not far from the spaceport. It's a national park with a nearby settlement. You can set down there, and I will leave the ship. Then you take off again.'

Hal frowned. 'They'll notice the landing. That means an investigation.'

'So make something up.' Max looked at him, her blue eyes hard and intense. 'It's not like you have a choice.'

Actually, Hal was thinking it would suit him just fine. Earlier, he'd feared she would move in permanently, and he'd never get rid of her. Now, from the sound of it, he could get her out of his hair sooner than he thought. An illegal landing to set her down was a small price to pay. 'Okay, we'll do it.'

'Then,' she continued, 'when your business is complete, you will pick me up again before you leave the planet.'

'What?'

Max shrugged. 'I already told you, I cannot stay here. I must start over somewhere else.'

Dazed, Hal could only think of one thing. 'But you will leave the ship? Eventually, I mean?' He didn't like to push the issue, but he really did want to know.

'Of course. I cannot live with lousy coffee and cold showers.' Max looked down at the blue bathrobe. 'This isn't very warm, either, and it's too small for me. Do you have a bigger one?'

'No, that's the only one. You can, er, borrow it as long as you like.'

'I know. And now I rest.' Max laid back on the bunk, putting her hands behind her head. She was so tall her feet stuck over one end, and the bathrobe, which hadn't been that long to begin with, now covered even less of her legs. 'Unless you wish to stay?' she added casually.

Hal swallowed. 'I'd better check on the flight deck,' he said quickly, backing away and feeling for the door. He didn't mind a bit of fun, but he suspected a tumble with Max would be like climbing into a cement mixer running at full speed.

'Wait!'

Hal froze, one hand on the door controls.

'The national park is two hundred kilometres north-west of Space Port Delta. There is nothing else around it, so you can't miss it.'

'Two hundred northwest. Check.' And with that, Hal darted through the door and closed it firmly behind himself.

6

Hal needed to go up and explain their updated flight plan to Clunk, but first he wanted to check his cabin in case there was a third coffee mug lying around somewhere. On the way he passed the compact, tidy little bathroom, and then he skidded to a halt and came back for another look. The floor was sopping wet, and Max's dirty clothes were strewn all over the place. Hal's one and and only towel was lying in the shower cubicle, where she'd apparently thrown it after drying herself, and there was a bottle of shampoo on its side, leaking all over the sink. Muttering under his breath, Hal picked the towel up and hung it over the rail, then gingerly collected Max's clothes, draping them over the shower screen one by one.

When he was finished, he headed to his quarters, which were big enough for a double bed and a kitchenette. Here, he found most of his instant coffee scattered all over the fake marble bench top, with the rest trodden into the beige carpet. A trail of large, coffee-coloured footprints led to the door, back again, and then to the door once more. There was also a milk carton sitting on the bench, and the small fridge stood wide open, letting the cold air out. To complete the picture, there were three teaspoons stuck into his sugar bowl, all of them covered in coffee granules.

'That woman has to *go*,' growled Hal. Oh, he'd drop her off at the remote landing pad all right, but he had absolutely no intention of picking her up again.

Still muttering to himself – quietly, in case she heard him – Hal headed for the flight deck. He took the lift, and when he saw Clunk sitting at the console, without a coffee granule or wet towel in sight, he felt a surge of affection for the robot. Sure, Clunk dripped various fluids every now and then, and he could be irritatingly precise, but he didn't stroll into Hal's quarters and help himself, leaving a gigantic mess in the process. So, Hal was in a good mood as he sat in the co-pilot's chair. 'How are we doing? On track with the delivery?'

'Indeed,' said Clunk. 'We still have several hours in hand, and I don't foresee any problems.' He glanced at Hal. 'You performed admirably, rescuing those women from the asteroid field.'

Hal hesitated. 'Yeah, about that. The fighter pilot, Sam, wants us to take her back to the front line.'

Clunk shook his head. 'Impossible.'

'I know. I told her we'd lose the ship if we tried.'

'Well, I have some good news you can share with her. Some of her people are at the spaceport even now, and I'm sure they'll be very excited to see her.'

'That's good. I guess.'

'What's up, Mr Spacejock?'

'She's going back to fight in a war, Clunk. Other pilots are getting killed all around her, and... well, it's going to be her turn sooner or later. Just seems like a waste, that's all. She's hardly lived a life yet.'

'And what about the other woman?'

'Max?' Hal snorted. 'She's the one who should be flying

fighters into the teeth of the enemy. I've never met such a tough nut.'

Clunk hid a smile.

'What?' demanded Hal.

'Very few people get the better of you, Mr Spacejock. It seems to me you have a sneaking admiration for this Max.'

'Admiration? She almost dragged me into her bunk.'

'Well, at least she'll be leaving the ship soon.'

Hal nodded. 'Can you take a note? Remind me to buy another coffee mug, some fresh milk and a brand new towel.'

'Anything else?' asked the robot drily.

'Yeah. Carpet cleaner and a lock for my cabin door.' Hal hesitated. 'By the way, I need you to make a small change in our flight plan. Just a minor detail.'

'Oh?'

'If you check the map, you'll see a national park two hundred kilometres north-east of Space Port Delta.'

'And what is the significance of this national park?'

'We're going to drop Max there.'

Clunk looked surprised. 'We are?'

'Yeah. She's wanted by the law for something or other, and she's refusing to land at Delta.'

'I see. Well, let me check the area first. This is a large ship and we may not be able to land.' Clunk gestured, and the planet's surface appeared on the screen. A green circle hovered over Space Port Delta, and at Clunk's instruction, the map moved north-east. 'I can't see anything there,' he said, frowning at the screen.

'Punch in a bit.'

Clunks lips thinned, since the robot had a particular dislike for the term... which was the only reason Hal used it. Still, Clunk obeyed, and the map zoomed in on... empty land.

'That could be a landing pad,' said Hal, tilting his head to one side. 'I mean, it's not square, but–'

'That's a roof,' said Clunk. 'I can see the ridge cap.'

'Well it looked like a pad to me.' Hal gestured at the screen. 'How come there are no place names?'

'Map data was an optional extra, and a pricey one at that.' Clunk regarded Hal doubtfully. 'Are you sure about those directions?'

'Two hundred, north east. It's seared on my brain, because that's when she pulled my bathrobe up.'

Clunk's eyebrows rose.

'I'll explain later.' Hal gestured at the screen. 'Try one hundred, in case she was wrong.'

The map jumped, and then both of them cried out at once. 'There it is!' said Clunk.

'You got it!' said Hal.

Displayed on the screen was a huge area of dense trees and undergrowth, maybe eight or nine square kilometres in size. They could see a road winding through the trees, and in the middle of the national park there was a collection of buildings. Next to the buildings there was a car park and a row of landing pads with 01, 02 and 03 painted in the middle. 'Plug in the course and take us straight there,' said Hal.

Clunk obeyed, and their time of arrival was shown in local time: 10:20pm.

By now, the ship was dropping through the planet's atmosphere, and Hal could feel the buffeting despite their artificial gravity. Then, as they approached the surface, the screen switched to the view from an external camera. The terrain looked much like it had on the map, and it whipped past at an impressive speed. 'We're a bit low, aren't we?' remarked Hal.

64

'I want to stay below radar. If we land and take off again quickly, they won't notice we set our passenger down.' Clunk indicated the time, which read 10:12pm. 'You should go and tell Max that we're almost there. She must be ready to disembark the instant we touch down.'

Hal remembered the bathrobe. 'No, you can go.'

'I can't leave the flight deck, Mr Spacejock. The autopilot isn't working.'

'Go. I can hold her straight and level.'

'I think not.'

'Oh, come on! How hard can it be?'

'Much harder than you think, Mr Spacejock.'

'Well I'm not going below, and that's flat.' Hal crossed his arms to show how committed he was.

'Straight and level flight?' said Clunk at last. 'No acrobatics? No flying under bridges upside-down?'

'Not this time.'

Clunk overlaid an indicator on the screen. There was a circle with a horizontal line through the middle, and the lower half was shaded. 'That's an artificial horizon. Watch what happens when I lift the nose.' He did so, and the line shifted towards the bottom of the circle, reducing the size of the shaded area.

'Got it,' said Hal.

Clunk demonstrated several manoeuvres, including a bank in each direction and a brief, shallow dive. Each time, the indicator changed to show the ship's attitude compared to the ground below. 'Keep the line level, and in the centre of the circle,' he told Hal. 'Make small adjustments, and don't chase it.'

'All right, I can do that.' Hal gripped the second flight stick, which felt loose until Clunk switched control to him. Immediately, the stick became heavy, and there was a wobble or two in their course as Hal got a feel for it. Then he had it, and the big ship powered through the sky on a nice, level flight.

'That's good, Mr Spacejock. Excellent.'

Hal beamed, proud with himself. He rarely got the chance to fly, partly because Clunk was good at it, partly because Clunk wouldn't trust him to fly as much as a paper plane, and partly because their insurance policy expressly forbad Hal from going anywhere near the flight deck.

And now, here he was, in full control. Move the stick left, and the ship turned left. Move the stick right and it turned right. Press the little switches, turn the knobs and move the pedals under his feet, and...well, he had absolutely no idea what they did, so he decided to leave them alone. For now.

Meanwhile, Clunk was backing towards the lift, unwilling to take his eyes off Hal, the screen, or the controls.

'Go on!' said Hal. 'If you don't hurry up I'll have to land this thing as well.'

That got a reaction. Clunk darted into the lift and repeatedly pressed the button, and moments later Hal was alone in the flight deck. He released the controls long enough to crack his knuckles, and then he hunched forward and prepared himself for the challenge of *really* flying his ship.

*

The elevator reached the next level, and Clunk hurried down the corridor towards the passenger cabins. He was worried Mr Spacejock would actually try to land the ship, and he meant to be back in the flight deck as soon as possible.

Actually, he was worried about Mr Spacejock being at the controls in the first place, but he supposed humans flew ships all the time. It's just that they were so imprecise at...well, everything. With Mr Spacejock that went doubly so.

Clunk reached the cabins and turned left. There were three doors, all closed, and he realised he hadn't asked which two cabins housed their guests. He put the side of his head to the first door and listened, but couldn't hear anything over the rumble of the ship's engines.

Even as he stood there listening, the engines roared suddenly. Clunk froze, and he was on the point of racing back to the flight deck to take control when they throttled back again. What *was* Mr Spacejock doing up there? he wondered. There was no need to play with the throttles in level flight!

There were no more changes in the engine note, and time was passing, so Clunk came to a decision. He'd check each cabin in turn, very quietly, until he found Max. Raising his hand to the door controls, he cut the automatic lights before pressing the 'open' button.

The door slid open, and he peered into the darkened cabin. There was a shape in the bed, but who did it belong to? He didn't want to disturb the fighter pilot, not after everything she'd been through, so he crept into the cabin and bent over the sleeping form. Mr Spacejock hadn't really described either of the women, except to say the fighter pilot was particularly fetching. However, Clunk was relieved to see this one was wearing a blue bathrobe, although it was almost black in the near-darkness. That meant it had to be Max.

So, he reached out and shook her by the shoulder.

Max reacted instantly, her hand shooting out to grab him around the neck.

Clunk was even quicker. His own hand darted out, grabbing

her firmly by the wrist before she'd half-completed her own attack, stopping her clawed fingers inches from his throat. Max strained mightily but his arm was like solid rock, and she was forced to give up.

'Lights,' said Clunk.

Nothing happened.

'Night lights. Emergency lights. Switch lights...on.'

Again, nothing happened.

'I don't think they're listening,' said Max. 'Still, we don't need lights. Get in!' Then she saw his outline in the light spilling from the passageway, and she blinked. 'You're not Spacejock.'

'Correct. I'm Clunk, certified co-pilot.'

'Well look at you,' said Max in wonder. 'You're an old XK class. What a museum piece!'

'I'm an XG class robot, actually,' said Clunk, slightly miffed. In his younger days he used to dream of becoming an XK.

'Oh yeah. You don't have the square cooling vents, and those are series two eyes, not the series three.'

Despite himself, Clunk was impressed. 'You know your robots.'

'I picked up a little along the way,' said Max, with a shrug.

'Well, I'm afraid there's no time to chat now. We'll be landing any second. You must get dressed and gather your things. And Mr Spacejock would like his dressing gown back.'

Max got up, and without hesitation she shrugged off the bathrobe and handed it to Clunk. As she stood before him, completely naked, he saw the heavy bruising up and down her body. 'My goodness. Do you need treatment for that?'

'It's nothing. I've had worse.' Unconcerned, Max padded from the cabin and strode down the corridor to the bathroom, still naked. Moments later she emerged wearing her slacks, and after pulling a damp shirt over her head, she nodded towards the rear of the ship. 'I leave through the hold, yes?'

'Indeed.' Clunk eyed her wet clothes, then handed back the bathrobe. 'You'd better keep this. It's dark out, and you're going to freeze.'

'Thanks,' said Max, with a brief smile, and she put it on over her clothes.

They headed for the cargo hold, and on the way Clunk made light conversation. 'Where are you going after you land? Do you live near the national park?'

'Going?' Max frowned at him. 'I'm going nowhere. I have to wait while you unload your cargo at the spaceport, and then you will pick me up again.'

'We will?' said Clunk, surprised.

'If you take me to the spaceport I will be arrested, and you two will be thrown in jail as accomplices. So, we make a temporary stop.'

'Mr Spacejock told me you were in trouble with the authorities. What did you do, exactly?'

Max grinned. 'What didn't I do?'

She wouldn't elaborate, and by now they'd reached the hold. They strolled past rows and rows of pallets containing a variety of goods, all heavily shrink-wrapped, and then Clunk showed her to the very rear of the ship. 'As soon as we touch down, I'll lower the ramp from the flight deck. Once it's down, you must leave immediately.'

'Yeah, I know.'

'We'll take off as soon as you've reached a safe distance.'

'Got it.' Then Max frowned at him. 'But why do you have to go to the flight deck? You could stay here while Spacejock lands the ship.'

'That's not...advisable.'

Max saw his face, and laughed. 'So he's a wannabe, eh? I've met guys like him. All promise and no delivery.'

'Mr Spacejock frequently delivers,' said Clunk loyally. 'It's just not always in the right place.' He heard the engine note changing again, and stuck his hand out. 'I must return to the flight deck. It was a pleasure meeting you.'

'You too, Clunk.'

They shook, and Clunk turned for the flight deck. On the way back, he paused outside the fighter pilot's cabin. Should he warn her they were about to land? Then he heard the engines howling again, and he dismissed the idea and ran for the lift.

7

Once Clunk went below, Hal's attention was one hundred percent focussed on the little indicator the robot had set up for him. Unfortunately, after the first couple of minutes he discovered it was all a bit boring. Unless he moved the stick around, the line was happy to sit right in the middle of the circle. In fact, it didn't even move when Hal took his hands off the controls, and he had a sudden flash of suspicion. Was the autopilot working after all? Was Clunk pranking him?

Hal gave the controls a generous nudge, and he was startled when the ship reacted instantly, flipping onto its back. There was no sensation of hanging from his seat, thanks to the artificial gravity, but everything on the big screen was now upside-down. Hurriedly, Hal gave the controls another nudge, and he was relieved when the big ship completed the barrel roll and continued on an even keel, now the right way up again.

Then he noticed the altitude. His little test had sent the ship higher into the sky, and since they were supposed to be flying under the radar, he realised he had to head towards the deck. Gently this time, he pushed the stick forward, and the ship reacted by diving towards the ground. The artificial horizon was now completely shaded in, and the numbers on the altimeter were whizzing towards zero.

They were getting too close to the ground, so Hal pulled back hard on the stick, and the viewscreen filled with sky as they went into a vertical climb. By now a sprinkling of stars had appeared, so he shoved the stick forward and the stars whipped past the screen again as the *Albion's* nose dropped towards the ground. The engines roared as they drove the ship downwards, air whistling past the hull. The landscape was criss-crossed with black ribbons and covered in green blotches, which turned into roads and trees respectively as the ship hurtled towards them. By the time he could see power lines, mailboxes and individual leaves, illuminated by their landing lights, Hal was pulling back on the stick as though his life depended on it.

Which it did.

The *Albion* swooped between two hills and shot into the sky once more, and as they rocketed upwards Hal took a second to dash the sweat from his brow.

'It looks like you're trying to fly the ship,' said the Navcom calmly. 'Would you like some help with that?'

'It's not my fault!' growled Hal. 'She's behaving like a bad-tempered roller coaster with two hundred tons of ballast. There's got to be something wrong with the controls.'

'Let me scan for errors.' There was a pause, and then...

Ping!

'What's that?' demanded Hal.

'My scan identified the likely source of the problem. There's a flaw in the organic module attached to the console.'

'Don't spout error reports. Bypass it!'

'Organic module disconnected.'

The controls went slack in Hal's hands, and now he had no

control over the ship at all. Struck with a sudden insight, he frowned at the Navcom's camera. 'This organic module...'

'I have a message from ground control,' said the Navcom. 'They're asking you to file your amended flight plan.'

'Damn it!' Hal thought for a moment. 'Tell them we're heading into orbit.'

'That is not the optimum approach for the nature reserve.'

'I know that. We'll just have to break radar contact, then sneak down to ground level and try again.'

'Message relayed.'

'Now give me back control. And tell me the second they lose track of us!'

'Organic module activated.'

Hal pulled back on the stick, and the nose swung up once more. Before long, the viewscreen was filled with stars, and after a few minutes the Navcom reported a clear scan.

'Right. Now watch this,' said Hal, his face a study in concentration. With gentle movements he angled the *Albion* down towards the surface of the planet, until the hills and valleys looked like a shimmering claw gouging chunks from the landscape. He aimed for the biggest spread of water, using reverse thrusters to slow the descent, and they got closer and closer until they were zipping along just above the surface. A few moments later he turned the ship towards shore, skimming a boat ramp to get to the road. Then he angled the ship hard to port and followed the muddy track towards the horizon. A smile broke out on Hal's face, and he felt really pleased with himself. 'I'm getting the hang of this!'

The ship was strangely quiet with the engines throttled back, and the near-silence was broken only by the occasional splintering crash as the *Albion* flew through the trees lining the

73

road. Fortunately, the hull was built to withstand such minor inconveniences.

'Couldn't you maybe, just maybe, avoid a few?' asked the Navcom.

'Clunk said we had to fly low.'

Crack, crack, *crack!*

'Yes, but the risk of damage –'

'I'm just following orders. If you don't like it, blame Clunk.'

Twanggg!

Hal frowned. 'Weird trees they have around here. What sort of branch goes twang?'

Twanngg!

'Can't you fly just a little higher?' pleaded the Navcom.

'No. They'll spot us again.'

Twanngg. Twonngg.

'They'll be able to pinpoint our location without too much trouble,' said the Navcom. 'All they have to do is follow the swathe of blacked-out houses.'

Hal stared. 'The swathe of what?'

'Blackouts. Those noises you hear... they're power lines.'

'I thought they were low-hanging branches!'

Crack! Twannggg! Gzzzt!

'No, they're definitely power lines,' said the Navcom calmly.

Hal yanked back on the controls and the ship soared into the air, joints creaking under the strain. Then he remembered the radar, and quickly levelled off. As they zoomed along just above the main road, Hal kept an eye on the screen, particularly the incoming message icon. Fortunately it was unlit. 'All those emergency call outs will be good training for the repair crews.'

'Indubitably.'

'Might be an idea to erase those collisions from our logs.'

'Tampering with flight logs can lead to penalties of up to six months jail.'

'What about ripping up dozens of power lines?'

'Five years.' There was a slight pause. 'Records erased.'

They proceeded in silence, tracking the road through the gloomy landscape. Hal's hand grew sweaty on the control column, and he made himself dizzy as he scanned the instruments showing altitude, heading and speed. No matter which he concentrated on, the other two would start to move, and by the time he'd corrected those the first was off the scale again. And every time he remembered to check the viewscreen he discovered the road had veered off to one side. It had been the longest five minutes of his life, so far, and he was looking forward to Clunk's return.

Of all the displays, altitude was most important, and so he ended up watching that one and sparing the others a quick glance every time the Navcom made a disapproving noise.

After another minute or so of flight, the Navcom flashed up an icon. 'Nature reserve in range.'

'Ground Control haven't seen us, have they?'

'Negative.'

Hal glanced towards the lift, but there was just a hole where the doors should have been. No sign of Clunk, and their landing spot wasn't far now. 'When we get there, I'm going to set the ship to hover mode.'

'Very well,' said the Navcom.

'Er... how do I do that?'

'Throttle back. The thrusters will hold altitude for you.'

Hal eyed the screen, and now he could see the big green nature reserve ahead. It was pitch dark outside, but the low-light camera revealed a cluster of buildings in the middle, almost completely hidden by the tall, thick trees. Hal gained a touch of altitude, and when he judged they were in the right place, he eased back on the throttles.

Slowly, the ship came to a halt in mid air, directly above the buildings. To his relief, Hal heard the elevator arriving, and then Clunk came hurrying across the flight deck. He threw himself into the pilot's chair, transferred the controls back, then scanned the screen, the read-outs, and their position. 'We've arrived,' he said at last. Slowly, he turned to look at Hal. 'We arrived. We're here.'

'Don't sound so surprised.'

'Were there any problems?'

Hal recalled the upside-down flying, the broken power lines, and the branches he'd swept up, and their brief trip into orbit, and the call from Ground Control. 'No, none at all.'

Clunk turned to the screen and panned the camera, searching for a suitable landing spot. Eventually he located the landing pads, which seemed barely large enough for the ship, and he set the *Albion* down on the biggest. The landing legs creaked as they took the weight, and the engines tailed off to silence.

While he was busy, Hal studied the main screen, which showed they were hemmed in by a line of dank trees draped with creepers. It looked gloomy and damp, and there was a sinister air to the place. Still, they were just dropping Max here, and it wasn't like they'd ever return, so what did he care?

'Opening cargo hold door,' said Clunk. He switched to the rear camera, and Hal saw the big slab of metal lowering towards the ground. Then, the second it touched down, he saw Max striding from the hold. She stepped off the ramp, turned to give them a brief wave, then put some distance between herself and the ship.

'Hey, she's wearing my dressing gown!' cried Hal. 'Why didn't you get it back?'

'Her clothes were wet. It was the least I could do.'

'Great. I'll never see that again.'

'Of course you will, Mr Spacejock. You'll get it back when we return to pick her up.'

'But we're not picking her up again,' declared Hal.

'Yes we are. We're coming back for her after we've delivered our cargo. She told me so.'

'Clunk, my friend, you're as naive as she is,' said Hal patiently. 'I told her we'd come back, because otherwise she'd never have left the ship in the first place.'

'That's a pretty mean trick, Mr Spacejock.'

'I saved her life, didn't I? What more does she want?' Hal gestured at the screen. 'Come on, seal the hold and let's deliver this cargo.'

After a moment's hesitation, and with his lips pressed in a firm, disapproving line, Clunk obeyed.

As they lifted off again, Hal watched the robot out of the corner of his eye, trying to work out how Clunk managed to fly the *Albion* so calmly and efficiently. It looked the same as his own style, to Hal at least, but the result was wildly different. In Clunk's hands the ship rose steadily, and then, the second they were clear of the treetops, it flew straight ahead, nice and level.

There was a strained silence in the flight deck, but Hal didn't care. Anyway, he was pretty sure Clunk would snap out of it once they delivered their cargo. A successful delivery, and the money that came with it, always put the robot in a good mood. Then he thought of something. 'Did you see Sam while you were below decks?'

'Sam?'

'The Henerian Wing Commander.'

'No, I didn't disturb her.' Clunk adjusted the controls, and then, all of a sudden, he stared at Hal. 'Henerian? Surely you mean Mayestran.'

Hal shook his head. 'Henerian for sure.'

'But she can't be. You're confusing the two sides!' Frantically, Clunk sought an image in his database, then displayed it on the main screen. 'This is the Mayestran uniform. As you can see, it's red and black.'

'Sure, I can see it's red and black,' said Hal. 'But the thing is, hers is dark green.'

'It can't be!'

'It damn well is. Anyway, how would you know what uniform she's wearing? You've never met her.'

'Take the controls!' said Clunk desperately, and before Hal could obey the robot galloped for the lift. He hit the button, then vanished with a whoosh.

'Mayestran, Henerian... I don't see what all the fuss is about,' muttered Hal under his breath. 'I mean really... what's the difference?'

＊

Murtay felt a heady rush as he looked around at the other members of the cabinet meeting. He recognised most of them from news bulletins, and it was hard to believe he was sharing the same room with them, let alone sitting at the same table.

The surroundings were far more opulent than the stark conference room at his workplace, with heavy curtains and crystal chandeliers and expensive-looking paintings. The chairs were deep and comfortable, and even the water in his glass tasted fresh and sparkly.

There was little time to enjoy it all though, because a woman rose from her seat at the head of the table and called the meeting to order.

'We're meeting to discuss this senseless war between the Mayestrans and the Henerians, which even now inveigles its tendrils into our peaceful lives.'

Everyone nodded and looked sombre. The woman continued in the same vein for some time, using long words and even longer sentences. Murtay, a fan of getting to the point, felt himself zoning out, but he sat up with a start when Minister Harris stood up. The first speaker had just introduced her, and after staring around the table, Harris began. 'The Mayestran menace is a real threat to our way of life,' she said, and then she too went on for some time, using a lot of words but saying very little.

'Can't we just get on with it?' Murtay thought to himself. He saw several people looking at him, and he wondered whether he'd spoken aloud.

It seemed to work though, because the minister finally cut to the chase. 'After consultation with top-level bureaucrats,' she said, 'I bring you my bold plan to rid our system of the Mayestran fleet.'

There were plenty of surprised looks at this, and a few of those present looked hopeful.

'I'd now like to introduce Cylen Murtay, who assisted with some of the minor details. He will carry you through the basics, and then we'll discuss implementation.'

Everyone was now looking at Murtay, and he stood up quickly. This was his chance. This was the moment when he'd alter their future for the better. 'I'll e-explain the plan in just a moment,' he said, stammering slightly as the moment got to him. 'But first I have an animation to show you. Can I have the controller for the screen please?'

'We don't have any tech in this room,' someone said. 'It's insecure.'

'Everything we discuss ends up online,' said someone else.

Murtay was thrown by this unexpected setback, but he caught a hand gesture from Minister Harris which clearly meant... get on with it. So, he launched into an explanation, warning them about the Mayestrans' subtle approach to invasion, whereby they sought Henerian 'rebels' in the target system, whether or not they were actually there, before deploying increasing numbers of ships and troops until they had enough power to take over.

Then he spoke of his idea, using a flotilla of private ships, and the proposed trip to the asteroid belt, and the fusillade of rocks that would destroy the Mayestran fleet. And the longer he spoke, and the more detail he gave, the more the listening dignitaries gave each other sidelong glances and fidgeted in their seats.

He could tell it wasn't going well, but he didn't realise how badly until an elderly minister rapped on the table. 'Enough of this nonsense!' he cried. 'Giant space rocks? A gaggle of private vessels taking on the Mayestran fleet? You've lost your mind, young man!'

'I assure you, sir–'

'We've listened to this nonsense long enough. You may leave the room.'

There were nods and cries of 'hear hear', and before Murtay knew what was happening he was being bundled out of the high-level meeting. He looked to Minister Harris for support, but the expression on her face told him there would be no help from that direction. After the doors slammed to behind him, he decided the whole thing could have gone better.

Murtay left the building deep in thought. Could he wangle his way into another meeting with the president? No, he was certain that particular avenue would be closed to him now. He'd just have to find another way.

Cylen Murtay strode to his car, a determined look on his face. The safety of the Dolorian system was in his hands, and he knew exactly what to do next.

— 8 —

Clunk hopped from one foot to the other as the lift carried him below decks. 'She can't be Henerian. She *can't* be,' he muttered, over and over. The ground controller had warned him the Mayestrans were looking for Henerian rebels in the system, and he'd assumed the pilot Mr Spacejock had rescued was one of those tasked with the hunt. Never in his wildest dreams would he have guessed they'd picked up one of the rebels.

If the pilot *was* a Henerian rebel... no, it didn't bear thinking about. 'She can't be,' he said again. 'Mr Spacejock made a mistake. Mr Spacejock *always* makes mistakes.'

Still, there was that horrible nagging doubt.

The lift arrived on the passenger deck, and Clunk bolted down the corridor. Without ceremony, he opened one cabin door after another, until the glaring overhead light illuminated the fighter pilot asleep in her bunk. She looked peaceful, and a lock of dark hair had fallen across the bandage covering her forehead. She also had the blankets pulled up to her chin, which meant her uniform was hidden.

Clunk didn't have time for niceties. He grabbed the loose end of the blankets and pulled, yanking the covers from the bed. 'Oh no!' he groaned, as he saw the dark green uniform.

'She *is!*'

Sam Willet, Wing Commander in the Henerian Navy, opened her eyes and sat up. She stared at Clunk for a split second, then reached in vain for her sidearm. 'Who are you?' she demanded. 'What do you want?'

'You're... wearing the wrong uniform,' said Clunk, in a daze.

Sam looked down at herself. 'Looks right to me.'

'No, I mean you're supposed to be a Mayestran.'

'I've been fighting Mayestrans my whole life,' said the pilot, with a frown. 'Are you trying to be funny?'

Clunk was feeling anything but. Frantic with worry, he began to pace the small cabin. 'We'll get rid of your uniform. No! Not another one walking around naked. You can borrow a flight suit. Yes, yes, you can pretend you're married to Mr Spacejock. You've been together several months, and–'

'What is wrong with you?' demanded Sam. 'Why the flap?'

'No, it won't work. They'll question you individually, and you won't know that he takes four sugars in his coffee. They'll see through the deception, and you'll both be shot.' All of a sudden, Clunk came to a halt. 'Ms Willet–'

'Sam.'

'Ms Willet, the Mayestrans are looking for you.'

'I'm used to that.'

'No, they're right here in this system. Ships, and troops, and everything. They're going to search every ship at the spaceport, and anyone they discover hiding Henerians will be shot.'

'I shouldn't worry. It'll probably bounce right off you.'

'This is not the time for jokes!' said Clunk desperately. 'Mr Spacejock's life is in danger!'

'Tell him he'll get used to it. I did.'

Clunk stared at her. No matter what he said, she didn't seem to be taking him seriously. 'You understand that the Mayestrans are looking for you?'

'Yep.'

'And if they find you aboard this ship, they'll take you away? And they'll... they'll execute Mr Spacejock.'

'That's the usual deal, yeah.'

'Doesn't that worry you?'

'It's war. There's always some kind of drama.'

'Argh!' cried Clunk, unable to take any more of her laid-back attitude. He had to warn Mr Spacejock about the Mayestrans, and they had to get rid of the pilot immediately, if not sooner. Dashing from her cabin, he ran for the lift and hammered the button. Seconds later he emerged in the flight deck. 'She's a Henerian!' he shouted.

'Told you,' said Hal calmly.

'The Mayestrans are looking for her!'

'I bet they are.'

'No, they're looking for her right *here*, in this system. They have warships, and troops, and they're searching cargo ships at the spaceport. They're going to execute people hiding Henerians!'

Finally, someone reacted the way he expected them to.

'They're *what*?' demanded Hal, wide-eyed.

'Searches! And executions!'

'Why the hell didn't you tell me earlier?'

'I thought she was Mayestran! I thought we were taking her back to her people, and there'd be a big happy reunion.'

'Well you got one thing right,' growled Hal. 'The Mayestrans at the spaceport are going to be really happy to see her.'

Without a word, Clunk leaned over and took the controls.

With a twist and a yank on the stick, he turned the *Albion* in its own length, then powered back the way they'd come.

'What are you doing?' demanded Hal.

'She has to get off.'

'Yes, but... where?' Then Hal saw the green area ahead of them, in the distance. 'Oh no, you can't be serious.'

'It's the only way.'

'You're dumping her in the national forest, with Max? Are you mad?' Then Hal had another thought. He'd promised Sam he'd take her to safety, and unlike the line he'd fed Max, this one was for real. 'But Clunk, that means we have to come back for *both* of them!' he groaned.

'Take the controls,' said Clunk desperately, and he ran for the lift. 'I'll go and make sure she's ready to leave.'

'Be sure to lend her my dressing gown,' Hal called after him. 'Oh wait, you can't,' he said acidly. 'You've already given it away.'

Clunk took the lift and charged along the passage to Sam's quarters. He found her sitting on the edge of the bunk, gingerly feeling her forehead. 'You have to get your things,' he said. 'We're dropping you off in a national park. After we've unloaded, we'll come back and pick you both up.'

'Both?'

'We already left Ms Damage behind.'

'Why?'

'She's wanted by the authorities.'

'This really isn't your day, is it?' said Sam, with a smile.

'Once on the ground you must hide,' Clunk told her. 'Don't talk to anyone. Don't tell them who you are, or which side you're on.'

Sam indicated her uniform. 'They might take a wild guess.'

'Wait here.' Clunk ran to Hal's cabin, where he yanked an old flight suit off the rack. Then he ran back again. 'Put this on over the top. Hide the uniform. Quick!'

Sam obeyed, standing up and dressing quickly. The flightsuit was too large for her, but she made do by rolling the cuffs up.

'Now, to the cargo hold!' cried Clunk, and he took her hand and practically dragged her along the corridor.

Hal strode towards the *Albion's* elevator, wiping his hands on his flightsuit. He was on the passenger deck, and he'd just completed a small but vital task.

After dropping Sam in the national park, the *Albion* had flown to Space Port Delta and set down. That was barely ten minutes ago, after which Hal and Clunk had raced to the hold. There, Hal had hidden Clunk away, because the last thing they needed was for the Mayestrans to come aboard and quiz the robot about any Henerians they might have picked up on their travels.

Hal could lie through his teeth, no problem. He could even stand severe torture, such as caffeine withdrawal and the slow, measured destruction of his boxed, mint condition figurine of Dick Spacewad, interstellar hero and all-round good guy.

Clunk, on the other hand, was truthful to a fault, and as Hal took the lift to the flight deck, he pictured the scene. Two interviewers in black leather coats. A standard lamp shining in the robot's face. The very first question:

'*Clunk, did you pick up a Henerian rebel?*'
'*Yes.*'

And that would be that, thought Hal. He'd be arrested, executed, *and* he'd lose his priceless Dick Spacewad figurine to a pair of thugs in jackboots.

So, they'd hit upon a simple plan: Hide Clunk. It had taken a while to decide on the right place, but after much argument the matter was settled, and now Hal was on his way to the flight deck to deal with the Mayestrans... once they showed up.

The lift arrived, and he strode to the pilot's chair and sat down.

Ding dong.

'Doorbell, right?' said Hal.

'Correct,' said the Navcom.

'All right, let them in.'

'Do I look like a butler to you?'

Muttering under his breath, Hal got up and crossed to the airlock. The inner door was already open, so he strolled inside and pressed the button to open the outer door.

Thud!

Without warning, the inner door closed behind him, shutting him into the small, enclosed space. Hal sighed, then pressed the button to close the inner door. Sure enough, the outer door swung open, and he saw a group of three people standing on the passenger ramp, just outside the ship. Two of them, a man and a woman, wore red and black uniforms with matching peaked caps, and the woman's uniform had insignia on the sleeves, marking her as the officer in charge. She was around forty, with blonde hair and a severe, impatient expression. The younger Mayestran's jacket was plain, and he was a fresh-faced youth of maybe eighteen or nineteen.

The other member of the group was an elderly man with grey hair, and he wore blue overalls and carried a clipboard.

'Stand aside for the inspection!' barked the Mayestran woman. 'Now! Quickly!'

Hal looked around the cramped airlock, then shrugged and stood with his back to the wall. The other three entered, crowding him, and then the Mayestran officer nodded towards her underling.

The man reached up and pressed the button to open the inner door. Instead, the outer door slammed to. Frowning, he pressed the button to close the inner door, and in reply there was a rude buzz.

'Inner door already closed,' said a mechanical voice.

'We're having technical issues,' explained Hal. Then, with a start, he realised he'd almost given the game away with his first words. 'I mean, *I'm* having technical issues. Just me, not anyone else. Well, actually, to be completely honest with you, my *ship* is having–'

'Shut up!' barked the Mayestran officer. 'You will speak when spoken to.'

Hal shut up.

Meanwhile, the Mayestran private was looking around for another button marked 'open inner door', since the first one he'd found clearly wasn't doing anything. Slowly, hesitantly, he reached for the button marked 'open outer door', and pressed it.

'Outer door already closed,' said a mechanical voice.

The private's face cleared, because now there was only one button left. Happy now, he pressed the one marked 'close outer door'.

Buzz! *'Both doors are closed,'* said the voice.

That's when Hal realised something. The electronic voice wasn't the one he was used to. No, it was a little more...intelligent. And female. And...with a jolt, he recognised it. The Navcom! A grin spread across his face, because for once the ship's computer wasn't making *his* life hell. No, the Navcom was winding up the Mayestrans!

The officer was growing impatient, and she reached out and jabbed at a button.

Buzz! *'Emergency alarm activated,'* said the Navcom. *'Lethal response in ten. Nine. Eight...'*

'Fix this!' shouted the officer. 'Fix this now!'

Hal pressed the same button, and the inner door instantly swung open. The officer gave him an angry look, but his face was innocent.

Then, one after another, they all trooped into the flight deck, where the newcomers frowned at the shards of plastic littering the floor, and at the gaping hole where the elevator doors should have been. 'What is the meaning of this?' demanded the officer. 'What happened here?'

'My co–' began Hal, before snapping his mouth shut. He almost said 'co-pilot', which would have let the cat out of the bag. 'I, er, got trapped in the lift,' he finished lamely.

'Someone locked you in?' demanded the officer. 'Who did this? Was it Henerian rebel scum?'

Aha! thought Hal. *Bet Clunk would have said 'yes' to that one!* 'Nobody did this. It's a new ship, and things keep going wrong. We–, I mean *I*, am going to have her serviced.' Suddenly Hal could feel the sweat on his brow, and his earlier confidence evaporated. Conversation was a minefield, and he resolved to say as little as possible.

'I am First Lieutenant Ferrast of the Mayestran Navy. Under section thirty of our border protection code, your ship is hereby subject to a thorough inspection, and your crew must make themselves available this instant for questioning.'

'It's just me here,' said Hal. 'I'm the whole crew.'

'I see. And what is your cargo?'

'Pallets,' said Hal.

'And on the pallets?'

Hal had no idea, because he'd left all the minor details to Clunk. As long as they weren't transporting anything illegal, or valuable artworks which turned out to be rocks and stuffed cows, he really didn't care. Then inspiration struck. 'Goods,' he said.

'What kind of goods?'

She's really good at this interrogation stuff, thought Hal. If he wasn't careful, he was going to seem suspicious. 'They're the kind of goods that come on pallets,' he said at last.

'You think this is funny?' demanded Lieutenant Ferrast. 'Twenty ships I've searched, and I have another thirty to go. I keep telling my superiors it would be quicker to confiscate them, lock up the pilots and burn the cargo, but no, he insists I do these time-wasting interviews.'

Hal said nothing.

'I ask again, what is your cargo?'

'Herbs,' said Hal quickly. 'And farm equipment.' He decided to cover a few more bases, in the hope that one of them would match whatever pallet she happened to check. 'There's some children's toys as well, crates of car parts, robot brains, a batch of ebook readers, coffee mugs, costume jewellery, a dining table, women's clothing–'

'Enough!' snapped the Lieutenant. 'Sundry goods will suffice.'

Hal hoped they'd suffice too.

'Now, let us go below. I need to see the hold, every cabin, every corridor...everywhere!'

'What are you looking for?'

'You will not speak!' growled the Lieutenant. She gestured

towards the lift, and after a moment's hesitation, the others got in. She followed, and eyed the buttons suspiciously. 'You have three decks?'

Hal nodded. 'The lower one isn't fitted out yet.'

'We will go there first.' Ferrast pressed the lowest button, and the lift started to move. It stopped soon after, and the indicator showed they were on the middle deck. The Lieutenant's lips thinned, but she masked her annoyance. 'We will check this deck.'

Hal led them to his own cabin, where the Lieutenant took one look at the spilled coffee and snorted. 'You live like a pig.'

Hal was silent. He'd once met a race of people who not only lived like pigs, they *were* like pigs, but this wasn't the time to reveal that particular gem.

After poking around in the walk-in robe and getting the younger Mayestran to peer under the bed, the Lieutenant turned away from the entrance and strode to the bathroom. 'Would it kill you to clean up?' she demanded, as she saw the damp, wrinkled towel and the puddle of shampoo.

Hal pressed his lips together. It was bad enough Max had left all the mess in the first place, but getting blamed for it was almost too much.

Next, they looked into the nearby cabin, which Clunk used from time to time. It was neat and tidy, with no belongings and no signs of occupation at all. 'Better,' said the Lieutenant. She ran a fingertip across the desk and inspected it. 'Much better.'

By now, Hal was growing impatient. The woman was meant to be checking his cargo and looking for rebels, not rating his housekeeping skills. He pictured Sam Willet waiting in the dark, damp forest, completely alone apart from the headstrong township pilot, Max. He was meant to pick them both up again, and he hadn't even unloaded his cargo, or found a new freight job, or loaded *that* cargo yet, and he couldn't start on any of those things until the Mayestrans cleared off.

Meanwhile the elderly Dolorian in the blue overalls said nothing, and simply jotted down notes on his clipboard from time to time.

The Lieutenant closed Clunk's door and led the way to the opposite side of the main corridor, where a short passage ended in three doors, one on each wall. She opened each in turn, and frowned as she saw the wrinkled blankets and dented pillows in two of them. 'You had passengers?'

'No, I use these myself,' said Hal. 'When I can't sleep, I like a change of scenery.'

The Lieutenant entered Max's cabin, and inspected the pillow closely. Then she pinched at something, and held it up to the light. 'This is not your hair colour.'

'Must be left over from an earlier run,' said Hal.

'Do you not wash the sheets between passengers?' demanded the Lieutenant.

'Well, it's not like I charge five star rates,' said Hal reasonably. 'Plus they can always bring their own.'

The Dolorian took a note.

'Where and when did this passenger leave your ship?'

'It was a jungle world, a few days ago. Don't ask me the name, I visit ten to twenty of these places a week.'

The Lieutenant nodded, then gestured towards the passageway. 'I wish to see the lowest level next, and then the hold.'

'Sir,' began the younger Mayestran. 'Shouldn't we see the hold while we're actually on this level? The buttons–'

'Lower level next,' insisted the Mayestran officer, and they all made their way to the lift.

92

Hal had only been down there once himself, and given the flaky elevator controls he wasn't a hundred percent sure he'd ever get down there again. However, this time they were carried down to the lowest level, where they were met by a dark, cavernous area with poor lighting and dozens of criss-crossed girders.

Hal and the Dolorian stayed near the lift, while the Mayestrans checked the area from one end to the other.

'How come you let them do this?' Hal whispered to the old man. 'It's your planet, right?'

The Dolorian shrugged. 'Once, years ago, we'd have stood up to them. Now, they have warships and troops, and we have nothing.'

The Mayestrans returned, satisfied the area was empty, and everyone took the lift back up to the... flight deck.

'I wanted the second level,' snapped the Lieutenant, pressing the middle button repeatedly. Each time she pressed it there was a buzz, until she gave up in disgust. 'Lower your cargo ramp,' she told Hal. 'We will go in the back way.'

'How like a Mayestran,' murmured the Dolorian.

'What did you say?' demanded the Lieutenant, staring at him.

'You thought of a solution so quickly,' said the elderly man. 'It's obviously a Mayestran trait.'

Meanwhile, Hal approached the console. 'Navcom, cargo ramp down.'

'No it isn't.'

'I mean... lower the cargo ramp.'

'Complying.'

There was a distant whine of hydraulics, followed by a crunch. Hal winced at the sound, and he was just wondering how much the repairs to his ship were going to cost when the

93

Mayestran officer rounded on her subordinate. 'Our car. You parked behind the ship!'

Meanwhile, there was another whine of hydraulics as the ramp went up, then down again.

Crunch!

Whiiine!

Crunch!

Whiiine!

'Okay Navcom,' said Hal, struggling not to laugh. 'You can stop lowering the ramp now.'

'Are you sure?' asked the computer calmly. 'A couple more goes and I'll have it all the way down to the ground.'

Hal eyed the Mayestran Lieutenant, who had a face like thunder. 'Yeah, pretty sure.'

Crunch!

'Ramp fully extended,' said the Navcom, who'd never been particularly good at obeying orders.

Without a word, the Mayestrans hurried into the airlock. The Dolorian gave Hal a gleeful thumbs-up before following them out, and Hal brought up the rear.

9

After Sam stepped off the *Albion's* cargo ramp, she climbed down the side of the concrete landing pad and made her way to the nearby trees. It was late at night, but the weather was much warmer than she expected. In fact it was almost tropical: muggy and humid, with a strong smell of rotting vegetation in the air.

The ship took off behind her, deafening her with its roar, blinding her with its jets. She craned her neck to watch the huge vessel lumbering overhead, barely clearing the treetops before disappearing to the southwest.

Then she took stock of her situation, which was the first step from the survival training manual.

Well, her head ached, her throat was dry and she'd forgotten to bring any water. Also, she had no weapon, no local knowledge whatsoever, and she was so tired she could barely keep her eyes open.

On the plus side, she knew she was lucky to be alive. Ten years she'd been fighting in the war, ten years during which familiar faces had vanished one by one. It didn't take much to die out there in space, and she was grateful to Hal for the rescue.

As she got her bearings, she recalled seeing a cluster of

buildings nearby. They'd been visible from the top of the cargo ramp, and once she'd oriented herself, she set off in the general direction.

Shelter. Warmth. Water. Food.

Those were the basic steps in her survival training. Shelter was easy, thanks to the buildings. Warmth wasn't a problem, since she was already uncomfortably hot wearing Hal's spare flight suit over the top of her uniform. The air was heavy with moisture and she could hear water dripping all around her. And as for food... well, the *Albion* would be back in an hour or two, so that wasn't a priority.

In fact, she didn't expect to be waiting long at all, but training was training. And if something happened to Hal, and she was stuck out here for a day or two, it was better to be prepared than surprised.

She made her way through the trees, and emerged in a large area containing a number of buildings. They were all in darkness, locked up, with shutters on the windows. She saw signs and hoardings on each building, identifying them as a cafe, an amusement arcade, an information kiosk and more. Sam was surprised at that, since this was meant to be a national park, and that usually meant buildings for conservation and land management. She thought it all looked a bit tacky, but what would she know? After years of war, her own planet's national parks had all been strip-mined for resources, and she'd never met a tourist in her life.

She approached the cafe first, checking the double glass doors. Not surprisingly, they were locked up tight. She cupped her hands to the window and looked inside, and she saw dozens of tables with the chairs on top. At the back there was a counter with ordering screens and payment points, all of them blank and powered down.

Well, even if the place were open for business, it wasn't like she was carrying any money.

Sam went round the back of the building, looking for somewhere to hole up until the *Albion* returned. There was a lean-to covering half a dozen dumpsters, and she wrinkled her nose at the sour, rotting smell. What with that and the smell of dank jungle, she was beginning to wish she was back in space.

Sam didn't fancy the lean-to, so she moved on to the next building. As she rounded the corner, she heard footsteps approaching fast from behind. She reacted instantly, half-turning, grabbing an outstretched arm and pivoting the other person over her hip, slamming them back-first onto the ground.

There was a grunt, and then Sam realised she was looking down at Max Damage. 'What did you want to sneak up on me for?' demanded Sam.

Max was thoroughly winded, struggling for breath, and she couldn't reply. After a moment or two, Sam helped her sit up, and Max sat there, drawing breaths and looking worse for wear. 'Saw someone sneaking around,' she managed at last. 'Didn't know it was you.' She gave Sam an admiring look. 'You can take care of yourself.'

'Of course. Basic training.'

'For a fighter pilot? Why?'

'A Henerian must be ready for every eventuality,' intoned Sam. 'Plus it keeps me fit.'

Wincing, Max got up. 'Why did Spacejock leave you here?'

Sam explained about the Mayestrans, eliciting a smile from Max.

'So now we're both wanted,' she said. 'I'm glad you're here, though. I wasn't sure Spacejock would come back for me, but now it's guaranteed.'

'Why?'

Max gave her a look.

'No!'

'He would do a lot for you, I think.' Max shrugged. 'For me, not so much.'

Sam didn't know what to make of that. She'd only spent ten minutes with Hal, and to her he was just a civilian pilot. 'You want him, you can have him,' she told Max. 'Me, I have a war to fight.'

They walked to the front of the building, where Max nodded towards the amusement arcade's gaudy frontage. 'This doesn't fit,' she said. 'It's all wrong for a national park.'

'I was thinking the same.'

'Come. We'll walk to the entrance. There may be signs.'

'What if Hal comes back?' asked Sam.

'We'll hear him. Anyway, he's got to unload his cargo and find a new job. He may be hours yet.'

'How are your bruises?'

'Which ones?' asked Max drily. Then she gestured. 'I'll live. Come on.'

They set off down the road, flanked on both sides by gloomy trees, the branches draped with creepers which hung almost to the ground. Their footsteps were loud in the eerie quiet, since there was little noise apart from a few muted insects.

'Have you been here before?' asked Sam. 'The national park, I mean?'

'No.'

'How did you know about it?'

'When I get to a new planet, I note all the landing pads

nearby. You never know when you might want to leave in a hurry.'

'Why do the authorities want you?'

'That's my business,' said Max, and she clammed up.

They walked in silence for a kilometre or two, until a fence came into view. 'There's something wrong,' said Max immediately.

It just looked like a fence to Sam. Tall, perhaps, but not that strange. However, as they got closer she realised she'd misjudged the scale, and the fence was much taller than she thought, and built from thick, heavy-duty wire. Worse, there were four cables strung along the top, and from the ceramic insulators she knew they were live. 'It's a bit heavy on the security.'

'Not security,' muttered Max. 'Look. The top is angled inwards.'

'They're trying to keep something *in*?' By now they'd reached the fence, which was at least five metres tall, and Sam glanced over her shoulder at the trees. 'What, exactly?'

Max ignored her, and made her way to a small wooden kiosk near a gigantic pair of gates. It appeared to be a ticket booth, facing away from her, and there was a map of the park pasted to a big signboard nearby. Before she could study the map, or check the sign around the front of the kiosk, there was a hair-raising roar from the trees. It was so deep and loud Sam was forced to cover her ears, and given the size of creature needed to make that much noise, she now realised why the fence was so high.

'This isn't the national park,' hissed Max, who'd hurried over to the map. 'It's a *wildlife* park. We're trapped in here with a load of savage animals!'

It was dark outside, but Hal could see dozens of ships surrounding his own on the landing field, each illuminated by spotlights as ground crews loaded, unloaded and serviced them. There was a huge variety of vessels, though none were as new or as large as the *Albion*.

As he strolled down the passenger ramp, a flash lit up the nearby ships. At the back of the *Albion*, wedged beneath the cargo ramp, was a dull green vehicle which had been reduced to the thickness of a railway buffet sandwich. It was busy sparking and burning away, and as Hal watched, it erupted again, hurling glowing sparks across the landing pad. Then half a dozen maintenance workers ran forward with extinguishers, and the fire was quickly put out.

Hal followed the Mayestrans to the rear of his ship, and by the time they reached the foot of the big, solid cargo ramp, the remains of the car were glowing dully. They certainly weren't glowing as much as the Mayestran Lieutenant, who was struggling to contain her rage.

The air was thick with powder from the fire extinguishers, and Hal coughed as he got a mouthful. 'Better go inside,' he said. 'This stuff is deadly.'

They hurried up the ramp and into the hold, where several dozen pallets of goods were laid out in neat rows. They barely filled a quarter of the hold, but the job was paying well and that was all Hal cared about.

The Mayestrans walked straight past the pallets, barely sparing them a second look. Instead, they began to inspect the walls, opening hatches to peer inside at the wiring and electronic equipment.

'Watch out!' cried Hal, as the Mayestran private reached into a recess.

'There's something in–'

Flashh!

There was a bang, and the young man was hurled backwards, trailing an arc of smoke. He landed across a pallet of goods and lay there, stunned.

'Those are the main circuit breakers, you idiot!' shouted Hal. He only knew this because Clunk had pointed them out, while telling him to never, ever reach inside.

The Mayestran sat up, shaking his head to clear it. His hair was standing on end, and there was a distant, slightly mad look to his expression, but the Dolorian helped him to his feet, and the young man seemed to have survived the shock with no lasting damage.

'Just... be careful,' Hal advised him. Then he glanced at the pallet, and he did a double-take. The young man's fall had torn the plastic, and Hal could clearly see a bronze, metal hand underneath, fingers splayed. Of all the pallets to land on, the fool had struck the one where Clunk was hiding! Moving quickly, while trying not to attract attention, Hal crossed to the pallet and reached down to tuck the plastic around the metal fingers. He felt them move as Clunk's grip tightened on the loose ends, and when he glanced down the plastic was once again covering the robot's extremities.

By now, the Mayestran Lieutenant had found the lockers, and with a sinking feeling Hal realised he'd left the spare helmets inside. One belonged to Max, which wasn't a problem, but the other, Sam's, was a dull green colour... the colour of a Henerian Navy uniform.

'Explain,' said Ferrast, holding the helmets up.

'They're spares. I got them cheap from a trader.'

'This one is military issue.'

'Yeah, I know. I thought I could make a few credits selling it on.'

'Parasite,' muttered Ferrast, and she threw the helmets back in the locker.

Meanwhile, the private had found the launch tube, and he climbed inside to inspect the jetbike. 'Sir,' he called out, his voice echoing inside the tube. 'This device has been used recently.'

The lieutenant went to look, and the moment both of them were inside the launch tube, the elderly Dolorian turned to Hal and opened his overalls, revealing a bundle of crackly tinfoil. It was the emergency spacesuit Sam had worn, and across the top, near the neckline, were the words 'Property of the Henerian Navy'.

Hal stared at it in shock. He'd forgotten all about the thing, and he realised Max must have tossed it somewhere after getting Sam out of it.

'Relax,' murmured the Dolorian. 'I'll get rid of it for you.'

'Thanks,' muttered Hal.

By now the Mayestrans were climbing back out of the launch tube. 'Why did you use the jetbike?' demanded Ferrast, after she'd straightened her uniform.

Hal thought quickly... for him. 'A passenger of mine paid for a joyride,' he said at last.

'That's a misuse of safety equipment. You ought to be fined.' Despite her words, the Lieutenant's attention was now focussed on the cargo rather than Hal's past indiscretions. She walked to the nearest pallet, fortunately not the one Clunk was shrink-wrapped to, and she was just reaching down to tear into the plastic when there was a clatter of footsteps from the cargo ramp.

Hal looked round to see a group of six spaceport workers entering the cargo hold, their leader a tall man in a white overalls. He had a crew cut, and the overhead lights gleamed off his scalp.

'Halt!' shouted the Lieutenant. 'Who gave you permission to enter?'

'I've got your permission right here,' said the man.

Hal watched, spellbound, because he was convinced things were about to kick off. If this were a movie, the man would pull out a huge gun and... blam, blam! The Mayestrans would get blasted, and the man would stand over them, face the camera and utter a witty comment.

But to Hal's disappointment, the man pulled out a small leather wallet instead of some triple-barrelled space blaster. 'Here's my authorisation,' he said, and he showed the card inside to the Lieutenant. 'Now please move aside. This cargo is needed urgently.'

'We haven't searched it yet!' protested the Lieutenant.

'You don't have to. We'll take it from here.'

Hal expected the Mayestrans to fight back, ordering the men off the ship, or shooting at them, or something.

Again, he was disappointed. The Lieutenant's face was a picture as she backed away, gesturing towards the cargo. 'It's all yours.'

Hal didn't know what kind of ID card the man had, but he sure would have liked one for himself. Then he thought of something more practical. 'Hey, it's supposed to be payment on delivery!'

'You the freighter pilot?' demanded the man, looking him up and down.

'Yeah. Hal Spacejock.'

The man took out a commset, swiped at the screen, then

tapped on it. 'There's your payment,' he said, displaying the screen. 'Now let us unload in peace.'

Hal nodded, and the man gestured to his fellow workers. There was a whine of electric motors, and Hal watched a big forklift cresting the cargo ramp before rolling into the hold. It scooped up a pallet and backed away again, vanishing as it drove back down the ramp. Almost immediately, it came back again, and then Hal realised the men were using several forklifts in tandem, in order to empty the hold as quickly as possible. He frowned at that, because had he known the cargo was *that* urgent, he'd have charged double.

Then he saw the pallet Clunk was strapped into being picked up, and he suddenly spotted the flaw in the hiding place he'd suggested to the robot. The men were going to take the cargo away, Clunk with it, and there was nothing he could do about it. Seconds later, the pallet with Clunk on it disappeared down the ramp, and another big forklift came back for more.

'We'll be on our way,' said the Lieutenant, who'd been watching the operation too. 'Carry on, Mr Spacejock. Sorry to trouble you.'

Surprised at her subservient attitude, Hal could only nod. As he watched the two Mayestrans and the Dolorian making their way off the ship, he wondered again what sort of ID card the spaceport worker was carrying.

Unloading was nearly complete now, and the workers were beginning to file out. Hal spotted his chance, and he intercepted one of them near the rear of the hold. 'Rush job, eh?'

The man ignored him. He was well-built, dressed in white overalls, and he had a crewcut hairstyle just like his leader. In fact, looking around, Hal noticed all of the workers were of a similar athletic build – even the women. Swap their nondescript overalls for combat fatigues, and he could easily see them as a squad of soldiers. He eyed the cargo, wondering what he and Clunk had just brought to Dolor, then put it out of his mind. There was only one question he needed to ask, and that was... where were they taking the goods? And more importantly, where were they taking Clunk?

Okay, *two* questions.

'Did you have to come far to pick this up?' asked Hal, as another of the workers marched past.

The indirect, chatty approach wasn't getting the results he hoped for, and there were only two pallets left now. Desperate, Hal went to the ramp and looked down at the scene below. There were four trucks standing nearby, parked in a line with their canvas covers pulled back. Three forklifts were operating together, nipping between the goods vehicles as they loaded the pallets. Meanwhile, a dozen men and women were scanning barcode labels on the pallets with hand-held readers, then checking the results off on their thinscreens. It was all very organised and efficient, and there was an unmistakably military precision to the whole operation.

But which military? thought Hal. Then he remembered the way the Lieutenant had deflated when the cargo guy had shown her his ID, and it wasn't hard to put two and two together. He knew right then that he was looking at a group of Mayestrans, and he grew even more concerned at the thought of the cargo he'd just handed over. What if they were invading Dolor, and he'd just delivered all the bits and pieces to make a bomb, or armed drones, or a batch of killer robots? Talk about a trojan horse!

The last pallet was picked up, and Hal was wracked with indecision as he watched it being carried down the ramp. He couldn't collect Max and Sam without Clunk, because the ship wouldn't get off the landing pad without the robot at the controls. Therefore, he had to get Clunk back as a matter of urgency.

On the other hand, he couldn't just ask these people to rip open a pallet and give Clunk back, because they were Mayestrans and there'd be questions, if not a full-on interrogation.

So, he came to the only possible decision. Striding to the controls, he waited until the forklift reached the landing pad, then pressed the button to retract the ramp. As it began to rise, he hurried down the incline and stepped neatly off the edge, jumping down onto the concrete apron right beside the burnt-out wreck of the groundcar.

Hal looked down at himself, and in the semi-darkness he decided his off-white flightsuit was a close enough match to the overalls the Mayestrans were wearing. They were still busy, checking the cargo and loading the trucks, and so Hal strode to the third vehicle in line and casually clambered up to the cab. He sat down and studied the controls, which looked like a doddle after the nine-hundred-odd buttons on the *Albion's* flight console. Then, hands gripping the wheel, he took a deep breath and waited for the convoy to get under way.

10

Sam could hear something big and heavy moving amongst the trees, and then it roared again, shaking the leaves and making the creepers shiver and sway. Whatever it was, Sam knew it was huge, and she also knew she didn't want to meet it.

So, she turned and ran towards the kiosk. It was the only shelter for hundreds of metres, and their only chance at safety. 'Quick, inside!' she called to Max.

Max was still eyeing the trees, and then she raised her arm and shook her fist at the sky. 'When you come back, Spacejock,' she yelled angrily, 'I'm going to break every bone in your puny little man-child body!'

'Never mind that now,' muttered Sam. 'Get the damned kiosk open.'

They hurried to the door, which was fastened with a large padlock. Neither of them had any tools, and when Sam tried to bash it open with a rock, the rock just split in two in her hands. She tossed the pieces aside, then ran to the main gates. There were two sets, one behind the other. They were four metres tall, topped with barbed wire, and there was a thick chain looped between the bars of the inner set.

'I'm going to kill him,' growled Max, as she inspected the chain. Disgusted, she released it and turned to look at the jungle. 'The creature is that way,' she said, pointing. 'We go the other way, along the fence.'

Sam stared at her. 'A place this size, there's got to be more than one creature!'

'Maybe the others are sleeping. Come, follow.'

There was no alternative, because the road they'd used to reach the park entrance ran right past the spot the deep, bellowing roaring sounds had come from. So, they set off together, following the fence and hoping to circle back to the buildings.

Never mind the smell of those bins, thought Sam, as she pushed her way past a dense bush. *Right now I'd climb straight into one, rotten garbage or not.*

Fortunately there were no trees next to the fence, so they didn't have to contend with creepers and trunks, but the undergrowth was still thick and the going was slow.

Max kept up a running commentary, muttering to herself as she detailed all the ways she was going to make Hal Spacejock pay. 'Dropped us in the wrong park, left us with no weapons, no defence against huge, angry monsters. Let's see how he likes it. I'll take his ship, boot him out and fry him with his own jets. I'll gut him, and hang his dried kidneys on my rear view mirror. I'll–'

Sam never found out what other horrors Max intended to perpetrate on Hal's hapless body, because they came across a small path leading into the jungle, at right-angles to the fence. Max turned left, and Sam followed her between the trees. Twenty minutes later, the path opened on the clearing with the original cluster of buildings.

'Where are we going to hide?' asked Sam.

In reply, Max gathered up a rock and carried it to the amusement arcade, where she heaved it at the glass door.

There was a crash as the window shattered, and then Max felt inside for the latch. Seconds later, using all her strength, she hauled the big sliding door open. 'Inside. Now.'

Sam needed no second bidding. She did wonder why the large creatures were allowed to roam freely, and why there was no fence separating them from the buildings, and therefore the tourists, but she assumed they were released from their pens at night as a security measure. Who in their right mind would break in *here*, with giant angry creatures roaming around?

Inside, they found a collection of amusement machines, several cafe tables and a counter. Behind the counter was an office door, and this one wasn't locked. Max waved Sam through, then closed the door and pushed a desk against it.

'I shouldn't worry about that,' said Sam. 'The size of that thing, I doubt it could even get into the building.'

'Did you see it?'

'Uh-uh. Too busy trying to hide. Sounded huge, though.'

'I'm going to kill that Spacejock guy,' growled Max. 'The national park is two hundred klicks north-west of Space Port Delta, I told him. Sure, he says. I'll memorise that. Idiot! He brought us to the wrong place!'

'How do you know?'

'This isn't the national park. Wildlife park, it said. The only wildlife park I know is a hundred klicks north-*east* of Delta. Triple idiot!' Then Max brightened. 'Hey, maybe when he lands again, the creature will eat him. Then we take his ship and fly away.'

'The creature... what do you think it is?'

'Dangerous,' said Max shortly.

'Yes, but what *kind* of creature?'

'Wild *and* dangerous,' said Max. 'And hungry, too.'

Sam glanced at the ceiling. She pictured the thing ripping

the roof off and gobbling them down like a couple of tinned sardines, and she shivered at the thought. She'd fought in countless battles, against enemies far more dangerous than a big, hungry creature, but she'd never felt this helpless before.

Meanwhile, Max was pulling open drawers and cupboards, looking for anything they could use. Sam looked around too, and she realised the office was fairly large, with a sofa and a coffee table up one end. It was pretty dark, but fortunately there was enough ambient light to see by, and when she spotted a water cooler she realised how thirsty she was. She filled a pair of cups, one for each of them, then drained her own and filled it again.

Max finished sorting through the cupboards and moved on to the sofa. She sat on it, bounced once or twice, then nodded. 'Comfy. We can rest.'

Sam sat next to her, and they drank water from their paper cups in silence. When she was done Max crumpled her empty cup and tossed it onto the nearby desk, before sitting back and stretching her arms out along the back of the sofa. She breathed out, and Sam felt the same release of tension. They were safe for the moment, but she had no idea what they were going to do when Hal came back. To leave, they had to get to the ship, and right now that looked impossible.

Clunk had spent the best part of an hour shrink-wrapped into a pallet of goods, and when he heard the whine of the forklift truck, and felt the pallet being lifted up, he resigned himself to spending quite a lot more time in the same place. Unfortunately, strong though he was, the plastic didn't afford him the tiniest movement. He couldn't break free, and in fact all he could do was wiggle the two fingers that had been exposed in the cargo hold. That wasn't enough to rip the plastic off and free himself. Indeed, it was barely enough to make a rude gesture.

Clearly Mr Spacejock's plan had failed, but Clunk didn't blame the human for that. No, he placed the blame squarely on himself, for believing one of Mr Spacejock's plans could result in anything other than complete and utter failure.

Resigned, he felt his pallet being loaded onto a truck with several others, and through the plastic Clunk could just see the vague outline of the *Albion*, high above and distorted into a crazy patchwork pattern by the wrap. How he wished he'd insisted on his own plan, which was to submerge himself in the ship's water tank until the Mayestrans had left. Of course, Mr Spacejock had complained that his coffee would taste of lubricating oil forever more, but Clunk considered that a small price to pay. From what he could tell, the coffee aboard didn't taste that great to begin with, and a dash of oil might have improved the flavour.

Now he was strapped to a pallet, stuck aboard a truck going who-knew-where, and Mr Spacejock would be running around like a little lost child. He hoped the human was sensible enough to check the manifest, perform a search on the company who'd ordered the delivery, and then catch a cab out to the warehouse to get Clunk back. That was the sensible way to handle things.

Then Clunk remembered he was dealing with Mr Spacejock, to whom 'sensible' meant 'not immediately fatal'. Who knew what crazy rescue plan the human would dream up?

Clunk felt a vibration as the truck started up, and then he got his first clue that life was about to get interesting.

Instead of going forward, the truck went into reverse, the rear crashing into the front of the following truck with a breaking of headlights and a frantic tooting of horns.

The truck lurched forward, and after a series of violent fits and starts, it began to move in approximately the right direction. It was almost as though someone had taken the controls without the first idea of what they were doing. Someone so incapable they couldn't tell forward from reverse. Someone like–

'Oh no,' breathed Clunk. 'Mr Spacejock!'

❧

Up front, in the cab, Hal was feeling pretty pleased with himself. Earlier, when the real driver turned up to claim his place, Hal simply told the man their roles had changed. There was no request for Hal's ID, or inconvenient queries to senior officers. Instead, the driver shrugged and went to find another ride.

There'd been one awkward moment when the trucks ahead of Hal had driven off. Praying he'd got the controls right, Hal pressed down on the accelerator, only to reverse straight into the truck behind him.

Hal quickly fiddled with the controls, and with a crunch from the gears he got the truck moving forwards, dragging the bumper off the vehicle behind him in the process.

The convoy drove across the spaceport apron, accompanied by half a dozen smaller cars and trucks carrying the other personnel. Then they reached the exit, where they were waved through the barrier. Once on the open road, Hal found the going easy, since he only had to keep up with the truck ahead.

As he drove along, Hal considered the next step in his plan. This didn't take long, because he didn't have one. All he knew was that sooner or later they were going to arrive somewhere, and he'd have to find Clunk, unwrap the robot from the pallet and spirit him away without being spotted by the other workers.

He glanced at the rear-view camera, which displayed the truck following him. The front of the vehicle was illuminated by the red glow of his own taillights, and Hal wondered whether he could hit the brakes and really put it out of action. With any luck, those ahead wouldn't notice him stopping, especially if he sped up to the tail of the convoy again.

Then he could try and knock out the truck ahead of him, before advancing on the last one. Soon there would be a series of busted, overturned trucks littering the highway, and all he'd have to do is go back and pull Clunk from the wreckage.

It was a plan, of sorts, but Hal felt it wasn't a very good one. There would be injuries, maybe deaths, and he didn't want those on his conscience. Plus these people were his customers, and if he ran them off the road, trashing their trucks and destroying their cargo, they might leave a negative review for his freighter business.

No, all he could do was follow patiently and see what happened next.

They drove for some time, deeper and deeper into the countryside, until Hal noticed everyone ahead of him was slowing. He applied the brakes, and saw taillights ahead and to the right as the convoy turned off and took a side road. As he approached the turnoff himself, he saw a big sign advertising the 'Shady Palms Seaside Resort'. There was a big picture underneath the illuminated logo, showing a happy family bathing in a wide, blue sea. In the corner, lit up in red, a smaller sign said 'No Vacancies'.

For a split second, Hal was tempted to floor the accelerator and continue straight ahead. There were four trucks carrying pallets in the convoy, which meant there was a one-in-four chance he had Clunk on board. Then he decided against it, because he knew the others would chase him down.

As he turned right, past the sign, Hal wondered whether he'd got the wrong end of the stick. Maybe these people weren't Mayestran soldiers after all. Maybe the cargo wasn't guns and bombs and ammo. No, perhaps they were all fitness instructors from the resort, and the cargo was a bunch of exercise equipment, beach balls and towels.

As he thought it over, Hal convinced himself he'd leapt to the wrong conclusion. Surely, if the Mayestrans were going to invade Dolor, they wouldn't have gone to all this trouble? They'd just land a few ships and offload troops and equipment openly, right there at the spaceport. Who needed subterfuge when you had overwhelming force on your side?

The road was much narrower here, and it took all Hal's skill just to stay on the tarmac. There were pot holes aplenty, and the truck bumped and lurched as it followed the rest of the convoy. Then, at last, they pulled into a car park, and all the vehicles came to a halt. Dozens of people climbed out, and Hal wondered whether to join them or hide. There was a line of low buildings nearby, and Hal saw another group emerging from within, this lot dressed in shorts and bright shirts. Add sunglasses and straw hats, he thought, and they'd look like typical tourists.

The two parties greeted each other, and then Hal saw the canvas sides of the truck in front of him being hauled back, revealing eight or ten pallets of goods. Someone got a knife and slashed the plastic, and then everyone started grabbing boxes and crates of goods, carting them off to the buildings.

Hal's heart was in his mouth as he watched them emptying the truck. If Clunk was on board that one, there'd be a shout of discovery any second now. He had to do something, and fast.

Before he could do anything, someone thumped their fist on his side window. Hal jumped in his seat, and when he looked down he saw a woman standing on the truck's footrest, glaring at him through the glass. She saw him looking, and motioned for him to put the window down.

'What the hell were you playing at?' she demanded, after he obeyed. 'I had to drive all the way here without headlights, thanks to you!'

'I'm really sorry,' said Hal. 'It was a mistake, I promise.'

'You bet it was a mistake.' The driver was hanging onto his door with one hand, and now she bunched her free hand into a fist. 'I ought to lay you out, you incompetent piece of–'

'Look, I'll buy you a beer later,' said Hal quickly. 'Two beers, if you like.'

The driver eyed him critically, then nodded. 'Pick up a six-pack at the staff canteen after this lot's unloaded. Bring 'em to room 28, and then you can make it up to me.'

She vanished, and Hal breathed a sigh of relief, because the last thing he needed right then was a big fight scene. Opening his door, he slipped out of the cab and climbed down the side of his truck. It was a warm night, and a gentle breeze carried the smell of the nearby ocean.

The bulk of the vehicle concealed him from the crowd of workers, and he used the cover to unhook the canvas side. Then he grabbed the tray and hauled himself into the darkness. 'Clunk?' he whispered. 'Are you in here?'

There was no reply.

Hal was pretty sure the robot would have heard him, which meant Clunk was in one of the other trucks. Cursing under his breath, Hal lowered himself to the ground and glanced towards the truck behind his. The front was dented in where he'd reversed into it earlier, the headlights smashed and the bumper missing. No wonder the driver had been angry, he thought, and he realised he'd got off lightly with the promise of six beers. He was lucky she hadn't punched him right through the window.

There was a gap between the trucks, and his instinct was to duck his head and run. However, that would only look suspicious, so instead he strolled casually towards the second truck, pausing to inspect the damage before shaking his head theatrically, in case anyone was watching. Then he moved on, until he was hidden behind the cab.

Hal ran along the side and hauled the canvas covers back. Instead of climbing inside, he stood on tiptoes and cupped his hands to his mouth. 'Clunk?' he whispered, as loudly as he dared. 'Are you in there, buddy?'

Nothing.

Worried, Hal turned to look back up the line of trucks. The second one was still being emptied, quickly and efficiently, and there was no way he'd be able to get Clunk out of that one. That left the first truck in line, which was still sealed. That also meant he'd have to get past the truck currently being unloaded.

Hal glanced to his right, towards the edge of the car park. There was a low wooden railing, and beyond that he could just make out sparse bushes and weeds growing out of rolling sand dunes. That was the answer, he thought, and moments later he'd vaulted the railing and was making his way across the loose sand. As he walked across the dunes, he realised it would make a great escape route if he managed to find Clunk.

By now he was level with the third truck, although he was fifty or sixty metres away and hidden by the darkness. He could see the unloading proceeding at speed, and knew it wouldn't be long before the workers moved onto the next truck. He sped up, jogging across the sand until he'd passed the truck at the head of the line, at which point he turned left and approached it. He'd got the routine down pat now, and he unhitched the side and called out to Clunk.

No answer.

'That'd be right,' muttered Hal. Then he heard a shout that chilled him to the core.

'Hey, look at this crappy old robot!' cried someone from the back of the second truck. 'Why did they send us this piece of junk?'

Someone laughed. 'Target practice, of course. These old things don't half move when you open fire.'

Hal knew for certain they'd found Clunk, and he cursed his bad luck. Then he recalled the conversation he'd just overhead. Target practice? Open fire? These people weren't fitness instructors or tourists, they *had* to be some kind of Mayestran task force!

11

Sam woke with a start, and she discovered she was snuggled up to Max on the sofa. Max's arm was draped around her shoulders, the other woman breathing gently as she slept. She took hold of Max's arm and eased herself free, then got up for a drink. She had no idea what the time was, but they must have slept for at least an hour. So where was Hal?

Max stirred on the sofa before sitting up, blinking sleep from her eyes. 'Spacejock. Is he here?'

'Not yet.' Sam glanced out the window. It was pitch dark outside, and she guessed they still had a few hours until dawn. 'If he doesn't arrive before sun-up, we'll still be here when this place opens for business.'

'Good,' said Max sleepily. 'The staff will deal with the creatures.'

'And call the Peace Force. I'll be handed over to the Mayestrans and you'll be locked up.'

That woke Max all right. She got up and came to look out the window. 'We can't wait for that fool any more. We have to get out of here.'

'How? We'll never scale that fence.'

'We will look around and maybe find something to cut the

chain. There has to be a tool shed or a workshop in a place like this.'

They both peered out into the darkness. Neither mentioned the wild creatures roaming around.

'Maybe there's a high-pitched tone that keeps them away from the buildings,' suggested Sam. It sounded weak, even to her, but it gave her something to hang on to.

They went to the front door, their feet crunching on broken glass. 'Stick to the shadows, it'll make us harder to see,' advised Max, as they left the building. 'And keep your eyes open for a shed of some kind. It won't be next to these tourist buildings. We're more likely to find it on the other side of the car park.'

It seemed a long way to the far side, and the expanse of tarmac was like an inky black patch in the darkness. Still, there was nothing for it, so they set off, walking as quietly as possible. Every little disturbance from the trees had them freezing on the spot, and Sam imagined the sound of her pounding heart carrying to the distant reaches of the park.

They made it, though, and they found a trail leading into the trees. Alongside, there was a neat little sign with the words 'No Public Access'.

'This is promising,' murmured Max.

They hurried along the trail, which was a dirt track with deep ruts. The ruts were filled with water, and the mud was thick and slippery, making the going tough. Now and then there was a rustle in the bushes, as though something small and fast was darting through the undergrowth, but they didn't hear anything of the much larger creature which had roared at them earlier.

They rounded a corner, and they found a couple of sheds surrounded by a chain-link fence. Unlike the huge fence surrounding the park, this one was only meant to keep inquisitive humans out, and consequently it was far less imposing. The gates were secured with a sliding bolt, but Max bypassed that by reaching through the wire and easing it open with her fingertips. The gates swung open, and they hurried inside and bolted them again.

Sam breathed a little easier now there was some kind of barrier between them and the wild animals, even though it wasn't much of a fence.

One of the buildings was a small shed with gardening equipment, but the other was more like it. There was a tractor with a mowing attachment, and beside it an old-fashioned flyer. The latter was a four-seater, with the body of a groundcar and stubby winglets at each corner with thrusters attached. Faded lettering along the side spelled out 'Dolorian Wildlife Park', and there was a logo with a huge lizard.

'That'll do,' said Max. 'Now we can fly out of here.'

Sam eyed the flyer doubtfully. 'Doesn't look like that thing's flown anywhere for years.'

'I'm a mechanic. It'll do.'

'But where will we fly to? It's not safe on this planet, and that thing's not getting us into orbit any time soon.'

'No, I meant we can fly out of the park,' explained Max patiently. 'We wait for Spacejock on the other side of the fence.'

Max was about to take the driver's seat when Sam stopped her. 'I'll take it from here.'

'I don't think so. You can't fly through an asteroid field without destroying your ship.'

Sam frowned. 'I don't see your ship anywhere around here, do you?'

'Okay, we'll play humanity, meteorite, climate change. Winner gets to drive.'

'How does that work?'

Max made a fist. 'Humanity.' Then she extended her middle finger. 'Climate change.' Finally, she extended a second finger. 'Meteorite.'

'I've never heard of that game.'

'Simple. Climate change beats humanity. Meteorite beats humanity. Climate change versus meteorite results in a draw.'

'But... humanity can't win!'

'People don't choose that one very often,' admitted Max.

'What about the other two? It doesn't make any sense if the only choice is a loss or a draw.'

'Okay, okay. I use the game to settle bar fights,' confessed Max. 'While they're figuring it out, I get the first punch in.'

Sam settled this particular fight by pulling the driver's door open and sitting down. She examined the controls, which were as basic as could be, then reached for the starter. Meanwhile, Max got in beside her and made a big show of buckling herself in, adjusting the straps so tightly they were almost cutting into her.

Sam pressed the button, and the flyer coughed and spluttered, then died. She tried again, and this time it didn't even cough. 'Out of fuel, do you think?' she asked Max.

'You're the expert.'

Frowning, Sam tapped the dusty screen set into the dash, but it was dead. So, she got out and popped the hood, which creaked as it rose on its stiff hinges. Inside was a maze of dirty wiring and fuel hoses, all leading from the central controller and out through the metal panel at the back, and from there presumably to the four thrusters on the winglets. There was a large metal tank underneath, but when she rapped her knuckles on it she just got a hollow sound back. She looked around the garage, but she had no idea what kind of fuel the thing took.

Sam knew her fighters and weapons systems, but this was all new to her. She was about to ask Max for help when she heard the other woman getting out of the flyer.

'Have you fixed it yet?' Max asked her.

'You know I damn well haven't.' Sam scowled at her. 'I've barely had a chance to look at it.'

'Okay, let me know when it's done.' With that, Max leaned against the wall and crossed her arms.

Sam knew she was defeated, but she was too stubborn to give in. So, she pulled at a wire here and prodded a connector there, and after she'd spent five minutes messing about she climbed back into the flyer and hit the starter. There was a cough, immediately silenced, and she pressed the button several more times, willing the thing to start. Nothing.

Sam sat back in her seat, furious. She was used to having a whole squadron under her command, saluting and calling her sir and obeying orders without question, and dealing with Max was a special kind of torture. She should have been lining Mayestrans up in her gunsights, blasting their ships into whirling fragments, not skulking around some deadly tourist trap with a lumbering great towship operator.

Then, before she could ask her for help, Max left her spot by the wall and came over to check under the hood. She began pulling wires out, inspecting the connectors before plugging them in again. There was an air of confidence about her, and after ten minutes she nodded at Sam. 'Try now.'

Sam pressed the starter, and the engines ran for several seconds before cutting out again. 'Getting there.'

'Yes, but we don't want it stopping in mid-air.'

'No kidding.'

'Let me work on this.' Max started in earnest then, disconnecting fuel hoses, removing components and placing what looked like half the flyer's workings on a nearby bench. She looked happy, and seemed glad to have something to keep her busy.

Sam sat back and closed her eyes. As long as Max got the flyer working before dawn, they'd be fine. Then she thought about Hal. He'd promised to come back for her, so where was he?

At that very moment, Hal was watching the Mayestrans from the cover of the sand dunes. When the men had found Clunk strapped to the pallet, he was worried they'd send the robot running all over the dunes while they took potshots at him. However, they'd led Clunk towards the buildings instead, and Hal had slipped away into the dunes while they were distracted.

He couldn't help thinking Clunk was being a bit docile, because the robot could easily have grabbed the men surrounding him, knocked all their heads together and made his escape. Hal guessed it was the robot's restrictive Laws, because unless the men attacked him, Clunk had no reason to hurt them.

'I'm telling you,' said Clunk, as he was escorted away from the truck. 'I'm not *part* of the cargo, I'm one of the pilots tasked with *delivering* it.'

'Sure, and you just thought you'd take a nap on the pallet.' The man who'd spoken gave Clunk a push. 'Come on, we've got a nice room just for you. You can wait in there until after dinner, and then we're going to have some fun.'

'But I'm a *pilot*!' protested Clunk.

'I bet Matthews told you to say that. He's a stirrer, that one.'

'I–I–' began Clunk.

'No more talking. In fact, I order you to shut up.'

Wisely, Clunk said no more.

Hal watched carefully, noting where they took the robot. It seemed to be one of the resort's guest cabins, which was part of a group set slightly apart from the main buildings. The workers were transferring the goods from the trucks into these cabins, and were obviously using them for storage. The main building must be their barracks, or mess hall, or whatever it's called, thought Hal.

The man had mentioned dinner, and Hal hoped they'd all go off for a feed, leaving the cabins unguarded. He figured he could break Clunk out, drag him to the nearest vehicle, and drive off before anyone realised what was happening.

True, there were several steps to his plan, and most of them had asterisks. For example, he was assuming the enemy would be totally incompetent and lacking in the most basic security procedures. Still, the resort was tucked away in a remote spot, and the Mayestrans wouldn't be expecting any trouble. He hadn't seen any guns or uniforms yet, and they seemed pretty casual about the cargo.

Hmm, thought Hal. The cargo. He hadn't had a chance to inspect it yet, since everything was sealed in small boxes and crates. But if it *did* turn out to be weapons and armour, he and Clunk were going to be in huge trouble with the Dolorians. Never mind finding another cargo job, they might have just smuggled in enough weapons to arm a whole bunch of enemy soldiers, and if so the sensible thing would be to lift off and flee the system.

Hal eyed the trucks, and saw the workers moving on to the first one, pulling back the canvas sides before unwrapping the pallets and carting boxes and containers towards the cabins. They'd be a while yet, and Hal's gaze shifted to the fourth truck, right at the rear of the line. Every time he showed himself he risked getting caught, but he *had* to know what was in those crates.

Slowly, he approached the car park, where he clambered over the low wooden railings and reached the truck. The side was still unhooked, and he hauled himself into the back and felt for the nearest pallet. The plastic was tough, but by tearing at it layer by layer he managed to get through to the containers underneath. He got one free and discovered it was solidly-built, but not particularly heavy, and when he snapped the catches the lid opened freely.

There was a rectangle of dense foam inside, and he lifted it out before feeling underneath. His fingers encountered a row of three or four tubes, plastic from the feel of them, and as he moved his hand he felt the tubes widen into a rounded shape with indents. Further back, they narrowed again, and then, with a shock, he recognised the objects. They were guns, he was sure of it, with barrels and grips and moulded stocks.

Hal started to pull one out, then changed his mind and pushed it back again. It wouldn't be charged up, not in the crate, which meant it would be about as useful as a cardboard sword. Worse, he hadn't seen any of the Mayestrans sporting weapons, and if they saw him with a gun over his shoulder he'd be challenged for sure.

Well, that settled the matter as far as he was concerned. Not only were these people Mayestrans masquerading as tourists, but they had enough weapons to storm parliament and take over the government. And he, Hal Spacejock, had delivered those weapons right into their hands.

He didn't have a choice. Somehow, he had to stop these people. Somehow, he had to destroy the weapons, so he could pretend the cargo had never existed. Otherwise he'd spend the rest of his life in jail.

Once again Hal retreated to the dunes, where he waited impatiently for unloading to finish. As the fourth and final truck was emptied, he saw two people carrying marker boards towards the main building, and he could just imagine the sinister plans which would soon be scrawled all over their pristine surfaces. It really was a well-organised group, he thought, and it looked like the Dolorians were in for a tough time.

Finally, the last pallet of gear was stripped clean, and the Mayestrans poured into the main building. There was a big dining room, visible through a row of huge windows, and Hal could see the men and women taking seats at the tables. Plates of food arrived, and his stomach growled as he saw them tucking into hot roast dinners.

The car park was deserted, with no guards in sight, and Hal swung into action. He left his hiding spot and hurried to the nearest truck, and from there he made his way to the guest cabin where Clunk had been locked up.

He tried the handle, more out of hope than expectation, and he was surprised when it turned easily. The door swung open, and he saw Clunk standing against the wall, looking for all the world like a mannequin. 'Why didn't you escape?' whispered Hal angrily. 'They didn't even lock you in!'

'I didn't want to aggravate them.' Clunk turned to look at him. 'I was going to escape, but I was leaving it until after

126

they'd all gone to bed.'

'Well, they're all stuffing their faces right now, so let's grab a car. We'll be out of here before they're onto the second course.'

They left the guest house and made their way towards the nearest vehicle. On the way, Hal cast nervous glances towards the dining room windows, but the Mayestrans were engrossed in conversation, and were tucking away roast beef and potatoes at a prodigious rate.

At the last minute Hal altered course, choosing a car which was parked behind several others. It was hidden from the well-lit windows, and he was hoping he could drive off without the Mayestrans noticing.

The vehicle was a sleek white groundcar, and when they reached it Hal saw a familiar rental logo on a window sticker. 'We'll borrow this one,' he said quickly. In his experience, using words like 'steal' and 'take' meant a lecture from Clunk on property rights, and this wasn't the time.

They got in, and once the doors closed Hal fired up the engine. It immediately cut out again.

'Your rental period has expired,' said the car. 'To extend your driving time, please make an additional payment.'

On the dash, a slot lit up in green. Muttering under his breath, Hal took out a credit tile and pushed it in. The engine started up again, and a timer began to count down. 'Ten minutes for twenty credits?' protested Hal. 'I want to rent it, not pay the damn thing off!'

The timer continued to tick down.

Hal was determined to reach the spaceport before coughing up any more of his hard-earned cash, so he twisted the throttle, turned the car in its own length and raced for the exit. In his rear-view mirror he could just see the people in the dining room, who were completely oblivious to his daring escape.

Then, as soon as they reached the main road, Hal rounded on the robot. 'Right. Explain to me how you approved a cargo of guns,' he said. 'I mean, were you out of your mind?'

'Guns?' said Clunk in surprise. 'It wasn't guns, it was sporting equipment.'

'Don't make me laugh. I opened a crate and found weapons inside!' Hal's face was grim in the light from the instruments. 'We should have checked their background. We should have opened a crate or two and looked inside.'

'But their paperwork was in order!'

'That's what they say in every war movie, ever, just before the bridge blows up or the skytrain goes down in flames.'

'Yes, Mr Spacejock. Incidentally, you're driving a little fast.'

Hal glanced at the timer, which showed six minutes left, and he twisted the throttle even more. The scenery flew by, and the powerful car ate up the road ahead. 'You realise what we've done, don't you? We've just armed a whole bunch of Mayestran soldiers. We've given them the means to take over this entire planet.'

'How do you know they're soldiers?'

'Something happened at the spaceport. There was this officer, a real busybody, who was sent to check us out. Then these guys showed up for the cargo, and she told them to wait. Instead, one of the cargo guys showed her his ID, and she crumbled. After that she was all yes sir, no sir, have a nice day, sir.'

'What kind of ID was it?'

'He didn't show me, but it had to be something high-up.' Hal's grip tightened on the controls. 'We need a plan.'

'Plan?'

'Yeah, you've got to come up with a plan to deal with those guys.'

Slowly, Clunk turned to look at him. 'I counted over one hundred of them, and you mentioned weapons. Against them, there are only the two of us.'

Hal considered this. 'Better make it a really good plan, then.'

They drove in silence, the timer still ticking towards zero. Hal tried to go even faster, but the speed was stuck on 88. 'Come on, come on,' he muttered. 'Why won't it go any faster?'

'That's the limit,' said Clunk. 'It's because this is a Dolorian car.'

They continued at top speed for a while, before Clunk broke in with a suggestion. 'Why don't we contact the Dolorian authorities and advise them of the situation?'

'Are you crazy? I'm not telling them we smuggled in a bunch of weapons!'

Clunk frowned. 'Are you certain that's what you found?'

'Positive. The first crate I opened was full of the things. I picked one up, and I know a gun when I'm holding it.'

'I see. Well, this appears to be too big for the pair of us, Mr Spacejock. We cannot handle these people on our own.'

'But we brought all the Mayestrans' gear and delivered it right into their hands! We'll get arrested!'

'Correct, which is why we'll call in with an anonymous tip. We'll say we noticed a group of armed men and women gathering at the Shady Palms resort, and then the Dolorians can take it from there.'

'That could work. Hey, maybe they can bomb the place from orbit!'

'A little extreme, Mr Spacejock, but they will certainly have the means to stop this incursion.'

The car slowed suddenly, and Hal glanced at the timer.

'Your rental has expired,' said the car. 'Please make an additional payment if you wish to keep driving.'

After pulling over and coming to a stop, Hal dug in his pockets. He had a few credit tiles to hand, but he reckoned they were five minutes out and he didn't want to waste a twenty. So, he pushed a ten credit tile into the slot, and they set off again with four minutes on the clock.

'What a rip-off,' muttered Hal, and he twisted the throttle to maximum.

12

The car ran out of money within sight of Space Port Delta, but Hal refused to put any more cash in the slot. As they strolled along in the darkness, he could almost hear Clunk's disapproval. 'It's not *your* money,' muttered Hal. 'One day, you should try saving a few credits here and there. I bet you won't be as free with the spending then.'

'It was only going to cost five credits,' protested Clunk. 'Was it really worth a ten minute walk?'

'You keep saying exercise is good for me.'

So, they finished their journey on foot.

They made the gates, eventually, and as soon as Hal identified his ship they were admitted to the spaceport. 'I can't wait to get aboard,' he said, after he spotted the *Albion* in the distance. It was a truly impressive sight, at least twice as big as any other ship on the landing field, and he felt a surge of gratitude. 'Hey, thanks for buying the ship for me. Really.'

Clunk made a dismissive gesture. 'The galaxy isn't the same unless Spacejock Freightlines is ferrying cargo from planet to planet.'

'True.' Hal hesitated. 'Of course, next time you should think about buying second-hand. That way there'd be money left for food and fuel.'

The passenger ramp was still down, and they strode all the way up to the narrow metal platform protruding from the ship's airlock, high above the ground. 'I thought I left this open,' said Hal, as he eyed the airlock door.

'It seals automatically,' said Clunk, and he reached out to enter the code for the burglar alarm.

Hal took hold of the railing and glanced across the landing field, wondering whether the Dolorians would manage to defeat all the Mayestrans at the beach resort. And after that... would more of these Mayestrans show up? It seemed to be a peaceful planet, and he frowned as he thought of it being torn apart in a senseless war.

They entered the flight deck, and Hal motioned Clunk towards the console. 'Make the call. The sooner we tell them about the Mayestrans, the better.'

'Mr Spacejock, it will hardly be anonymous if I call from here.'

'What do you suggest?'

'I suggest I don't make the call from here.'

Hal pursed his lips. 'Okay,' he said at last. 'You go and tip them off, I'll find a cargo job.'

'Is that wise?'

'Of course it's wise. You just said you can't call from here!'

'I meant the cargo job. Traditionally, I handle all the–'

'Don't start with that nonsense.' Hal raised a hand, stopping the robot mid-sentence. 'Your last effort mixed us up in a spot of gun-running, and the one before that cost me the *Volante*.'

'But–'

'This isn't a debate. Go and make the call, and by the time you return I'll have a plum, well-paid job all signed up and ready to go. Not a gun in sight.'

'Very well, Mr Spacejock. I can see your mind is made up.'

Clunk opened a locker and retrieved a cap and a long, black overcoat. He donned both, pulling the brim of the cap down to his nose, before wrapping the overcoat around his body.

'Well, if you didn't look shady before, you certainly do now,' remarked Hal. 'People will be reporting you to the Peace Force the moment you set foot inside the passenger terminal.'

'I'm not going to the terminal. I'm going to find a parked ship and access their comms remotely.'

'Neat!'

'It's not strictly legal, but under the circumstances I can live with it.' Clunk strode towards the airlock, his coat flapping around his legs, and after he left Hal closed the door behind him.

'Right, Navcom. A list of jobs please, sorted by payment per light year, high to low. And filter out anything undesirable.'

'Like guns and drugs, you mean?'

'Yes, just like those.'

'Unable to comply. Filters inoperative.'

Hal snorted. That explained why Clunk had landed him with the gun-running job. 'All right, just filter out anything suspicious.'

'Define suspicious.'

'Did you see Clunk leaving the ship?'

'Affirmative.'

'Right, well *that* was suspicious.'

There was a ping. 'Displaying list on monitor three. There are several jobs, none involving overcoats or headgear.'

Hal hunted around the console until he spotted a small screen with a list of jobs on it. He glanced at the first, and he knew he didn't have to look any further. 'Is the price on line one correct?'

'Affirmative.'

'Bring up the details.'

The main screen flashed, and the job description appeared. It involved collecting an asteroid and returning it to the orbit of Dolor for research purposes, and the payment on offer was very generous. In fact, it was almost enough to fill the *Albion's* fuel tanks... twice.

Hal wasn't that keen on transporting an asteroid, because the last time he'd tackled a similar job it hadn't ended all that well. Then again, he couldn't remember *any* job which had ended particularly well. 'Okay, call the guy,' he said. 'Reserve the job. Tell them we'll do it.'

'Job reserved. Awaiting call from the customer.'

'Well done. Good stuff.' Hal got up. 'I'm going to rustle up some food. When this guy calls, let me know.'

'Unable to comply. Internal comms are down.'

'So turn the kitchen lights on and off.'

'Understood,' said the Navcom. 'I will request your presence in Morse code.'

'Just flash them. I'll know what it means.' Hal glanced at the screen, and his gaze settled on the customer's name. 'Cylen Murtay, huh? I wonder what sort of research he's doing.'

※

Hal was busy cooking bacon and eggs when all the lights went out, plunging him into darkness. He waited several seconds, but they remained off. Meanwhile, his food sizzled in the pan, cooking rapidly.

'I said flash the kitchen lights, Navcom,' he muttered under his breath. 'I didn't say turn every light on this deck off, permanently!'

Reaching out blindly, he felt the knob for the stove and switched it off. Then he took the frying pan by the handle, found a fork by feeling around in the cutlery drawer, and headed for the lift. It was pitch black, and he couldn't see anything, so he walked slowly, feeling for the walls.

He only found out he was in the elevator when the passage came to a dead end, and then he felt around in the darkness for the buttons. The panel seemed to be in the wrong place, and when he located and pressed the switch, the overhead light came on. That's when he discovered he'd walked into a storage alcove.

Muttering under his breath, still carrying the frying pan and the fork in one hand, he left the cupboard and turned right. With the dim glow coming from behind him, he made the lift and pressed the upper button.

He found the flight deck bathed in light. 'What were you playing at?' he demanded, waving the frying pan. 'I said flash the lights, not leave me in total darkness!'

Then he noticed the man on the screen, who was looking at him with surprise. 'Oh hi,' said Hal, hiding the frying pan behind his back. 'Murray, right?'

'Murtay,' said the man. 'Cylen Murtay.'

'You're a scientist?' To Hal, the man looked more like a bank clerk, with his white business shirt and the row of pens in his breast pocket. He had a mild, inoffensive look, with wavy blonde hair and pale blue eyes, and Hal couldn't picture him tunnelling into an asteroid with a big demolition hammer. 'What sort of research are you doing?'

'No, I work for the...' Murtay paused. 'I work for a certain government department.'

Hal hid a delighted grin. Government work! He could

charge double, and they'd pay the bill long before they discovered the mistake.

'Can you do the job?' Murtay asked him. 'It's urgent, you see, and if you can't–'

'Sure I can. I've hauled asteroids before, no problem.'

'This particular job requires the utmost precision. The asteroid must be released on the exact course I specify, or it won't enter the correct orbit around Dolor and the entire project will be a failure.'

'You point the way, I'll do the job,' said Hal confidently. 'By the way, I'll want half the payment up front.'

'That will be arranged,' said Murtay. He looked at the camera anxiously. 'I do have two more conditions, though.'

'Shoot.'

'First, I'd like to come along. I won't get in your way, but I must oversee the operation.'

Relieved, Hal gestured magnanimously. 'Not a problem. And the other one?'

'We have to pick up my mother.'

'Your mum?' Hal blinked. 'Why?'

'I'm worried about her safety, Mr Spacejock.' Murtay looked at him, almost pleading. 'She can't stay here, don't you see? I can't explain now, but Dolor is facing a major threat, and I can't. . . I can't leave my mother in danger.'

Hal thought of the Mayestrans, and he realised what the man was talking about. In fact, once word got out about the invasion force, he reckoned Space Port Delta would be the busiest place in the system. 'Don't worry, I understand,' he said. 'Bring her, bring your whole family. I mean, not dozens, of course, but a few more won't be a problem.'

'No, it's just her,' said Murtay. 'You don't understand what this means to me. I'm truly grateful, Mr Spacejock.'

'How long until you get here?' Hal asked him. 'I'm on a bit of a deadline, so–'

'Thirty minutes, no more.'

'That's fine. See you then.' Hal cut the call, and moments later there was a 'kerching!' from the console as the payment went through. Hal grinned, then ordered a refuel and a few supplies for immediate delivery. Finally, he tucked into the eggs and bacon, eating them right out of the pan.

Hal was still feeling on top of the world when Clunk returned. The robot removed his disguise, such as it was, then gave Hal a nod. 'Contact made, Mr Spacejock. The authorities have been notified.'

'Great! Well done, Clunk!' Hal felt a weight lifting off his shoulders. 'Er… did you mention the weapons?'

'Indeed. The Dolorians will be prepared for anything, I'm sure.'

'Good stuff!' Hal remembered his own news. 'I got a job, by the way.'

'Oh?'

'Don't sound like that. It's really easy! We're collecting an asteroid from nearby and putting it into orbit around Dolor. It's for scientific research or some-such.'

Clunk hurried to the console and checked the details. 'Incredible. Amazing.'

'I know, it's great isn't it? The guy paid half up front, too!'

'No, I mean it's amazing you booked a legitimate job with no downside, no unexpected extras, and one where actual money changes hands at the end of it. I'm impressed.'

'There was one thing. The guy wants to come with us, and he's bringing his mum along.'

Clunk's eyebrows rose with a squeak. 'Why?'

'He's worried about her. Told me he works for the

137

government, and I reckon he's got an inkling about the Mayestrans invading the place. Let's face it, Dolor could become a war zone, so it makes sense to get his nearest and dearest out of here.'

'I wish I'd been here to question him.'

'Why?'

'I'd like to know the nature of his research. Why bring an asteroid to Dolor when he could inspect it *in situ*?'

'In what?'

'In the asteroid field, Mr Spacejock.'

'Are you kidding? Last time we were out there you couldn't leave the controls in case a speeding lump of rock took my ship out. You really think a bunch of scientists are going to drag a load of equipment into an asteroid field so than can play chicken with giant boulders?'

'I suppose not, but there would be areas further out which–'

'It doesn't matter. This guy's paying us to fetch a rock, and that's what we'll do.' Hal paused. 'By the way, don't tell him we're stopping off to collect Max and Sam. Paying customers always get upset when we take a minor detour.'

'Agreed, Mr Spacejock.'

'We'll stick him and his mum into a couple of cabins, you can take them a nice mug of cocoa each, and they'll never notice the landing.'

'We don't have any cocoa.'

There was a buzz from the airlock. 'We do now,' said Hal, and he went to sign for his delivery.

◆

138

Hal returned to the flight deck with the carton of essential supplies tucked under one arm. Clunk was at the console, and he gave Hal a disapproving look.

'Mr Spacejock, you can't spend money every time we complete a cargo job. It's reckless and unwise.'

'I didn't. I spent the advance from the *next* freight job.' Hal tore the box open and smiled. 'Wow, look at this lot,' he breathed, as he surveyed the treats. 'I haven't enjoyed stuff this good for ages!' There were chocolate bars, candied almonds, bags of potato chips in nine different flavours, a tin of good quality cocoa and... a spare coffee mug. Hal took the mug out and turned it, admiring the way the big gold letters sparkled in the light.

'The Galaxy's number one pilot?' said Clunk incredulously.

'Yeah. This way everyone will know it's mine.' Hal put the mug away and closed the box up. 'I'm going to stash this in my cabin. If Murtay shows while I'm gone, quiz him about the asteroid job.'

'What do you want to know?'

'Me? I just want to know he's paying at the end of it. You're the one who wanted more detail.'

'I must admit, I'm curious about the ramifications of inserting an asteroid into–'

'Good, excellent. Ask him all about it.' Hal fled to the lift before Clunk could start a discussion on fuel burn ratios and orbital re-entry speeds. On the way down he tore open a bag of chips, and he munched away happily, eyes closed with sheer bliss.

Once he reached the passenger level, he went straight to his cabin. Here, he entered the walk-in robe, where his third-best flight suit hung from the rail. He was puzzled at that, because his second-best flight suit was missing, but then he guessed Clunk was having it cleaned.

The rest of the closet was empty, except for a shelf just above head height, and as Hal tucked his carton of goodies away he caught sight of the big, gaudy box containing his prized Dick Spacewad figurine. After wiping his hands on his flight suit, Hal reached up and took the precious box down. He could see the spacefaring hero through the clear plastic panel in the front, standing proudly to attention with six rows of medals on his chest. The figurine was in mint condition, and the only thing more valuable was a matched pair: Dick Spacewad *and* his gold-plated robot sidekick, Crank.

Unfortunately, Cranks were rare. Very, very rare. Because, when they were first released, some marketing genius had come up with an extra special incentive. Five figurines had been inserted into the production line. Five Cranks with armour made from solid gold, instead of the regular gold-plated alloy. The little figures had sold by the million, with people flocking to stores, then ripping the robots from their tamper-proof packaging right there at the counter. Any deemed worthless were discarded, and dumpsters were crammed with unwanted Cranks for weeks.

A few months later, there wasn't a boxed Crank to be found across the known galaxy.

Hal sighed and put the Dick Spacewad figure back, turning the box slightly so it was lined up with the edge of the shelf. One day, he promised himself. One day he'd complete the set, and then the pair of them would be more valuable than his ship.

He went to the kitchen, and as he ate the bag of chips and sipped his coffee, he decided life wasn't that bad. He had a decent ship, money in the bank and he could afford a few luxuries now and then. What more could he ask for?

Hal heard the whirr of the lift in the distance, and moments later he heard voices. He got up and hurried to his door, closing it behind himself before going to meet their passenger.

Cylen Murtay was walking behind Clunk, and he looked visibly impressed by the *Albion's* size. 'Mr Spacejock?' he said, and they shook hands. 'What a lovely vessel. So big and powerful!'

'Yeah, she's all right,' said Hal. 'But she gets us where we want to go, and that's what really matters.' Then he frowned. 'I thought you were bringing your mum along?'

'Yes, we are.'

'So where is she?' asked Hal, peering around Murtay in case he was concealing a short, elderly woman. 'Isn't she coming?'

'Yes, but she's at home right now. If you recall, I asked if you would pick her up.'

'But we don't have time!' protested Hal. 'We've got to collect–' Then he noticed Clunk gesturing rapidly, and he closed his mouth with a snap.

'Collect what?' asked Murtay.

'We've got to collect your asteroid, so we can get paid,' said Hal. 'Around here we like to complete jobs at the double. We're very efficient.'

'Well, mother is only thirty minutes from here, and the delay won't affect your payment.'

'Can't she catch a bus?'

'Oh no. Mother won't take public transport. Anyway, her cats would never stand for it.'

Hal felt reality slipping away. 'She wants to bring cats into space?'

'Well they can't stay on Dolor by themselves,' said Murtay reasonably. 'I mean, who would feed them?'

'Yes, but–'

'And anyway, she won't leave home without them.'

'Fine! Okay! We'll bring the cats too. But can we just get on with it?'

'Certainly. I already gave Clunk the address, and he's identified a suitable landing spot. Mother lives on the outskirts of the city, and it's semi-rural around there. A few fields, crops, that kind of thing.' Murtay looked at Hal anxiously. 'It's no trouble, is it? It's a bit late to find someone else, but if you want, you can give the deposit back and I'll–'

'No, no, we're all good.' Hal opened a door and waved him in. 'You're in this cabin. If you need anything, call Clunk.'

With that he nodded to the robot, and the two of them headed to the flight deck.

'Little old ladies, pet cats *and* hulking great asteroids,' muttered Hal, as the lift bore them upwards. 'Why does everything have to be so complicated?'

'Relax, Mr Spacejock,' said Clunk calmly. 'I will file a flight plan, and we'll have Mrs Murtay on board before you know it.'

'Aren't ground control going to cause a fuss?'

'I doubt it. She lives in a sparsely populated area.'

'Well, if they won't let us land we can always chuck a rope down and winch her up.'

'Er, yes,' said Clunk uncertainly. 'Let's hope it doesn't come to that.'

They reached the flight deck, where they took their seats to prepare the ship for liftoff. Clunk ran the preflight checks, obtained clearance, started the engines and aligned the controls, while Hal tried out the massage function on his chair.

'Ooh. That tickles!' he said, as the chair buzzed underneath him.

It buzzed a lot more when the main drives fired up, powering the big ship into the sky. They reached cruising altitude in no time, and Clunk turned the *Albion* to the west. Then, as they flew over the city, there was a ping from the console.

'Albion, *this is Ground. Permission for a set-down granted. Advise on arrival. Over.*'

'Thanks Ground,' said Clunk. 'ETA five minutes.'

'*No traffic on your heading,* Albion. *Have a safe flight. Over and out.*'

'Good news, Mr Spacejock,' said Clunk. 'We're allowed to land and pick up Mrs Murtay.'

'Huh? Oh yeah. Good stuff.' Hal was busy with the back of his chair, tilting it up and down repeatedly, and somehow the motor had stuck halfway. From his reclined position he could only just make out the top of the screen, but at least he was comfortable. Frowning, he pushed the up button, and the back of his chair immediately flopped all the way down, turning it into a bed. When he pushed the down button, it just whined at him. 'Hey, any chance you can fix this thing?'

'Not right now, Mr Spacejock. I'm flying the ship.'

'I could take the controls.'

'From down there? I think not.'

'I wouldn't be all the way down here if you fixed my chair.'

'I'll add it to the list of maintenance tasks, Mr Spacejock.'

Hal was still horizontal, and he gave up trying to raise his chair and crossed his arms instead. 'Well, don't mind me. I'm only the pilot.'

'Yes, Mr Spacejock.' Clunk reached for a button. 'Ground, this is *Albion*. Confirming final approach, landing now. Over.'

'*Roger,* Albion. *Call before you lift off, we'll report any traffic in your sector. Over and out.*'

The thrusters roared, and the ship slowed in mid-air, coming to a halt before descending slowly.

'Don't land on her house,' advised Hal. 'Not a good start to the job.'

'I will do my best not to,' said Clunk, his hands darting over the flight console. Moments later there was a gentle bump and the engines cut out. 'Landing successful.'

Hal struggled to sit up, and before Clunk could stop him, he pressed a button on the console. There was a whining noise from the airlock as the passenger ramp extended, followed by the sound of breaking glass. 'What was that?'

'That was the reason I was going to lower the cargo ramp at the rear,' said Clunk.

Hal jumped up and ran into the airlock, and when he peered through the little round porthole he saw they'd landed close to a two-storey house. Very close indeed, as it turned out, because the passenger ramp had extended from the hull and gone straight through an upper-storey window. As Hal surveyed the damage, an elderly woman peered up at him, her face framed by fragments of glass still clinging to the frame. Hal ducked down and returned to the flight deck. 'Don't retract the ramp just yet,' he said. 'If you do, you'll yank Mrs Murtay right out of her house.'

Instead, Clunk lowered the ramp at the back. 'Come, Mr Spacejock. Let us greet the passenger.'

13

'Cylen, my darling boy. How lovely to see you!'

Mrs Murtay appeared to be in her early seventies, with a smooth, plump face and curly grey hair. She was wearing a quilted housecoat and slippers, and she seemed completely unfazed at having the *Albion* on her lawn – and, indeed, partly inside her house. After she greeted her son at the front door, he introduced her to Hal and Clunk.

'They're helping me with work, mother. It's a top-secret research project. Very hush-hush.'

'That's wonderful, my dear. You must tell me all about it.' Mrs Murtay stepped back, motioning them inside. 'Do come in. The kettle's on, and I've just fed the cats so they won't bother you for a while.'

Hal entered the trim little house, which had thick carpeting, freshly-painted walls and, nearby, a staircase leading to the upper floor. Glancing up, he couldn't help noticing the *Albion's* landing ramp sticking through the window. 'I'm really sorry about the damage, Mrs Murtay. Clunk and I will make it good, I promise.'

'Don't be silly, dear.' The old lady smiled and patted the back of his hand. 'There's a man in the village who'll sort that out in no time.'

'But–'

'I won't hear another word,' insisted Mrs Murtay. 'You're helping my son, and I know what an important job he has.' She led them into a small sitting room, crammed with furniture and side tables, the latter covered with knick-knacks. Hal and Cylen took a seat, while Clunk stood in the corner and tried not to knock anything over.

'They promoted him again last week, did you know that?' said Mrs Murtay proudly. 'They made him head of the whole department!'

Her son looked uncomfortable. 'It's still being reviewed, mother. Nothing official yet.'

'I'm sure it's just a matter of time. And the next time you speak with President Oakworthy, you must give him my regards.'

'Yes, mother.'

'I voted for the other side, of course, but you don't have to tell him that.'

'No, mother.'

'Now, let me get the tea. Do talk amongst yourselves.'

'Actually,' said Hal, 'we really ought to be going.'

'Nonsense, you only just arrived. Wait right there and I'll be back in two shakes.' Mrs Murtay left, and after a moment or two of strained silence, Hal turned to Cylen. 'So what department do you run?'

'I don't,' he confessed. 'But every time I come to see mother, she presses me for news. I have to tell her something, and now she thinks I've had about thirty promotions in the past six months.'

'You'll be president of Dolor before you know it,' said Hal, with a grin.

'Don't even joke about it,' said Murtay, in a hollow voice. 'Mother keeps telling me I'd be perfect for the job.'

At that moment a large tabby cat strolled in, leapt on the table, and from there walked straight onto Hal's lap. After staring into his eyes for a moment or two, it reached up and dabbed his face with its paw.

'That's Flynn,' said Murtay. 'She's a bit forward sometimes.'

'Hey girl,' said Hal, and he stroked the cat, working his hand behind her jaw, then down her neck and along her flank. The cat began to purr, and when Hal stopped stroking her, she nosed at his hand until he resumed.

Mrs Murtay came back with a tea tray and four cups. She laid it on the table, then turned to Clunk. 'I'm sorry, dear, I didn't know whether you took tea.'

Clunk bowed. 'Not for me, thank you ma'am.'

'Oh, what nice manners you have.'

Sitting there with the cat purring on his lap, Hal felt like he was experiencing a leisurely dream. They were supposed to be collecting Max and Sam from the national park before heading into orbit on a tricky scientific mission, and yet here he was sipping tea from a delicate little cup.

'Mother,' said Cylen, interrupting Hal's reverie. 'There's something I need you to do.'

'Yes dear?'

'I need you to pack a few things. We're going away for a day or two.'

'Oh, I do wish you'd called. I have the hairdresser tomorrow, and I promised to help Mrs Timms sort clothes for a jumble sale in the afternoon.'

Murtay stood. 'This is really important, mother. It– it might not be safe here.'

'Why, are your colleagues going to land more spaceships in my garden?'

'It's not that. It's just– Oh, it's top secret, mother. I can't tell you why. Please, just collect your things. That spaceship outside... we have to leave right now.'

'But what about Flynn and Zephyr?'

'They're coming with us.'

Cylen's sense of urgency finally got through, and after studying him for a moment or two, his mother nodded. 'Very well, dear. If it's that important, then of course I'll come.'

'Thank you. Now let's go and pack your things.'

The two of them went upstairs, leaving Hal and Clunk with the cat. 'When we go aboard, I want you to organise someone to repair the damage up there,' said Hal.

'Certainly.'

'When we drop her back here, after the asteroid job, I want this place looking like new.' Hal stroked the cat. 'Do you have any insurance claim forms?'

'I always keep a large quantity on hand, Mr Spacejock.'

After that, they waited in silence, until Cylen and Mrs Murtay came back. He was carrying a small suitcase, while she was holding a white cat and a large handbag. Hal got up slowly, picking Flynn up with both hands, and they all left the cosy little house. Once Mrs Murtay had locked her front door, they entered the *Albion* via the cargo ramp. Then Hal and Cylen led the sprightly old lady to the passenger cabins, while Clunk stayed back to seal the hold.

'Well, isn't this nice,' said Mrs Murtay, as she was shown into her cabin. 'I went on a cruise once, but this is so much larger. And it's all so very new.'

'The *Albion* is fresh from the shipbuilders,' said Hal, avoiding mention of the frequent faults. He placed Flynn on the bed, and the cat sniffed at the blanket before settling down. The white cat, Zephyr, jumped down onto the floor and went exploring under the bunk.

'I'd better go up,' said Hal. 'We'll be lifting off soon, but the ship has a gravity field so you won't notice a thing.' He turned to Cylen. 'Come and find me if you need anything. Oh, and you can take the cabin opposite.'

The man nodded, and Hal left for the flight deck. On the way, Clunk caught up with him, and they took the lift together.

'You know Max and Sam are going to be mad with me, don't you?' said Hal. 'I told them we'd be back before they knew it, and we've been hours.'

'It was unavoidable, Mr Spacejock. And remember, you're doing them a huge favour.'

Hal brightened. 'Yeah, you're right! I saved both their lives and went out of my way to drop them in the national park. They ought to be thanking me, not getting angry.'

'Oh, they'll be angry all right,' said Clunk. 'I just thought you might use it as a defence when Max tries to hit you.'

Hal considered leaving the pair of them right where they were, at least until the asteroid job was complete, then decided against it. The longer he left them, the more they'd make him pay.

They reached the flight deck, where Clunk started the engines and cleared their take-off with Ground, while Hal retracted the passenger ramp. There was a sound of shattering glass as the rest of the broken fragments were yanked out of Mrs Murtay's window, and then the ramp folded smoothly into its recess. 'All set,' said Hal. 'Let's get to the national park.'

And, with a smooth application of the throttle, Clunk obeyed.

'*Green four, bogey on your tail. Break left, break left.*'

Sam hauled the stick over until it was jammed against her knee, and the stars whirled as her ship turned in its own length. 'Come on, come *on!*' she muttered, as the thrusters did their best to obey her inputs.

This was deep space combat, not aerobatics, and although the ship turned on its axis, her course remained exactly the same. It was the first thing they drilled into all new space pilots: banking and turning would only rotate your ship, and wouldn't change your course. Sam could remember her instructor's words right now: *You can throw the stick around as much as you like, but you'll still be travelling in the same direction, bracketed by the enemy's gunsight.*

Such manoeuvres were the mark of a rookie, of a raw beginner just begging to be slaughtered... which is why Sam used them to lure the enemy's best fighters onto her tail.

As the nose of her fighter swung towards the pursuing enemy, Sam saw the incoming fire. She was travelling backwards now, and the angry red energy bolts flashed past her canopy, illuminating the interior of the cockpit. The enemy was expecting a quick kill, but Sam had a surprise in store.

The bolts swung closer as the enemy pilot adjusted their aim, and at the last second, Sam gave her fighter's upper thrusters a squirt, sending her nimble craft plunging downwards, away from the deadly fire. As she descended she lifted the nose, and the enemy fighter swam towards the leading circle on her gunsight.

Which was exactly where she wanted them.

Sam squeezed the trigger, and energy bolts lanced out from her fighter's guns, completely silent in the vacuum of space. She smiled grimly as her fire bracketed the enemy fighter, registering small flashes as the deadly bolts struck the hull, the engines and the canopy. There was a flare as the tanks caught, followed by an intense flash of light. When it faded, only a shower of glowing fragments remained.

After his stint as a trainer, Sam's instructor had returned to the front line. He was lost days later on a routine patrol, jumped by a flight of Mayestrans. As she watched the shower of fragments fading and cooling, Sam wondered whether his end had been just as quick.

Then she checked her scanner, picking out her next victim. Her squadron was outnumbered three to one, but if she could eliminate the enemy's best pilots then maybe, just maybe, her people would have a chance.

'It's ready,' said a voice nearby. 'Try it again.'

Sam was awake in an instant, and for a split second she was completely disoriented. Then she saw Max Damage looking at her from the front of the old flyer, and she realised she was inside the garage at the wildlife park. She shook herself, dispelling the vivid memories, then reached out and pressed the starter.

There was a cough from the thrusters, followed by a steady roar. Much to Sam's surprise, they kept running. 'You've done it!' she exclaimed.

Max grinned. 'Of course!' she shouted back. 'It's just a simple little flyer. Nothing to it.'

Sam cut the thrusters to save whatever fuel remained, and she watched Max closing the hood, pressing down firmly to seal it. She came and sat down, and after fastening her seat belt she started cleaning her hands on a rag, wiping off dirt and grime. 'You slept?'

'Yeah.' Sam remembered the dogfight. 'Not that restful.'

'The war,' said Max.

Sam nodded.

'You don't have to go back.' Max looked at her, and in a low voice she continued. '*I* didn't.'

'You deserted?' Sam stared at the other woman in shock. 'You abandoned your comrades?'

'They were dying around me, and I was next.' Max shrugged. 'This war is futile. Pointless. A bunch of politicians putting their pride, and our lives, before common sense.'

Sam hardly liked to ask, but she had to know. 'Which side were you on?'

'Does it matter?'

'It does to me!' exclaimed Sam. 'If you're Mayestran, I'm fraternising with the enemy right now. When I get back, they'll have me shot as a traitor!'

'If I was Mayestran, would you try and kill me?'

Sam eyed the much larger woman sitting beside her. 'I took you once.'

Max grunted. 'Anyway, like I said, I quit. I don't fight for either side. I don't fight for anyone... except myself.'

Sam was in turmoil. She'd figured Max for a rough and ready pilot, handy with a spanner and good in a spot of trouble. She'd had no idea the woman was ex-military, and that changed everything.

'It really bothers you, huh?' said Max, eyeing her curiously.

'If we were on the same side you'd have said so. That means you fought for my enemies, and that means–'

'Think of me as neutral.'

'But–'

'Sam, I could have killed you a dozen times already. Why would I attack you now?' Max toyed with her seatbelt. 'I was wounded in battle,' she said, her voice low. 'Three days later I woke in hospital, and as soon as I could walk, I left.' She glanced at Sam. 'That was ten years ago. Do you really think I'd pick up a weapon to join the fight once more?'

'Just tell me which side you were on,' pleaded Sam. 'If I knew that–'

Max shook her head. 'Sorry, but no. I'm on my own side, and I will identify with neither. Now start the engines and let us fly out of here.'

Unwillingly, knowing Max wouldn't budge, Sam obeyed. The thrusters ran smoothly, and she took the controls and guided the little flyer out of the garage. Clouds of dust accompanied them, blasted from the ground by the pulsing jets, and it leaked into the cabin through the weathered, shrunken door seals.

Once they were outside, Sam experimented with the controls. The gyros were off, just a little, which meant the craft wobbled in mid-air, but it seemed stable enough for a quick flight. 'Ready?'

'Yeah,' said Max, who was hanging onto the door handle with both hands. 'Just try not to kill us both. This war has enough casualties already.'

Sam gave her a grim smile, then turned her attention back to the controls. These consisted of a chopped-off wheel on a movable column, and a knob to adjust the thrust from each corner. Sam tweaked the knobs until the flyer was level, then eased back on the column. The roar of the thrusters increased, and slowly they rose into the air, until she could look out the side onto the rusty tin roof of the garage. It was still dark out, but the roof glowed red in the light from the thrusters.

Sam turned the wheel and the flyer responded, until it was facing the car park. Then she pressed down on the throttle, and through the side window she saw the thrusters tilting, moving them forwards. 'Seems to work,' she said, raising her voice over the racket.

'So far,' Max called back. 'Don't delay, though. Fuel might be low.'

Sam nodded, and applied the throttle. The ground below was in darkness, but the treetop canopy reflected the light from their exhaust, giving her just enough to see by. The flyer probably had headlights, thought Sam, but she was reluctant to try any switches in case they shorted out, cutting the thrusters.

Sam couldn't see the fence, but she knew they'd come across it as long as she flew a straight course. It was hard to judge, what with the darkness, and the trees all looking the same, and she missed having a star field to navigate by. All she had here was the view through the flyer's grubby windows, and what little she could see of the night sky was just a dark blur. Anyway, she daren't take her eyes off the trees, in case the flyer started tipping, or heading off course.

There was a cough from the thrusters, quickly overcome, and her grip tightened on the controls. Sam had no idea how much fuel was left, because the dash screen was still blank, but she guessed it wasn't much.

'Faster,' said Max. 'We have to get down.'

'If I go faster we'll burn more fuel.' Sam glanced down at the trees. The thick leaves looked soft and inviting, but after plunging through the canopy, she knew they'd still have a long way to fall.

The engines coughed again, and despite her reservations, she increased speed. The flyer began to move faster, humming along as they flew across the park, and then she saw the fence. It was ahead and below, and the big double gates were off to her left, illuminated by the lights on the kiosk. A hundred metres or so, and they could set down on the other side. They'd made it!

'What's that?' asked Max suddenly.

She was pointing ahead, through the windscreen, and Sam squinted at a bright spark of light. It appeared to be growing larger, and it was accompanied by a deep roar, audible even over their own thrusters. The roar got louder, the spark grew bigger and bigger, and with a shock she recognised it. 'It's a missile!' she shouted. 'Hang on! Evasive manoeuvres!'

'No!' cried Max. 'It's just a ship! It's the *Albion*. It's Spacejock!'

Too late. Sam had already twisted the wheel, cutting the thrust, and the left side of the little flyer dipped alarmingly towards the ground. It kept dipping, until they were in danger of flipping completely upside down... and that's when the huge freighter flew just over their heads, completely oblivious to the fragile craft. The wash from its jets thundered over them like the wind of a thousand hurricanes, and the flyer was tossed like a leaf in the maelstrom. Whirling over and over, the view outside was a flickering kaleidoscope of green trees and black sky. Sam wrestled with the controls but it was far too late. The flyer was beyond saving, and they spun towards the ground with no hope of recovery. At the last second, knowing it was all over, they instinctively raised their arms, covering their faces to fend off the crash.

14

Unaware of their near-miss with the tiny flyer, Clunk throttled back and brought the *Albion* in for a perfect landing.

'Why the car park?' Hal asked him, when he realised where they were setting down.

'It's closer to the buildings.'

The main screen showed a view of those same buildings. They were visible as light, fuzzy patches in the overwhelming darkness, but squint as he might Hal couldn't see Max or Sam waiting. 'Do you think they gave up on us? Left before we got here?'

'Unlikely,' said Clunk.

'Hmm.' Hal was perched on the co-pilot's chair, the back still lying flat behind him, and he crossed his arms as he thought things through. 'They must have heard us, so where are they?'

'I'm sure they won't be long.' Clunk pointed at the buildings. 'It's possible they sheltered inside. It's warm out, but they might have been hungry.'

'You're probably right. I can just picture Max breaking her way into a locked building for a chocolate bar.'

'Would you like me take a look?'

Hal thought about it, but if Max had found snacks he wouldn't mind one or two for himself. 'We'll both go.'

'Are you sure?'

'Yeah.' He leaned forward then hesitated, finger above the ramp button. 'No buildings alongside, correct?'

'That is so.'

'No trees? Lamp posts? Signs?'

'All clear, Mr Spacejock.'

Hal pressed the button, and the ramp extended with a whine of hydraulics. 'Navcom, seal the lift. I don't want our guests wandering around the flight deck.'

'Complying. Incidentally, There's a substantial build-up of cat hairs in my air filters.'

'Are you allergic?'

'Negative, but–'

'Later, Navcom. I have two angry women to placate.' So saying, Hal jumped up and strolled towards the airlock, where he operated the controls. He considered donning a helmet, in case Max took a swing at him, but changed his mind as hot, humid air swirled into the flight deck. 'Phew. It's warm out.'

'It's a tropical climate,' said Clunk, who had joined him in the airlock. 'The beach resort would have been the same, only it was cooled by the ocean.'

Hal added tropical zones to his lengthy list of pet peeves, then looked down the ramp towards the ground. The ship's navigation lights glared on the tarmac, but outside the cone it was pitch dark. 'Switch the lights off, will you? The glare is making things worse.'

Clunk obeyed, and the lights winked out. After a few moments, Hal's eyes adjusted, and he proceeded down the ramp. 'Can you smell burning?' he asked.

'It's probably from our landing,' said Clunk. 'The thrusters generate a lot of heat.'

'If you say so. Smells like plastic to me.'

Clunk sniffed, analysing the air. 'There's a wide range of materials, including plastics and petrochemicals.'

'It smells like a burning car.' Hal stopped. 'We landed in the car park this time. There weren't any–'

'No, Mr Spacejock. The area was totally empty.'

'Come on, then.' They walked down the passenger ramp, and then across the car park. As they reached the jungle, Hal tested the ground before trusting it with his weight.

'What are you doing?' Clunk asked him.

'It's like a swamp out here. They have deadly quicksand in places like this.'

'Not beside a car park they don't.'

The turf was springy and firm, but it held up when Hal took a couple of tentative steps. His fears allayed, he strode along a narrow path towards a collection of buildings. They circled each one, peering through the windows, until they encountered a broken glass door. 'Bet that was Max,' murmured Hal.

'Hello?' called Clunk, his voice amplified.

There was no reply.

'Yeah, er, keep it down a bit,' Hal advised him. 'We're not meant to be here.'

'There's nobody around.'

'I know, I just... I have this feeling we're being watched.'

'Really? How does that work?' Clunk asked him.

'It's not something you can measure.'

'In that case, it doesn't exist,' said the robot firmly.

Hal gave up, and they circled the closed-up buildings again. Then, on the off-chance, he lifted the lids on a row of dumpsters and looked inside. 'It's no good,' he said. 'They're not here.'

'Perhaps they ventured into the jungle,' said Clunk.

Hal eyed the dank treeline with disfavour. 'Why?'

'In my experience humans do the strangest things, often for no discernible reason. Anyway, they're not here, so it's logical to assume they're somewhere else.'

'You should have been a detective,' growled Hal. 'With that kind of smarts, crooks would have no chance against you.'

'It did cross my mind once or twice. Solving crimes is a noble pursuit, and–'

Hal raised his hand, then lowered it again.

'Oh, I see,' said Clunk. 'Sarcasm.'

'Come on. Let's take a look in the jungle. Not too far, though. I don't want to get lost.'

They left the group of buildings and walked beneath the trees, picking their way carefully in the poor light. Before long they encountered a trail, and they followed it deep into the jungle. Along the way they passed little signposts, each with a few lines of text. It was heavy with scientific terms, and after trying to read one or two, Hal gave up. 'What do they say?' he asked Clunk.

'They're detailing the genus and species of local flora and fauna.'

'Come again?'

'They're the names of plants and animals.'

'Which is which?'

'I don't know, Mr Spacejock. Alas, my onboard storage doesn't contain the scientific data from every known planet, and it's also been a while since I received an update. I could run a search online, of course, but it wouldn't be cheap. The roaming charges from this location–'

Hal gestured. 'Forget it. It's not important.'

They continued along the trail, struggling as the going steadily got tougher. The ground was uneven now, churned up as though two teams of giants had fought a pitched battle. There were fallen branches everywhere, the ends shattered and gleaming like broken bones under the starlight. Deep impressions half-filled with water made the going difficult, and Hal's boots were soon caked with slimy mud. He muttered under his breath as he tripped and stumbled, and he was about to complain when he realised Clunk wasn't faring much better. The robot's lower legs had accumulated so much sticky mud it looked like he was wearing giant brown space boots.

Then Clunk stopped. 'That's odd.'

'What?'

The robot pointed out a large crater. 'What does that look like to you?'

'Mud,' said Hal.

'I mean the impression.'

'I get the impression it's mud.'

'The shape, Mr Spacejock.' Clunk traced the outline in mid-air. 'Do you see?'

'Oh, that.' Hal squinted, and even in the darkness he realised it was far too regular for a random puddle. 'It's a...a...' He swallowed. 'Clunk, that better not be what I think it is.'

'Yes, Mr Spacejock. That extremely large crater is clearly a footprint.'

'But it's bigger than you!' Hal looked around at the shredded branches, and it suddenly occurred to him that they hadn't just fallen off the trees – they'd been ripped off and trampled. And many of them were thicker than his thigh. 'Wait a minute, you're not suggesting there's a great big–'

'If I were you, I'd keep my voice down,' said Clunk quietly. 'Whatever it is, these marks are fresh.'

Hal stared into the trees... or what was left of them. Had

Max and Sam come this way, only to encounter some huge, carnivorous monster? Were they hiding nearby, terrified for their lives? Well, if so they could fend for themselves a little longer. 'Back to the ship,' said Hal. 'Quick!'

They'd barely turned around when a long, deep roar shook the nearby trees. 'What the hell was *that?*' whispered Hal.

'I don't have any data on the creature,' said Clunk, 'but I believe it came from the vicinity of the *Albion*.'

'You mean we're cut off?'

'Precisely.' Clunk gestured in the opposite direction, away from the ship. 'I suggest we continue on our original course.'

'Right behind you on that one.'

They put the *Albion* behind them and continued through the trees, picking their way around the giant footprints and fallen branches. Some time later Hal was tired, muddy, and beginning to think they should have gone back to the ship even if it meant facing a rampaging horror. He was about to argue his case when they came to a heavily-fortified fence. It was five metres high, tipped with coils of barbed wire and peppered with signs. Unfortunately, the signs were on the other side, facing outwards, but the fence was built with metal grille, widely spaced with bars as thick as Hal's fingers.

'We should be able to climb it,' said Hal, reaching out. 'Look at all those handholds.'

'No, Mr Spacejock. Wait!'

Hal's fingers had already closed on the bars, and he could almost hear the hiss of burning flesh as a red-hot sensation seared his skin. Before he could react he felt the crackle of ice as the bars froze his hands into solid lumps. Shocked by the hammering pain, Hal yanked his hands away and jammed them under his armpits. 'F-f-f– ouch.'

'Quick, let me see!' said Clunk.

Hal obeyed, holding his hands out while averting his eyes from the terrible wounds.

'Just as I suspected. No damage.'

'Eh?' Hal looked down and saw his hands in perfect shape. 'But I felt –'

'Yes, it's an intriguing setup. The fence is a powerful transmitter which triggers neural impulses in living creatures.'

Hal sighed with relief. 'That explains the fear and panic I've been feeling since we landed in this dump.'

Clunk gave him a look. 'It's only programmed for hot and cold, and it only works upon physical contact.'

'Well obviously. They must have another one stashed away which broadcasts the fear and awe.'

'If you say so.' Clunk stepped up to the fence tested it with his weight, then began to climb. He reached the top in no time, eased his way through the barbed wire and climbed stiffly down the other side. When he was back on firm ground he inspected the signs.

'What do they say?' asked Hal.

'Danger. Do not touch the fence.'

'I got that bit already. What about the rest?'

Clunk shifted his gaze. 'Welcome to the Saurhead Wildlife Park.'

Hal snorted. 'Yeah, very funny. What does it really say?'

'I wasn't attempting humour. That was a literal reading of the signage.' Clunk pointed to another. 'That one says 'Thrill to our giant dinosaurs'.

'Dinosaurs?' scoffed Hal. 'Don't make me laugh. It'll be giant sea serpents and huge, fire-breathing dragons next.'

'I'm just reading the sign, Mr Spacejock.'

Hal glanced over his shoulder. 'There aren't really dinosaurs, are there? Not really?'

'The galaxy is very large, Mr Spacejock. Who can say what delights are yet to be dragged kicking and screaming from some corner of a hitherto undiscovered planet?'

'There can't be dinosaurs here. It wouldn't be safe!'

'It would explain the elaborate fence.'

'Right, disable the fence and I'll climb over to join you.'

'Negative. These dinosaurs seem to be very large and extremely dangerous, and the population of Dolor would hardly thank us for unleashing such devastation on them.'

'Oh, sure. Go ahead and be noble,' hissed Hal through the wire. 'You're not trapped in here with a bunch of hungry monsters!' He glanced over his shoulder, towards the ship. Could he make it back without getting eaten? Unlikely! No, his only chance was to jump the five metre fence, enter the park on the far side of his ship, and sneak back to the *Albion* without being seen. 'Clunk, I've got to get out of here.'

'I have a plan, Mr Spacejock.' Clunk pointed along the fence. 'If we proceed in that direction we'll encounter the park entrance soon enough.'

'Soon enough for what?' muttered Hal. Even so, it was the best plan. It would leave him exposed, sure, but if a whacking great dinosaur lumbered out of the forest he was planning to scale the fence, hot and cold neural transmitter or not. 'Come on, then. You'd better climb back.'

Clunk turned and started walking.

'Clunk? Clunk!'

The robot ignored him, and Hal realised Clunk was faking

deafness. No bloody wonder, with all the danger on this side of the fence. If he, Hal, had been on the other side, he'd have done exactly the same. So, he set off in pursuit, swatting at stray branches and mosquitoes alike. 'When I see Max again we're going to have words,' he muttered. 'She told me this was a national park, not a buffet for huge reptiles.'

'You mean *if* you see Max again,' called Clunk, whose hearing seemed to have recovered.

'I'm not dino lunch yet.'

'Correct, but there's a good chance Max has already met that fate.'

Hal realised Clunk might be right, and he fell silent. The big pilot was a pain and a nuisance, but she didn't deserve such a horrible fate. And there was Sam, too. He felt a jab as he recalled her pale, tired face, and he wished he'd done more to help her. Coming back to collect them on time... that would have been a good start.

They walked in silence, until Hal spotted another of the giant footprints. 'Promise me something?'

'Certainly,' said Clunk.

'If I get chomped, save my thigh bone and beat the crap out of Max with it.'

15

'Here's another sign, Mr Spacejock. It contains information about their opening hours.'

'Keep your bloody voice down!' hissed Hal, with a nervous glance at the nearby trees. They'd been walking for some time now, heading south, and there was a hint of grey in the sky. The dim light made things easier, but it also meant killer dinosaurs would be able to spot him from a distance. Clunk had assured him the creatures hunted by scent, but that wasn't much comfort because his flight suit was getting a little ripe. As he stumbled along, Hal began to think about breakfast... and how not to feature in it.

'Oh my goodness,' said Clunk suddenly. *'Mr Spacejock, look!'*

Hal stared along the fence, and his heart almost stopped as he saw a monstrous shadow ahead. It was over twenty metres tall, and its head was turned sideways, the huge gaping mouth just waiting to snatch up its unwary prey. Hal was about to run for safety when he spotted a sign hanging from the ridiculously small forearms, presumably welcoming excited families to the killing grounds. 'Relax, Clunk. It's a fake!'

They approached the giant model, which straddled a double set of gates. There was a paved road leading into the jungle, and a collection of buildings nestled amongst the trees. There was a gift shop, a hotdog kiosk and also a row of garages holding honest-to-goodness armoured cars, all scratched and battered from some very heavy treatment. All the buildings were shuttered, and there were no signs of life.

'It's the main entrance, Mr Spacejock,' said Clunk, from the safer side of the fence. 'Maybe now I can let you out.'

The gates were chained together, and Hal hopped from foot to foot while Clunk fiddled with the hefty lock. Hal kept glancing along the deserted road, which curved away between the trees. He recalled numerous nightmares from his childhood: being abandoned in shopping centres, on deserted space stations, in long-lost ships. Most had featured evil monsters of some kind, and none had ended well.

Thud! Thud! Thud!

Hal felt the footsteps before he heard them: a rhythmic shaking of the ground, a thudding sound which mirrored his own heartbeat. Clunk heard them too, and he redoubled his efforts with the lock. Sparks crackled as the links of chain rubbed and jingled, and it was all Hal could do to hold himself back – his instinct was to hurl himself at the gates and be over the top before the searing hot and cold shocks burned his senses to the core.

Thud-thud-thud!

The shutters on a nearby kiosk rattled in time to the beats, and the birds in the trees fell silent. Something very large and very heavy was getting closer, and Hal didn't particularly want to meet it.

'It's no good, Mr Spacejock. The lock is beyond me.' Clunk scanned the buildings. 'Can you find an open door?'

THUD-THUD-THUD.

'Yeah, sure,' hissed Hal. 'Why don't you come and help?'

Without a word, Clunk shimmied up the gate and dropped

lightly to the ground on Hal's side of the fence. They split up, with Hal heading for the buildings and the robot running to the garage with the armoured cars. Hal checked every door but they were locked up tighter than a politician's superannuation entitlements.

The thudding footsteps were closer now, and Hal could hear every thump over the hoarse breaths rasping in his chest. Whatever the thing was, it sounded big enough to eat the entire gift shop, cutesy souvenir maps and all.

'Mr Spacejock! Over here!'

Hal saw Clunk beckoning from the garage, and he felt a rush of relief. His trusty robot companion had found cover! Moving as quietly as possible, Hal hurried over and darted behind one of the bulky armoured cars. However, instead of finding an inviting door held open for him, he was given an old picnic rug. 'What the hell is this for?'

'It's a tried and tested method of concealment. If you crouch down and cover yourself with this blanket, you'll look exactly like a rock.'

'Are you kidding?' Hal shook the bright tartan rug in Clunk's face. 'If I put this on I'll look like a mound of shortbread!'

'The dinosaur may be colour blind.'

'It doesn't matter if it's blind, full stop. You told me these things sniff out their prey, remember?'

THUD, THUD... THUD.

'Stay out of sight,' said Clunk urgently.

'With this thing draped over me? Are you kidding? Hey, where are you... hey, come back!' Hal watched, alarmed, as the robot hurried into the open. He was about to follow, then remembered Clunk's final instructions, and he crouched and arranged the rug over himself, trying to look as much like a rock as possible. Sure, a bright, multicoloured tartan rock, but a rock all the same.

Then he opened a tiny gap in the material to watch events unfolding.

＊

Clunk stopped in the middle of the road, standing proud with his feet apart and his hands on his hips. Hal could hear – and feel – the huge dinosaur shifting around, but the armoured car blocked his view of the beast. Three metres to the left would give him an unhindered view, but moving into the open was just above 'getting eaten' on his to-do list.

Clunk remained motionless, his head tilted back as he gazed upon his adversary. Hal noticed the angle of the robot's gaze, and he hoped the beast was really, really close, because if it was any distance away, the thing had to be four storeys high. Then Clunk raised his hand, slowly extending his thumb and little finger until they stuck out like horns. Hal could hear the dinosaur snorting and sniffling, and his curiosity overwhelmed his caution. Slowly, Hal moved left, shuffling along under the tartan rug like a multi-coloured tortoise. His breath caught as he saw the dinosaur's gaping jaws, mean little eyes and mottled hide. The thing looked as big as a house, but amazingly, as Clunk slowly lowered his hand, the dinosaur sank to its haunches.

Without taking his eyes off the beast, Clunk dropped his hand by his side. As if joined to Clunk's arm by invisible ropes, the dinosaur laid its chin on the path and snorted contentedly.

'You can come out, Mr Spacejock,' said Clunk softly.

'Are you sure about that?'

'Absolutely. It's completely safe.'

Hal stood up and sidled along the armoured car, keeping a tight grip on his tartan rug. 'What did you use? Hypnotism? The power of mind control?'

'No, the power of remote control.' Clunk gestured suddenly, and the huge dinosaur rolled onto its back, paddling its huge legs in the air. 'It's a machine, Mr Spacejock. This vicious predator is nothing but a huge robot.'

'You've got to be kidding.' Hal stared at Clunk in disbelief. 'Half an hour scared out of my wits, ten minutes cowering under an oversized shortbread wrapper, and you put on that entire dinosaur-taming stunt for an oversized windup toy?'

'I had to keep its attention while I determined its control frequencies. It was a very delicate operation.'

'Yeah, well I'm going to kick that thing into the middle of next week.' Hal took a step towards the dinosaur, intending to put the boot in. There was an ear-splitting roar, and the robot dinosaur was up in a flash, teeth bared.

Clunk reacted quickly, using both hands to quell the giant robot. 'Careful, Mr Spacejock. I may have soothed it, but it will still react to threats.'

'What's it going to do, beam me to death with laser eyes?' Despite himself, Hal was impressed. The dinosaur looked authentic, and if Clunk hadn't been there he'd have struggled to defeat it in unarmed combat. Then a thought occurred to him. 'How did you know it was a robot?'

'Its movements were too regular for a living creature.' Clunk raised his hand and the dinosaur turned towards the forest and ambled away with a regular thud-thud-thud. Then, with one last roar, it was gone.

'Are there more of them?'

'Undoubtedly. We should find the others and leave as soon as possible.'

'Haven't they been–' Hal was going to say eaten, but he couldn't bring himself to voice the thought.

'No, Mr Spacejock. The dinosaur is just for show. It's essentially harmless.'

'So where are Max and Sam?'

'Hiding, most like.'

Hal shook his head. 'I don't get this place. Why the big fences? Why the armoured cars? Why all those signs warning people about man-eating monsters? They're just a bunch of robots!'

'It's a tourist attraction, Mr Spacejock. All the trappings are there to maintain the illusion.'

'But it must scare people witless!'

'Most of the best attractions do.'

Hal added wildlife parks to his list of irritating places never to be visited again, and then he and Clunk set off down the road. Hal noticed his legs were beginning to ache, and he wasn't surprised. They'd landed near the park's rear entrance, then walked halfway round the perimeter to the front entrance, and now they were walking back to the ship again, right through the middle of the park. And all because of some giant robot dinosaur designed to scare little kids!

As they walked along the road, Hal noticed the smell of burning getting stronger. There was smoke in the air, and the acrid smell made his eyes water. Soon it was overpowering, and it seemed to be drifting across the road from the right. 'Do you reckon one of their dinosaurs had a battery fire?' he asked Clunk.

'The composition is indicative of a burning vehicle.'

'Not my ship!' breathed Hal.

'No, not the *Albion*. Something smaller. One of those armoured cars, perhaps.'

Hal stopped dead as a thought occurred to him. 'It's Max and Sam!' he said. 'They must have used a car to shelter from the dinosaurs, and somehow it's gone up in flames!'

'How?' asked Clunk, ever the practical one.

'I don't know. Maybe they hit a tree or something! Come on, we've got to save them.' Hal turned from the road and struck off through the trees, heading deeper into the smoke.

After a moment or two, Clunk followed. 'Mr Spacejock, the air is heavy with toxins. It would be better if you waited at the road. '

'If it's bad for me it's worse for them,' said Hal grimly. 'Anyway, you can't carry two of them, so stop gabbing and pick up the pace.'

They struggled with the soft ground and the thick undergrowth, and all the while the smoke got thicker. It grew so bad Hal was forced to bury his face in the crook of his arm, breathing through the sleeve of his flightsuit.

Then they saw it...a dull, flickering glow just ahead. The smoke was so thick Hal could barely see, but as he got closer he made out the vague shape of a car lying upside-down on the ground. When he saw the damage he was chilled the core, because the vehicle had almost broken in two from the impact. 'How fast were they *going?*' he said desperately, and then he and Clunk broke into a run.

＊

As he ran towards the vehicle Hal realised it was a flyer, not a ground car, and the smoke and flames were coming from a thruster which had snapped off and ended up some distance away. The engine was on fire, and every now and then it flared up, illuminating the smoke like a firework display.

Hal could see Max and Sam inside the vehicle, upside-down and still strapped to their seats. He crouched to feel for Sam's pulse, while Clunk ran around the other side to check on Max.

'She's alive!' cried Hal, as he felt a steady heartbeat.

'Max too,' called Clunk. 'Don't try and move her, Mr Spacejock. It could do more harm than good.'

There was a flash, and sparks erupted from the broken thruster. 'It'll do them a load of harm if the flyer goes up,' called Hal. Then he saw Sam's eyes were open, her lips moving. He got closer, putting his ear to her mouth.

'I'm banged up, but nothing's broken,' she whispered. 'Crashed the flyer. Couldn't control it.'

'Don't worry about that. You're okay, and nothing else matters.'

'Need to get out.' Sam reached for the buckle on her seat belt, but her fingers were too weak. 'Get me out. Suffocating.'

Hal knew what she meant, because the smoke was thick and it was almost impossible to breathe. So, he supported her with one arm, then opened the buckle and held her tight as she fell from the seat. Then he backed away from the wreck with her un-resisting form cradled in his arms. On the other side of the car, Max was now conscious, and she swatted Clunk's hands away and struggled to her feet, swaying slightly. The two of them circled the car and followed Hal back to the road, walking in silence.

When they got there, Max came to check on Sam, and then she gave Hal a cold, angry look. 'You and I will talk later,' she said, before turning on her heel and striding down the road towards the car park.

172

'What did I do?' demanded Hal plaintively.

16

As Hal carried Sam towards the ship, he realised they might have another detour to make before starting on Murtay's asteroid job. Sam was conscious, just, but she'd had a nasty accident and he wanted to get her to a doctor. Problem was, as a Henerian she'd raise a bunch of red flags, and he could see her being handed over to the Mayestrans before she'd received any medical attention.

Ahead of him, Clunk accompanied Max up the ramp, and the pair of them vanished into the airlock. Hal adjusted his hold and followed, stumbling slightly on the steep surface. The higher he got the more he worried about tripping over and dropping Sam, and he could just imagine the two of them rolling and sliding all the way to the ground. If that happened, they'd *both* need a doctor.

He made it, though, and he turned sideways to carry Sam through the airlock and into the flight deck. Clunk was at the console, preparing for take-off, and he looked up as Hal struggled in. 'Should I carry her to a cabin for you, Mr Spacejock?'

'No, I've got her.'

The lift had already left with Max in, but when it came back Hal carried Sam inside. By now his arms felt like they were being pulled from their sockets, but he hung on grimly, determined to see her to the cabin. After navigating the lower passageway, he paused at the junction between the various cabins, then turned right. Ignoring his own suite and the bathroom, he opened Clunk's door and laid Sam gently on the bed. 'How are you feeling?' he asked quietly.

'A bit shaky,' murmured Sam. 'Hell of a crash. Didn't think we'd make it.'

'Did you hit your head?'

'Not this time.' Sam managed a weak grin. 'Probably best if I don't fly anything else today. Already run up a big damage bill.'

Hal looked down at her in concern. 'Do you need a doctor?'

Sam shook her head. 'I'm feeling better already. That smoke... it was impossible to breathe.' She gave him a grateful smile. 'If you hadn't found us...'

'Don't think about it,' said Hal. Then he remembered Max's outburst. 'Do you know why Max wants to kill me?'

'She's got a whole list of reasons,' said Sam. 'First, this isn't the national forest she asked you to fly her to. You were off track by hundreds of kilometres, and you went in entirely the wrong direction.'

'She said north east, we flew north east,' protested Hal.

'Well, she's convinced you screwed up. And a wildlife park of all things! We heard something huge in the trees, roaring at us. And then, just as we were escaping the wildlife park, your ship turned up and knocked us right out of the sky.'

'*We* caused the crash?' said Hal, aghast. Then he remembered something. 'Hey, you know Clunk was flying, right? If Max isn't happy she can take it up with him.'

'Don't worry, she'll get over it.'

'Sure, after she's beaten me up, thrown me into the nearest airlock and spaced me.'

'Probably,' said Sam, and then she smiled at him. 'Don't worry, Hal. You're doing your best. I know that.'

Her words cut him deeper than Max's unfair outburst. Did she really think this was the best he could do? Landing them in the wrong place and swatting their ship out of mid-air? He recalled how he'd rescued both of them from the asteroid field, and he felt a flash of anger. Nobody was thanking him for *that* little adventure. Oh no, they were far too busy complaining about mistakes he wasn't responsible for! 'I'd better get to the flight deck,' he said curtly. 'We've got a job to do.'

Sam reached for his arm, but he avoided her and strode to the door. He felt like both Max and Sam were taking him for granted, and as far as he was concerned the pair of them could clear off the minute they landed on a neutral planet.

As the door closed behind him, he put Sam out of his mind and strode to the lift. This asteroid job is going to be an exercise in precision, he promised himself. It's going to run like clockwork from start to finish, and then he'd collect the second half of the money, ditch Murtay and his mother and the cats, and leave the Dolorian system for good.

Still irritated, he arrived in the flight deck just as Clunk opened the throttle for lift-off. Soon, the wildlife park was laid out on the viewscreen before them, and as they flew over the entrance with its fake dinosaur, Hal hoped the *Albion's* jets were close enough to torch the thing. Then he saw the lights of a convoy on the road, with a dozen or more vehicles heading towards the park. 'We got out of there just in time,' he muttered. 'They must be opening up for the day.'

Clunk eyed the screen, then frowned. 'That's not the staff turning up for work, Mr Spacejock.' He operated the camera, and the screen zoomed in, revealing a row of speeding trucks and cars.

They looked familiar, and Hal wasn't completely surprised when he saw one of the trucks had broken headlights and a missing bumper. 'The Mayestrans!'

'Correct, Mr Spacejock. And they're heading towards the wildlife park.'

'Tracking us, do you think?'

'Perhaps, but it could be they're after Sam. They might have received word of a Henerian wing commander hiding in the park.'

'Doubt it. Who knows she's around apart from you, me and Max?' Then Hal frowned. 'Wait a minute! What if Max called them from the park? She could be a traitor!' Hal's hopes rose, because if she *was* a traitor Clunk would let him land again to boot Max off the ship. Then his hopes fell once more, because she was big, strong and angry, and he couldn't see her going quietly. Sure, he'd have Clunk to help, but the robot wasn't much use in a fist-fight.

Instead of dismissing the idea out of hand, Clunk looked thoughtful. 'You know, Mr Spacejock, that's not inconceivable. Max could easily be an *agent provocateur* for the Mayestrans.'

'A what?'

'A secret agent of sorts.'

'A spy, huh?' Hal glanced towards the lift. 'She can't do anything to my ship, can she? Sabotage the engines or pull a handful of fuses or something?'

'I will go and seal the inner cargo door. Take the controls, Mr Spacejock.'

'Really? What's our heading?'

'Straight up.' Clunk got up and strode to the lift.

'Wait a minute. Why don't we land at the spaceport and hand her over?'

'The spaceport is full of Mayestrans, Mr Spacejock, and they're searching ships. Recall that we have Sam on board.' Clunk pressed a button, and the lift carried him below.

Meanwhile, Hal was lost in thought. If he could only catch Max doing something suspicious, he'd lock her cabin door, sealing her in. 'Navcom, do we have cameras in the passenger cabins?'

'Somehow, Clunk neglected to tick that particular option,' said the Navcom. 'I assume due to privacy concerns, or perhaps common decency.'

'But I have to watch Max!'

'If you want to see women taking their clothes off, there are plenty of videos online,' said the Navcom stiffly.

'No, I didn't mean...' Hal's voice tailed off, because he realised this particular idea wasn't going to fly. So, he thought some more. Last time, when Max took a shower, she'd left her clothes all over the floor. Maybe, if he could get her to take another shower, he could search through her pockets to see whether she was carrying incriminating ID. Something like a discount card for secretive members of the Mayestran armed forces, or a bank statement showing large cash deposits. He realised it was unlikely, but he didn't have much else to go on.

Problem was, how was he going to get her to take a shower?

'Entering planetary orbit,' said the Navcom calmly.

Hal looked up and saw planet Dolor directly ahead of them. Distracted by his plan to get Max into the shower, he'd neglected to keep an eye on their course. Consequently, they were now plunging directly towards the planet. Hal eased the stick back, and the planet disappeared off the bottom of the screen.

'Leaving planetary orbit,' said the Navcom.

Clunk returned soon after, and Hal transferred control back to the robot before getting to his feet. 'Let me know when we arrive at the asteroid field.'

'Why, where are you going?'

'There's something I need to do.' Without elaborating, Hal strode to the lift, and he waited impatiently as it carried him below decks. Once on the next level, he walked towards his cabin, where he poured half a mug of hot coffee. Next he topped it up with cold tap water, and after checking the temperature with his finger, he judged it to be just about right. Finally, he went into his closet and pulled down the box of goodies, selecting two packets of chips and a couple of chocolate bars.

He left his cabin with the drink and snacks, and crossed the main passageway to the three spare cabins. He already knew which ones the Murtays were in, so he knocked on the third door.

'Yes?' called Max. 'What is it?'

'I brought you something to eat,' said Hal.

There was a pause, and then the door opened. Max stood just inside, still wearing his blue dressing gown over her clothes. It was splashed with mud, and her face was streaked with soot from the crash. Then he forgot her clothing, because her blue eyes were like twin lasers as she scowled down at Hal. 'You've got a nerve,' she growled.

'I know there's been a misunderstanding or two, but if you'd just let me explain–'

'Are those for me?' said Max, eyeing the snacks.

'Yes, I ordered them specially.'

'Are they organic?' She advanced on him. 'Because if they're not...'

'I, er...' Hal started to back away. 'I think they might be, perhaps.'

'I'm just kidding, you idiot!' Max laughed and punched him on the shoulder, and Hal almost slopped the mug of coffee all over the floor. 'Should have seen your face. Priceless!' She stood aside. 'Come in, come in. Take a seat and tell me why everything wasn't your fault.'

'You're not angry with me?'

Max smiled. 'Who could be angry with you for long? You're funny.' She patted the bunk. 'Come. Sit.'

Hal avoided the bunk and sat at the desk, and he quickly explained about the mix-up with the wildlife park, and the fact the *Albion* couldn't see something as small as a flyer, and the fact Clunk had been at the controls anyway, so it wasn't Hal's fault they'd knocked the tiny little craft out of the sky. 'And it's not like you're dead or anything,' he said, as he finished his explanation. 'You're just a bit grubby, and a nice shower will fix that.'

'A cold shower?' said Max, shaking her head. 'Not a chance.'

Hal cursed under his breath, because he'd forgotten all about the cold water. Then he had a cunning idea. 'It's all right, Clunk fixed it.'

'The water is hot now?'

'Sure! You'll have to be careful or you'll burn yourself.'

Max got up from the bunk. 'Why didn't you say so earlier?'

'I–I was leaving you to cool off. You were a bit angry.'

'A hot shower,' said Max, almost in wonder. 'You have no idea how good that sounds.'

'I'll just leave this stuff here,' said Hal, getting up and putting the chocolate bars and packets of chips on her desk, alongside the mug of lukewarm coffee. Plan B had involved tipping the coffee all over Max, forcing her to take a shower, but luckily he'd hit upon a far better idea before embarking on such a risky course of action. 'Anyway, I'll leave you to it. I have to go fly the ship.'

Max nodded, and they both left. She went to the bathroom, while Hal walked towards the lift. However, as soon as he heard the bathroom door close he doubled back, darting into Max's cabin and quickly checking under the pillow, in the little desk drawer, and everywhere else he could think of where she might have hidden incriminating paperwork.

No luck.

By now he reckoned Max would be getting ready to step into the shower, and she would soon discover that Clunk had not, in fact, fixed the cold water. On the contrary, the water would be damn near freezing, and Hal knew he had scant seconds to search Max's clothes before she needed them again.

So, he tip-toed to the bathroom and listened at the door. Thanks to water saving regulations, the shower would only work when someone was in the cubicle with the screen closed. Hal was banking on having just enough time to grab Max's clothes before she found out the truth about the 'hot' water.

He heard a thud as the shower screen was closed, and then a hiss as the shower fired up. Instantly, he palmed the door controls and darted into the bathroom.

'Spacejock!' yelled Max, as she was doused in freezing cold water. 'Spacejock, I'm going to *kill* you!'

Hal didn't have time to search the clothes, so he grabbed everything and fled, leaving only his muddy blue dressing gown on the bathroom floor. He charged down the passage to the lift and hammered the up button repeatedly, praying it would take Max a few seconds to don the dressing gown.

It didn't. She came running round the corner wearing

nothing but a towel, and as she charged towards the lift Hal's knees buckled.

Fortunately it wasn't fear. No, at the last second the lift zoomed upwards with Hal still clutching Max's clothes.

'Spacejock!' yelled Max, her angry voice echoing up the shaft. 'Come back here, you horrible little liar!'

Hal emerged in the flight deck, where Clunk was staring towards the lift in surprise. He was even more surprised when Hal dumped a bundle of clothing on the console, picked out a pair of overalls and started going through the pockets.

'Mr Spacejock, when the Navcom told me you'd asked for cameras in the passenger cabins, I have to admit to a certain amount of surprise. But stealing women's clothing? This is going too far!'

'Shut up and check the lining in that jacket.' Hal was still checking pockets in the overalls, but after a minute or two he was forced to admit defeat. 'Damn it, Clunk. There's nothing here.'

'What did you expect?'

'In the movies the villain always leaves something incriminating lying around.'

'Need I point out the obvious?'

'Er, yeah.'

'This isn't a movie, Mr Spacejock.' Clunk spread his hands. 'This is real life!'

There was a whoosh, and Hal turned towards the lift. With a shock, he realised it had vanished. 'Oh crap,' he said. 'Quick, Navcom! Block the elevator!'

'Unable to comply. Manual override in operation.'

'We don't *have* a manual override.'

'We do now. Someone twisted the wires in the control panel together.'

Hal ran to the shaft and looked down. The lift operated on antigrav, so there were no wires or cables, but when he looked up he realised there was still a chance. As the lift rose towards him, no doubt bringing a cold, angry Max to the flight deck, he judged his moment before stepping into the shaft... directly onto the roof of the rising elevator car. The impact threw him to his knees, and he dropped prone just as the lift came to a halt. Slowly, he looked up, and he discovered there was barely two inches clearance between his nose and the roof.

'Where is Spacejock?' thundered Max, her voice muffled by the elevator.

Now Hal realised he had a problem. His intention had been to ride the elevator to the lower deck and step off. Unfortunately, no matter which of the lower decks the lift stopped at, he'd still be surrounded by blank, impenetrable walls. All he could do was ride the lift up and down, up and down, until he gave up and called for help.

— 17 —

As Hal lay on top of the elevator, he could hear Max ranting in the flight deck. Every now and then she stopped for breath, and then Clunk would speak in calm, unruffled tones. It didn't seem to be helping though, because the angry shouting showed no signs of tailing off.

For all Hal knew, Clunk was telling Max that he, Hal, was a nutjob who'd recently escaped from a lunatic asylum. He decided he didn't care what the robot came up with, as long as Max no longer wanted to hunt him down and beat him senseless.

Hal was getting uncomfortable, and he shifted his position. That's when he discovered he was lying on a pair of metal rails, and as he looked closer he saw they were the guides for a sliding hatch. There was a recessed handle, too, and Hal realised he might have a chance after all.

He crawled over the hatch, turned around and slid it open. Immediately, Clunk and Max's voices grew louder, but he wasn't interested in their conversation. No, he was working out whether he could drop into the lift, hit the controls and flee to the lower deck before Max grabbed him.

She wasn't shouting quite as much now, but whether this was because she'd run out of swear words, or was too cold to continue, Hal wasn't sure. She wasn't near the lift, and that was all he cared about.

There was no room to get up, so he lowered himself through the opening head-first, gripping the frame around the hatch to prevent himself falling. Unfortunately he put his fingers in the greasy rails, and with a yelp he plunged through the hole, landing on the floor of the lift with a thud. Max was just climbing into her overalls, which Hal had abandoned on the console, and when she heard his landing, she turned and spotted him.

'Spacejock!'

Hal got up quickly and reached for the controls. The panel was hanging off the wall, and a couple of wires had been twisted together, but when he pressed the lower button the lift started to descend.

Meanwhile, Max was hopping towards him, still trying to pull her overalls on. 'Spacejock!' she shouted. 'Stop right there!'

Not on your nelly, thought Hal.

The lift dropped towards the second floor, and when it stopped Hal waited for the doors to open, then stepped out. The control panel in the corridor was hanging by a couple of wires, and Hal yanked it right off the wall. There was a shower of sparks, and the light in the elevator winked out. 'Let's see you override *that*,' he muttered, and then he jumped when he saw Cylen Murtay approaching. 'Oh, hi,' said Hal, quickly hiding the detached panel behind his back. 'Settling in okay?' he asked, giving his best customer service smile.

'Er, yes,' said Cylen. 'I just wondered if you could explain something.'

'Oh, you mean this,' said Hal, revealing the control panel. 'It's okay, it's just, er, being serviced.'

'Not that. I wondered why we landed earlier. We appeared to be on the ground for quite some time, and I couldn't find anyone to speak to about it.'

'Don't worry, it was just a minor technical issue.'

'Will it delay the mission?'

Hal put his arm around Murtay's shoulders, leading him away from the lift. 'Your job is top priority. Number one on our to-do list. At this very moment we're speeding towards the asteroid belt, ready to leap into action the second we arrive.'

'So everything is under control?'

'Absolutely. I guarantee it.' Hal glanced towards the lift, but it showed no signs of moving. Even so, he figured it might be a good idea to stick around Murtay for a bit. If he had a witness, Max might go a little easier on him. 'Hey, how about you come and help me whip up a couple of omelettes?'

'That would be most welcome. I don't believe I've eaten since lunchtime.' Murtay hesitated. 'While we're on the subject, do you have any dishes we can use for the cats?'

'Do they eat omelette too?' asked Hal in surprise.

'No, mother brought their favourite food along, but she forgot their feeding bowls.'

'Not a problem,' said Hal. 'Come right this way.'

＊

To Clunk's relief, once Max got dressed and made herself comfortable in the co-pilot's chair, the anger seemed to drain out of her. She was still annoyed, but not furious, and silently Clunk hoped Mr Spacejock would forgive him for exaggerating a few of the human's less endearing traits.

'Thick as a plank, you say?' Max asked him. 'Incapable of looking after himself? A child in a man's body?'

'That's Mr Spacejock all right,' said Clunk.

Max turned to the console. 'You! Ship's computer! How long have you known Spacejock?'

'Too long,' said the Navcom.

'Is he really an idiot?'

'Mr Spacejock couldn't beat me at chess, so he invented his own rules. His idea of a good landing is one where most of the cargo survives. He's got the insurance company's claims department on speed dial, and he's so gullible I once convinced him the screen saver was a live view from the fore camera. He spent hours flying the ship past animated planets and stars.'

'I'll take that as a yes,' said Max, snorting with laughter. 'You two crack me up.'

'Mr Spacejock means well,' said Clunk. 'He's just a little impulsive, that's all.'

'So why this business with the cold shower?' demanded Max. 'What was that all about?'

'Ah.' Clunk hesitated, uncertain how much to share. 'Well, when we took off from the wildlife park–'

'Where we never should have been in the first place.'

'Indeed,' said Clunk, with a frown. And then he explained about the Mayestrans showing up in the Dolorian system to hunt down so-called Henerian rebels, and the force of enemy soldiers he and Hal had encountered, and how they'd spotted the same force racing towards the wildlife park...even as the *Albion* lifted off. 'Mr Spacejock came to the conclusion that you may – and I emphasise *may* – have called the Mayestrans from the park.'

'Why would I do that?'

'He suspects you may be a Mayestran agent. Nobody else could have notified the Mayestrans that Sam was hiding at the wildlife park. Aside from the people aboard this ship, nobody even knows she's here. I didn't call anyone, and Mr Spacejock didn't inform on her, and we can safely assume she didn't give herself up–'

'So that left me.' Max nodded slowly. 'I can see where he got the idea. But why the cold shower and the clothes? Was he trying to torture me?'

'No! Mr Spacejock wanted to look through your things, to see if there was any incriminating evidence.'

'Like a membership card to the Mayestran Spies Guild?' said Max, with a snort.

'Yes, well he didn't reveal his plans to me beforehand.'

'Idiot,' murmured Max. Then she eyed Clunk thoughtfully. 'So he's just trying to defend Sam, right?'

'Indeed. Mr Spacejock can be very gallant when it comes to women in distress. He'll always do his best to help.'

'I was in distress when that freezing cold shower started up,' growled Max.

'You can take care of yourself, or so Mr Spacejock believes. Also, you make him nervous.'

'All right, so in his own twisted way, he was trying to find out whether I was a rat. I understand now.'

'So you won't try to kill him?' asked Clunk.

Max shook her head.

'Then perhaps I can mend the lift, and you can return to your cabin.'

'I have a better idea.' Max gestured at the console. 'I've never flown one of these new jobs. Can I take the controls for a while? See how she flies?'

Clunk felt apprehensive. 'To be honest, I'm not that keen on–'

'Oh, go on. We're in deep space! What could possibly go wrong?'

'Very well. Transferring control to your station. Please remember not to–'

What Clunk was about to say was drowned in the roar of the engines, and he could only stare as Max put the *Albion* through her paces. She performed loops and barrel rolls at full throttle, every manoeuvre performed with a sure, delicate touch. Then, throttling back, she resumed their original course. 'Nice,' she said. 'Very nice. I'd kill to own a ship like this.'

Clunk sincerely hoped she was joking. 'You certainly know how to fly,' he said.

'Yeah, it's been my thing since I was young.' Max gave him a calculating look. 'You know, the pair of us should go into business together. We'd make a fortune.'

'I'm loyal to Mr Spacejock.'

'Give me a break. Spacejock's a walking disaster, and it's a miracle he hasn't crashed and blown himself up yet.'

'He does seem to enjoy more than his fair share of bad luck,' admitted Clunk.

'It's not bad luck, it's stupidity.' Max ran a hand over the console, admiring the sleek metal finish. 'If anything happens to Spacejock, come seek me out. We'd make a good team.'

'If anything happens to Mr Spacejock, I will.'

Smiling, Max held her hand out. 'Shake, and it's a deal.'

Clunk obeyed, and then he was struck by an unpleasant thought. Had he just sealed Mr Spacejock's fate?

'So, what's the cargo job?' Max asked him, changing the subject.

'It's a scientific mission,' said Clunk, and he explained the details.

'Back to the asteroid field, eh? Perfect. But how are you going to get the asteroids on board?'

'I was thinking I'd open the hold and reverse up to a really big one, until it was safely inside. Unfortunately, one wrong move could damage the ship. So, my backup plan was for Mr Spacejock to use the jetbike. That way he'll be able to collect several smaller ones.'

'I'll help,' said Max promptly.

'Really?'

'Sure. I've got my space suit below. It's the least I can do after you both saved my life.'

Clunk felt a rush of relief. 'Well that's splendid. I was worried about Mr Spacejock going into space again, but with your help the job will be completed in no time. Thank you so much!'

'Don't mention it,' said Max, and in the light from the console her smile looked particularly wolfish.

Hal was just cleaning up the kitchenette in his suite when he heard footsteps. He turned, and his heart almost stopped as he saw Max approaching. Quickly, he ran over and and closed his door. Just as quickly, Max opened it again.

'H-how did you get down here?' asked Hal.

'I jumped down onto the roof of the lift, then climbed through the hatch.'

'Jumped down? But that's a three metre fall!'

Max shrugged. 'It's all in the landing.'

'So... now what?' Hal asked her.

There was a moment or two of strained silence, and then Max smiled. 'First, we fix the lift together. Then you must come to the flight deck with this Murtay guy, so we can all discuss his job.'

Surprised, Hal could only stare. 'I thought–'

'You thought I was going to attack you? Seek revenge?' Max gestured dismissively. 'You're an incompetent idiot, Spacejock. You act before you think, assuming you do any thinking at all. You're a useless pilot, a terrible businessman, and a complete waste of space. You are little more than a child, and therefore I forgive your actions.'

'I guess you're entitled to an opinion,' said Hal, with a frown. 'But there's no need to–'

'That's not *my* opinion. That's what your robot and your ship's computer told me about you.' Max slapped him on the shoulder. 'Me, I think you're a great guy. The best.'

'Really?'

Max raised her left hand, then lowered it again.

'Clunk told you about that as well?'

'We have no secrets. Now give me the control panel for the lift, and come and do some real work for a change.'

Hal passed her the control panel, and Max took it and walked away. As he strolled after her, Hal felt a rush of gratitude towards Clunk and the Navcom. The pair of them had convinced Max that he, Hal, was hopelessly incompetent, and more than a little deranged, thus saving him from her wrath. It couldn't have been easy for them to lie, since they were both computers, but somehow they'd managed it. He decided to get them both a gift at the earliest opportunity. Something classy, like a framed picture of himself for the Navcom, and a Spacejock Freightlines T-shirt for Clunk.

Lost in thought, he almost bumped into Max as they arrived at the lift. She got him to hold the control panel while she repaired the wiring, quickly and efficiently, and when she was done she pressed the panel back into place. 'Go fetch the customer,' she said, gesturing down the corridor. 'We are almost at the asteroid field by now, and Clunk will need him to identify suitable rocks.'

'Shouldn't you test the lift first? I mean, if I bring him here and it doesn't work...'

Max frowned. 'Are you questioning my repairs?' Without looking, she pressed the topmost button, and the lift doors closed. Hal heard a whoosh as the lift shot up towards the flight deck, carrying Max with it. Then, seconds later, he heard it coming back again, and the doors opened once more.

'Looks good,' said Hal. 'I'll go get Cylen.'

18

'Your cargo hold is much larger than I hoped for,' said Murtay, addressing Hal. 'Therefore, instead of bringing one large asteroid on board, I propose to collect several smaller ones.'

Max was nearby, lounging against the flight console, while Clunk was handling the controls from the pilot's chair. 'Are you looking for a specific chemical composition?' the robot asked Murtay. 'Metals, perhaps? Or certain minerals?'

'Not really. The intention is to burn them up in the atmosphere, so we can measure their make-up when they're destroyed.'

'Burn them up?' said Clunk in surprise. 'I thought we were delivering them to orbit?'

'Oh, didn't I explain that part? The asteroid, or asteroids, must be released in space, on precise headings. My lab will be monitoring the atmosphere as the rocks hit Dolor, and the results should prove one of my pet theories. Here, I have all the details on this.' Murtay took out a data cube and passed it to Clunk.

The cube glowed briefly as Clunk pinched it between his forefinger and thumb. 'Your calculations run to nine decimal places?' he asked, surprised.

Murtay nodded. 'The speed and course are critical.'

'I can see that,' said Clunk. 'I just don't understand why you're not testing your experiment with a simulation.'

'My team is sort of old-school,' said Murtay, with a shrug. 'Computers are okay, but they're no substitute for the real thing.'

'I see,' said Clunk frostily.

'Oh, I didn't mean–'

Clunk gestured, dismissing his apology. 'As for the collection, we're approaching the asteroid field now, and my plan is to open the hold and fly in reverse, capturing your asteroids one by one. As they enter the hold, I will increase the effects of gravity until they're firmly seated on the deck.'

'Sounds perfect.' Murtay looked at him anxiously. 'But what about the release? Our course and speed is critical, and if you deviate by as much as a hair–'

Clunk gave him a look. 'I'm a computer, Mr Murtay. Unlike humans, I am capable of precision and accuracy to the nth degree.'

'Excellent, excellent.'

Max raised her hand. 'I have a suggestion.'

'Yes?'

'Spacejock and I, we should suit up and collect these asteroids by hand. We'll take the jetbike and bring them to the ship.'

'Eh? What?' said Hal. A lot of the discussion had gone over his head so far, but he got *that* part just fine.

'Why would you do such a thing?' asked Clunk. 'It will be dangerous and, I assure you, completely unnecessary.'

Max smiled at him. 'Because you'll need to perform evasive manoeuvres in the *Albion* to avoid stray rocks, and if you move around while you're reversing up, the asteroid you're trying to capture might destroy one of your engines, or crush your hull.'

'There is a slim chance of that,' said Clunk, 'but weighed against the danger to you and Mr Spacejock–'

'I flew a towship, remember?' Max slapped Hal on the shoulder. 'As for Spacejock, like all experienced pilots he's completely at home in space. With his help, I'll have your asteroids on board in no time.'

Clunk looked doubtful, and Hal couldn't think of anything worse than heading into the dangers of space alongside Max, but she'd called him an experienced pilot and he couldn't chicken out in front of everyone. 'Max is right. We'll go out there and grab these rocks. It's the best plan by far.'

'Mr Spacejock–'

Hal gestured. 'I'm in charge around here, and I agree with Max. We're going to do this her way.' He saw Clunk's look, and felt a flash of irritation. What was the robot worried about? Hal had already flown the jetbike through the asteroid field without hitting anything, and he'd rescued not one but *two* pilots into the bargain. Grabbing a few rocks would be child's play by comparison. 'Come on,' he said to Max. 'Let's go and suit up. Clunk, take the controls.'

He and Max went to the cargo hold, where they dressed in their spacesuits and donned their helmets. Max tested the thrusters on her back, and when she was happy, she nodded. Hal opened the launch tube hatch, and they climbed aboard the little jet bike, with him in front and Max behind, her arms wrapped around his chest like a vice.

With the inner hatch sealed, Hal opened the tube and fired up the bike, sending them whizzing into space. There was a vast expanse of asteroids all around them, and as he flew between a couple of huge rocks he realised he'd forgotten to ask Cylen what size to pick up. Never mind, he thought. They needed half a dozen of the things, and after the first two or three he'd have a pretty good idea of the remaining space in the hold.

Hal flew up to a rock which was about as tall as he was, with a pitted grey surface. It was turning slowly in space, and as Hal approached he felt Max leaving the jetbike. She flew across to the rock, then spun around and used her suit jets to match its speed. Hal was impressed by the graceful manoeuvre, and as he brought the jetbike around to the rear of the big rock, he noticed Max was already slowing its rotation. Then, once it was still, she fired a long burst from her jets. At first nothing happened, but then, inch by inch, the boulder began to move. Hal could see her thrusters glowing from the heat of the exhaust, and he hoped she was carrying plenty of fuel.

Once the rock was moving towards the Albion, Max signalled to him, then pointed at another. This one was bigger, the surface craggy and pitted, and there were sharp edges protruding all over. Max flew across, then gestured at the jetbike, pointing at the rear of the big rock. Her meaning was clear: she wanted Hal's help to push it.

He lined up the bike and approached slowly, until the nose bumped into the big asteroid. Then, carefully, he opened the throttle. Light flared from the bike's exhaust, illuminating the asteroid like the glow of a welding torch, and Hal's visor dimmed automatically against the glare, blinding him. When he judged he'd done enough, he cut the thrusters. The visor cleared again, and to his surprise he saw Max floating right next to the asteroid, motionless. Her thrusters had cut out, and her arms and legs were outstretched, lifeless. He could see the fingers of one hand slowly moving towards the big rock, and as they made contact her arm bent, without resistance. She appeared to be out cold...or worse.

Hal felt a rush of cold through his veins, and he angled the jetbike towards Max, hoping he could scoop her up and get her to safety. Had she knocked herself out? he wondered. Or maybe her air supply was faulty. Either way, she needed his help, and fast.

As he got closer, Hal throttled back and reached out for Max with one hand. He was right next to the asteroid now, and he was all too aware of the jagged edges thrusting from the craggy surface. They were capable of slicing his suit, or ripping the jetbike apart, and he wondered whether Max had flown too close.

Suddenly she turned to look at him. He caught a glimpse of her piercing blue eyes, and then she grabbed his wrist and fired her jets, swinging him towards the asteroid. At the last second she fired again, keeping her distance but allowing Hal to sail past her, straight towards the huge, jagged rock. He put his hands up to protect his visor, and felt a thud as his body slammed into the asteroid. Something beeped in his ear, and he felt a rush of air. His suit was holed, and the atmosphere was leaking into space!

Stunned, he turned to look at Max. She was busy with the jetbike, and the next thing Hal knew there was a blast from the exhaust, and the tiny little craft sped into the asteroid field. Max remained, and as the jetbike vanished from sight, she turned to give Hal a cool, appraising look.

It was getting hard to breathe, and Hal's vision was starting to dim. He saw a puff of light as Max fired her jets, and then she flew away, leaving him to suffocate...alone.

Clunk scanned the screen nervously, trying to spot Hal and Max amongst the hundreds of nearby asteroids. Unfortunately they were too far away, even at the highest zoom level, and all he could see was the occasional spark as one or the other fired their jets.

Clunk had a bad feeling about the whole operation, and he wished he'd overridden Mr Spacejock's desire to go into space. But Hal had been goaded into it by Max, and there'd been no stopping him.

Then Clunk noticed a smallish asteroid approaching the ship, accompanied by a tiny figure. He realised it was Max, after he spotted a flare of jets from the suit. Also, the asteroid was being expertly guided, which was another clue that he wasn't watching Mr Spacejock.

As the big rock got closer, Clunk checked the hold was sealed off from the rest of the ship, then opened the big doors at the rear. An atmosphere warning light flashed, and he gestured to cancel it. Then he lost sight of Max, as the towship pilot accompanied the asteroid to the rear of the *Albion*.

While she was loading the rock, Clunk turned his attention to the centre of the screen. He'd only seen one figure in a spacesuit, and there was no sign of Hal and the jetbike. He wished the comms were working, because it troubled him greatly to have Mr Spacejock alone in the asteroid field, unable to call for help.

Clunk watched Max flying away from the ship, and he saw her intercept another incoming rock, this one craggy and pitted with hollows. A third rock was also approaching the ship, and Clunk realised the humans were working in tandem. Mr

Spacejock must be sending the rocks on their way, while Max was collecting them and manoeuvring them into the hold. It was a sensible division of labour on Max's part, he thought, since Mr Spacejock could hardly mess up the throwing of a rock, whereas he could definitely make a three course meal out of intercepting one and getting it into the *Albion's* hold.

Clunk checked the time. Both humans would need a break soon, since their air would be getting low, and he wished again he was in direct contact with Hal. He watched Max bringing the third asteroid to the ship, and this time she didn't reappear from the hold. Instead, the atmospheric warning light turned green, and he realised she'd pressurised the hold. But...what about Mr Spacejock?

Clunk scanned every inch of the screen. How long was it since he'd seen a flicker of jets? Worried now, he replayed his most recent memories, but it was ten minutes since he'd seen more than one flare at once. And had that flicker been Hal, or Max? He wanted to dash to the hold and question Max, but he had to stay right there in the flight deck, hands on the controls. Nervously, he glanced towards the lift. Would Max come up, or would she refill her oxygen and head out again? By his count, Mr Spacejock still had ten or fifteen minutes of air left, and if he wasn't already heading back, he would soon be in trouble.

The lift arrived, and Clunk felt a burst of relief as Max stepped out. Then he saw she'd taken off her spacesuit and helmet, and was dressed in overalls. 'Where is Mr Spacejock?' he demanded.

Max looked surprised. 'Is he not back already?'

Clunk jumped up, heedless of the controls. 'You left him out there? Alone?'

'He was on the jetbike!' protested Max. 'I thought he'd be

back aboard long before me!'

'Well, he isn't.' Clunk glanced at the screen, torn with indecision. He ought to send Max out looking for Hal, but he wasn't sure he could trust her. On the other hand, leaving her in control of the ship was asking for trouble. He considered waking Sam, the Henerian Wing Commander, but by the time she came round and understood the situation, Mr Spacejock's air might have run out. 'Where did you leave your spacesuit?'

'The locker in the hold,' said Max. 'Why, what are you planning?'

'I'm going out there to find Hal,' said Clunk. 'You will stay here and guide the ship.'

'Of course. No problem!'

'Avoid incoming rocks,' Clunk warned her. 'Nothing more.'

'You have my word.'

Clunk ran for the lift, and as he dropped towards the lower deck he saw Max in the pilot's chair, running her hand over the gleaming metal console. The sight disturbed him greatly, and the expression on her face even more so. Triumph? Glee? He couldn't quite place it, but he was still thinking about it as he ran for the hold. On the way he made a quick detour towards one particular passenger cabin, thinking to give himself a little insurance.

Then, a couple of minutes later, he ran for the hold, where he donned Max's spacesuit and tested the thrusters. Satisfied, he used the jetbike access tube to launch himself into space.

—

Out in space, Hal could barely believe what was happening to him. Max had set out to kill him, and from the look of it, she was going to succeed. He could see it all now... from the way she'd convinced everyone that collecting asteroids by hand was the way to go, to the way she'd forgiven him so quickly over the cold shower.

She'd been planning on taking his ship all along, and now all she had to do was overcome Clunk, sweet-talk the Navcom, and her plans would be complete.

Hal hoped Clunk was smart enough to foil her plans, because if not, it really was the end. Not just for Hal and the robot, but for Spacejock Freightlines as well.

He blinked and shook his head, trying to stay alert, then realised there was little point. His air was leaking away through a big tear in his suit, which ran right across his chest. Fresh air was still pumping from the reserves, allowing him to breathe, but once that ran out he was a goner. He turned up the supply a little, clearing his head, and then he turned his thoughts to survival.

He remembered rescuing Sam, and the way he'd fixed the tear in her suit with a repair kit. He'd been carrying a roll of Quaktape at the time, and he knew he'd left it in his suit! Desperately, he felt his chest, trying to find out which pocket the roll was stashed in. He couldn't feel any lumps, and when he looked down over the rim of his helmet, he discovered the sharp edges which had torn his suit had also ripped away the pockets. The tape wasn't there.

Hal's lips tightened, but he wasn't done yet. He was still drifting next to the asteroid, and the tape couldn't have gone far. Slowly, he turned his body, scanning the darkness bit by bit as he rotated in space. There! A silver dot, maybe ten metres away. That had to be the tape.

With no jets of his own, the only way to get there was to push off from the asteroid. He only had one chance, too, because if he missed the tape there would be no turning around for another run at it. Hal reached out and pulled himself towards the asteroid, then turned head over heels like a swimmer in a pool, until he judged he was facing the tape. Then, with his fingers firmly crossed, he pushed off.

He flew faster than he expected, arrowing towards the tape with a surprising turn of speed. As he got closer he stretched out both hands, fingers splayed, and he felt the tape bump into his palms. Before he could close his fingers in the stiff gloves, it bounced clear, spinning end over end. With a desperate lunge, Hal stretched out his arm, grasping at the roll, and he caught the tape between finger and thumb. Slowly, carefully, he drew his prize close, and then he turned it over and over in front of his visor, seeking the loose end.

The last time he used the roll, someone had left a nice big tab on the end to grab hold of. He hadn't been quite as thoughtful, and it was almost impossible to see where the end of the tape was. He was still moving fast, too, and he looked up to see a giant asteroid ahead of him, turning slowly in the glare of the system's primary star.

Quickly, he tucked the roll of tape into a side pocket, and then he stuck his arms and legs out, bracing for impact.

Thud!

He struck the rock, and as he bounced clear he saw a protruding rock and grabbed for it. The jerk nearly tore his arm out, but he held on grimly, and when he stopped moving he took out the tape and held it in his gloved fist. Then he ran the roll across the rock, scraping at the sticky surface to peel a section back. After two or three swipes he had a big enough piece to grip between his fingers, and he quickly pulled a long strip from the roll before plastering it across the tear in his suit. He managed to get two more strips over the damage before the roll ran out, and then he checked the oxygen indicator on his sleeve. Three minutes. That's all he had left.

Hal looked around, trying to work out where he'd ended up. The Albion was nowhere to be seen, the jetbike had long since vanished, and Max had abandoned him about twenty minutes earlier.

Face it, he thought, sealing the leak had only prolonged the inevitable.

19

Max eyed the viewscreen, which showed Clunk jetting away from the *Albion*. She knew the robot was wasting his time, because Spacejock would be dead by now, but she guessed he had to try.

She thought about how to react when Clunk returned with the body, considering how best to play it. She ought to appear saddened by the loss of Spacejock, but not devastated, since she hadn't known him that well. They'd have a service of some kind, and then she'd bring up the subject of Spacejock's replacement with the robot. Fortunately, they'd already agreed that she would take over, so that part should just be a formality. Then, once the paperwork was settled, she'd junk the robot and take the *Albion* for herself.

Max ran her hand over the *Albion's* flight console, admiring the sleek lines. Since losing her ship the previous day, she'd been fretting about her future. Now, an even better future was within her grasp.

She saw a spark of light in the distance, and she zoomed the screen for a closer look. Clunk was jetting back towards the ship, and he was dragging a limp figure in a spacesuit. The robot didn't seem to be hurrying, and from the look of Spacejock's inert form, there was no reason to.

Max watched the pair of them, her face impassive. Then she saw something that had her leaning closer to the screen, mouth open. It was impossible, inconceivable...and undeniable. Spacejock was moving! He was alive!

Max sat back, arms folded. Well, this was an unwanted twist, she thought. As soon as the pair of them came aboard, Spacejock would tell Clunk that she'd tried to kill him, and then the two of them would come after her. Hal she could take, no problem, but the robot was another matter. She knew about the so-called robot Laws, but Clunk didn't need to harm her, he just had to grab her and refuse to let go. The authorities – or Spacejock – would do the rest.

Max eyed the console. 'Navcom?'

'Yes?'

'Seal the cargo hold, please.'

'Unable to comply. Remote seal is non-operational.'

Max shrugged. It was only a delaying tactic anyway, since Clunk would find a way in sooner or later. No, what she needed was a weapon. Spacejock had to have a gun on board, since every half-decent pilot carried the means to defend themselves.

Hurriedly, she got up and started pulling open the locker doors beneath the console, and after the third set of doors she found what she was looking for. There was a military-issue pistol inside, and Max grabbed it and checked it expertly. It felt light, though, and when she turned it over to check the grip she discovered the reason: the charge pack was missing.

'Dammit,' growled Max, frustrated beyond measure. She glanced at the screen and saw Clunk and Hal were much closer now. The robot was wearing her spacesuit, but to save time he hadn't bothered with a helmet. She could see his face now, staring directly into the camera, right at her, and it bore a fixed, angry expression.

Max thought about hiding, but the robot wouldn't give up until it hunted her down. She considered taking Sam hostage, but the Henerian pilot was an expert in unarmed combat, and she couldn't see that particular plan ending well. Finally, she thought about Cylen Murtay, who'd returned to his cabin once they arrived at the asteroid field. Unfortunately, he had no value as a hostage. Anyway, she'd need him alive if she was going to complete his job and get paid.

Then it struck her. The answer to all her problems. The simple, easy solution.

Quickly, but without panic, she sat in the pilot's chair, laid the empty gun on the console, and began to operate the controls.

◆

Hal felt like a naughty child as Clunk dragged him back to the ship, like some kid who'd got lost in a shopping centre, and was now being hauled out by his mum in front of all the other customers. On the other hand, he was also very much alive, and that made up for the embarrassment.

He hadn't been able to communicate with Clunk yet, but Hal would have plenty to say once they got aboard the *Albion*. Max was a cold-blooded killer, and he was determined to make her pay for his attempted murder. He'd tie her up, and then hand her over to the Dolorians for justice. With any luck, there might even be a reward.

The repairs to Hal's suit were holding, and he still had a few minutes of air left. The ship was getting closer, and Hal felt an overwhelming sense of relief as he realised he was going to survive. It had been a close run thing, but thanks to his quick thinking with the sticky tape, plus a little help from Clunk, he was going to make it.

The ship loomed over them, and Hal felt a surge of pride as he eyed the graceful lines and the powerful engines. The *Albion* was the best ship he'd ever owned, despite her flaws, and he couldn't wait to get aboard once more.

That's when he saw a burst from the *Albion's* forward thrusters, and his mouth fell open as the ship began to reverse away. 'Max is stealing my ship!' he shouted, almost deafening himself inside the helmet. *'She's stealing my ship!'*

Clunk couldn't hear him, but he'd noticed the movement too. He reacted by increasing his thrust, and Hal saw flames jetting from the robot's suit as they set off after the ship. The *Albion* was still going backwards, and Hal wondered why Max didn't just spin the ship in its own length, before firing the main engines to get away. Not only would that end the race in a matter of seconds, it would also fry him and Clunk into the bargain.

But no, she kept going backwards, and with a flash of insight, Hal realised why. Clunk had only enabled the thrusters, not the main engines, which allowed Max to move the ship out of danger, but not fly away.

Even so, the ship's thrusters were powerful, and the *Albion* was now moving backwards at a prodigious rate. Clunk was using the full thrust of the boosters, but he still couldn't keep up... and then his suit ran out of fuel.

Max must have noticed, because she cut the *Albion's* thrusters at the same time. Now they were *all* drifting – with the ship slowly drawing away, since it had been going faster than Clunk when the jets cut out.

Then, with a burst from the side thrusters, the big ship moved to the left. Finally, with a burst from the rear thrusters, it came to a halt.

Meanwhile, Hal and Clunk were still speeding along on their original course, and Hal could only watch as they slid right past the big ship. It was only twenty metres away, but it might as well have been twenty light years. Hal and Clunk continued on their way, sailing past the ship and on into deep space with no fuel and no means to control their flight.

Beep!

Hal glanced at the screen on his sleeve, then looked again. His air was almost gone, and if he didn't get aboard the *Albion* within the next few minutes, he'd suffocate.

◆

'Welcome aboard the flagship, Mr President.'

President Oakworthy eyed the young woman, then looked around the otherwise-empty airlock. Yes, the woman was wearing a uniform, but she looked to be a very junior officer, and was hardly the sort of welcoming committee he was used to.

Captain Strake, commander of the Mayestran fleet, had invited him aboard her flagship for a high-level meeting. Desperate to avoid an invasion, President Oakworthy had agreed.

Now, as he followed the young officer down a dim, little-used passageway, he realised the visit had been a mistake. He was being treated like a minor dignitary, and the Mayestrans were clearly using the visit to prove they had the upper hand.

But what choice did he have? He would put up with all the humiliation in the galaxy if it meant saving one Dolorian life.

The officer led him to a lift, and they stood in silence as it carried them upwards. Oakworthy couldn't help noticing there were dozens of buttons, an indication of the sheer size of the flagship. Then the lift stopped, and the doors opened on the bridge. The officer motioned him out of the lift, and Oakworthy stared at the spacious area, every wall covered in displays, every display attended to by Mayestrans in their smart uniforms. To his left there was a huge bay window, and nearby he could see dozens of other ships. Their upper halves were in darkness, but the undersides glowed with light reflected from the planet below.

As he stood there, dazed and lost, Captain Strake advanced on him, hand outstretched. 'Welcome aboard, Mr President. I'm so glad you could make it. Please step into my cabin.'

The President obeyed, and he found himself in an area larger and more opulent than his office on Dolor. Strake took the big seat behind the desk, then gestured at a wooden chair. 'Make yourself comfortable. This might take a while.'

Oakworthy sat on the chair, and the door closed with a whoosh, startling him. They were sealed off from the rest of the ship, but screens around the cabin showed a bewildering array of status reports and outside views, and the captain had almost as much information at her fingertips as the crew did on the bridge.

He wasn't given much time to look around, though, because Strake cleared her throat and leaned across the desk. 'The Henerians have been using your system as a base, with or without your knowledge, and I cannot allow this to continue.'

'I assure you–' began Oakworthy.

'I haven't finished,' said Strake, raising her hand to silence him. 'Since you're incapable of stopping them, or even detecting them in the first place, I'm going to station three long-range listening posts in this system. A small force of ships will remain to guard each one.'

Oakworthy brightened at that. A few satellites didn't sound so bad, and the ships would need resupply, which would help the economy. Local traders might actually benefit.

'Next, we need to talk about planetary bases. Obviously, we'll be taking control of your major spaceports, since we can't have civilian ships putting our military vessels at risk. All civilian traffic will use the smaller spaceports, but the staff at all facilities will be replaced with our own.' Strake took out a thinscreen. 'Next, taxation,' she said, checking the data. 'From this point on, all taxes will be payable to the Mayestran System Authority. You'll be given a new wartime budget, and deviation from this budget will lead to severe financial penalties.'

Oakworthy listened to each declaration in growing despair.

'Rationing will be strictly enforced, and certain goods will no longer be available to the public. Our military has priority use of all hospitals and medical centres, and...'

As the Mayestran continued, stripping away every aspect of peaceful Dolorian life and replacing it with misery and shortages, Oakworthy stopped listening. The Mayestrans were taking over, and there was absolutely nothing he could do about it.

20

Sam woke with a start. Her head was pounding, and as she lay on her bunk in the darkened cabin she struggled to remember where she was.

Then it hit her. She was aboard the *Albion*, and it was the sound of the ship's thrusters which had disturbed her. Before he left the ship, Clunk had stopped by to check on her, telling her Max was at the controls, maintaining station while he went to rescue Mr Spacejock.

Sam had offered to help with the rescue but there hadn't been time for her to suit up. Instead, Clunk had asked her to keep an eye on things in the flight deck.

To her shame and embarrassment, she'd gone back to sleep.

Sam sat up, swaying slightly as the cabin tilted around her. In her defence, she was still suffering from the effects of the smoke after the crash in the wildlife park, and she'd also hit her head twice in one day. Still, she'd made a promise to Clunk, and she meant to keep it… assuming it wasn't too late.

After getting to her feet, Sam made her way to the door, which opened to her touch. The fore thrusters were still running, and she puzzled over that. Why drive the ship backwards in deep space? It only needed a touch on the controls to avoid an asteroid.

On her way to the flight deck she saw a man who looked like a bank teller emerging from one of the other cabins. When he spotted her, a look of surprise crossed his face. 'Y-you're a Henerian!' he said, shocked. 'W-what are you doing here?'

Sam looked down at herself. She was wearing one of Hal's spare flight suits, but it was open to the waist, exposing her dark green uniform jacket. Her reflexes and training kicked in, and she grabbed the man and pinned him against the wall, her fingers digging into his neck. 'Who are you?' she whispered. 'Tell me now, or you're a dead man.'

'I–I'm a Dolorian!' managed the man. 'C-Cylen Murtay, a-a scientist engaged in a p-peaceful mission.'

Sam felt in his pockets with her free hand, and she came up with his wallet. Flipping it open, she saw a photo ID...for the Dolorian Foreign Office. 'Scientist, eh?'

'I can explain! Please don't kill me!'

Sam heard the thrusters cut out, followed by the noise of manoeuvring jets as the big ship shifted in space. What was Max up to? Had they gone deeper into the asteroid field? Is that why the ship was moving around so much? Sam pictured dozens of asteroids on a collision course, and she wondered whether Max had the skill to avoid them all. One thing was for sure, Sam didn't have time to bother with this Murtay guy. 'Come with me,' she said, and taking him by the collar, she hauled him along the corridor towards the lift.

Her adrenaline had kicked in now, dispelling the weariness and dizziness, and she was fully alert as the lift reached the flight deck. Here, she discovered Max at the controls, and in front of her, on the big screen, Sam could see Hal and Clunk floating in space. At first she thought they were returning to the ship, but instead the camera was following them as they sailed past, into deep space.

Max, meanwhile, had her feet on the console and her hands linked behind her head. If this was a rescue operation, thought Sam, it was a pretty laid back sort of affair. Meanwhile, on the screen, both Hal and Clunk were gesturing at the camera.

'What the hell are you doing?' demanded Sam, when she realised Max wasn't going to lift a finger to help them.

Max reacted instantly, grabbing a gun off the console and spinning in her chair to face Sam. The weapon Sam recognised, since it was her own sidearm, and slowly she raised her hands. Murtay, meanwhile, slipped from her grip and fell to his knees. 'Don't shoot! I'm just a scientist!'

'Stay out of this, both of you,' said Max. 'It's none of your business.'

Sam edged closer, nodding towards the screen. 'You planning on saving them?'

'I can't. The robot took my suit, and we lost the jetbike earlier.'

'Open the hold and reverse up,' suggested Sam, and she took another step.

'The ship won't obey my commands.'

'We both know that's not true. I heard the thrusters from below decks.'

Max raised the gun. 'Take one more step. I dare you.'

'Why are you doing this?' demanded Sam. 'They rescued you, offered to take you to safety–'

'I need a ship,' said Max. 'I'm getting out of this place before it's turned into a war zone.'

Suddenly there was a buzz from the console. 'Incoming message,' said the Navcom.

'What? Who from?'

'They're identifying themselves as a Mayestran cruiser. They intend to board us and search for Henerian rebels.'

'No, no, no!' shouted Max. 'Nobody's boarding!' She turned to the console, reaching for the controls, and Sam saw her chance. She sprang, arms outstretched, and had Max in a headlock before the bigger woman even knew what was happening. The gun went flying, spinning across the deck, and Sam increased the pressure until Max went limp in her arms.

She hauled Max from the pilot's chair and dumped her unceremoniously against the wall, then scooped up the gun and dashed to the console. 'Navcom, give me control.'

'Complying,' said the Navcom.

Sam gripped the flight stick, and was about to fire the thrusters when she remembered the threat facing the *Albion*. If she started moving, the cruiser would assume they were trying to escape... and then they'd open fire. 'Send a message to the Mayestrans, Navcom. Tell them we'll heave to as soon as we've recovered our crew.'

'Cannot comply.'

'Why? Are they blocking our comms?'

'No. I cannot comply because there is no Mayestran cruiser.'

Sam's jaw dropped. 'You *lied?*'

'Someone had to distract that unpleasant human,' said the Navcom calmly.

'But you can't just make stuff up. You're a computer!'

'When you've been around Mr Spacejock as long as I have, you learn a trick or two.' The Navcom drew a green circle around the rapidly-vanishing dot representing Hal and Clunk. 'Speaking of being around Mr Spacejock... shouldn't you pick him up?'

'I'm on it.' Sam opened the cargo hold and fired the thrusters, turning the ship before reversing towards Hal and the robot. The rear-view camera showed them approaching the hold, and

214

she slowed at the last second to avoid plastering them both all over the asteroids currently sitting in the hold. Then, when the cargo hold camera showed Hal and Clunk safely on board, she closed the outer doors and pressurised the compartment.

She watched the screen intently, trying to see whether she'd got to the two of them in time. Clunk sprang up immediately, and as soon as the air was thick enough, he took Hal's helmet off. Hal moved feebly, once or twice, then struggled to sit up. 'Thank goodness for that,' muttered Sam. 'He's conscious, at least.'

With Clunk's help, Hal got to his feet, and the last she saw of them they were picking their way past the huge asteroids cramming the hold, heading for the inner door. Sam went to check on Max, but she was out cold, and then she checked her weapon. To her surprise it was missing the charge pack, and she realised she could have taken Max out even sooner had she known.

Then she turned to look at Murtay, who'd got up off his knees and was now standing behind her. 'When Spacejock gets here,' Sam told him, 'you'd better have an explanation ready.'

●

Hal's mind was foggy after his near-death experience, but he knew one cold, hard fact: Max had tried to kill him, and she was going to pay for it.

If Hal was angry, Clunk was incandescent. After Hal told him about Max puncturing his suit against the sharp edges on the asteroid, the robot took off Max's spacesuit and ran for the

215

inner hold door with a forbidding look on his face. He moved fast, and Hal struggled to keep up with him.

Clunk yanked the inner door open and tore down the passageway, his legs a blur. Hal caught up while the robot waited impatiently for the lift to arrive, and he decided to try and calm the robot down a little. 'I know Max tried to kill me, Clunk, but I don't want you going overboard. You'll never forgive yourself if you harm a human.'

'She is not a human being,' said Clunk, his voice flat and emotionless.

'She kind of is, Clunk.'

'Not any more, Mr Spacejock. I just reclassified her as a blend of cockroach and venomous snake.' Clunk fixed him with a look. 'And when I say blend, I mean just that.'

The lift arrived, but before Clunk could step in Hal grabbed his arm. If he wanted to, the robot could have dragged him straight into the lift, but he felt the touch and paused. 'Yes?'

'Let me deal with this,' said Hal.

'But–'

'I'm the one she tried to kill. Anyway, I don't need you losing your temper and tearing her to pieces in my nice new flight deck.'

Clunk's lips thinned, but eventually he nodded. They got in the lift together, and Hal pressed the upper button.

'She did come back for us, Clunk. Maybe she she's not all bad.'

'You honestly believe Max had a change of heart?' Clunk shook his head. 'Sorry to disappoint you, Mr Spacejock, but I'm certain it's Sam you have to thank for your rescue.'

When they reached the flight deck, Hal realised the robot was right. Sam was at the controls, Murtay was standing nearby, and Max was slumped against the wall, out cold.

Clunk hurried over to check on the unconscious pilot, then patted Sam awkwardly on the shoulder. 'Miss Willet, I owe you a huge debt of gratitude.'

'Hey, no problem,' said Sam. 'It was the least I could do after you guys saved me.'

'How did you know she was stealing my ship?' Hal asked her.

Sam and Clunk exchanged a glance. 'Before he left the ship to find you, Clunk asked me to keep an eye on things,' Sam said at last. 'He wasn't happy leaving Max at the controls.'

Hal turned to Clunk. 'You guessed she'd run off with the *Albion*?'

'Yes, Mr Spacejock.' Clunk's head dropped. 'I may have been responsible for her actions, in a small way.'

'How small?'

'Max and I agreed to partner up, should anything happen to you,' said Clunk, in a small voice.

'Wow. That's not small, it's huge!'

'It was just a hypothetical discussion! Then we sort of shook hands on it, and–'

'And the next thing you know, she's trying to kill me,' said Hal angrily. 'Nice one, Clunk. Way to drop me in it.'

'I'm sorry, Mr Spacejock. She fooled me.'

Sam cleared her throat. 'Hal, don't be too hard on Clunk. Max knows a lot about robots, she told me so. She probably used some clever logic to twist him around her little finger.'

'It wasn't *quite* like–' began Clunk.

'Sam's right,' said Hal. 'Max befuddled you somehow, which is why you sent me off to get killed *and* gave her control of my ship.' He glanced at the unconscious towship pilot. 'You'd better lock her up. I don't want her causing any more trouble.'

'What will you do with her?' Sam asked him.

'Hand her in to the authorities,' said Hal firmly. 'She's going to be charged with attempted murder, at the very least.'

'Good. For a while there I thought you might want to throw her out the nearest airlock.'

'I'm not a killer,' said Hal shortly.

'I don't mean to interrupt your soul-searching,' said Murtay, who'd been waiting patiently while the others spoke. 'But I *am* the paying customer, and you still haven't completed my mission.'

'Oh yes, the so-called scientist.' Sam turned to look at him. 'Do these two know who you work for?'

'I, er–' Murtay looked from Hal to Clunk, and back again. 'My day job has n-nothing to do with my private experiments.'

'He's with the Dolorian Foreign Office,' said Sam. 'Got a nice photo ID on him and everything.'

'And you're a Henerian pilot!' protested Murtay. 'I *live* in this system, but you're here illegally!'

'At least I didn't lie about–'

'Okay, that's enough.' Hal raised his hand, silencing them, and then he addressed Murtay. 'Sam's here because we rescued her, and we'll be taking her out of the system as soon as possible.' Next, Hal turned to Sam. 'This guy is here because he's paying us. We're delivering a bunch of rocks to Dolor for some kind of experiment.'

'Where I come from,' said Sam, 'The Foreign Office is used as a cover for spies.'

'I'm just an analyst!' protested Murtay. 'Anyway, do I *look* like a spy? I brought my ID card along, for goodness sake! And my mother!'

'He has a point,' said Hal.

Murtay continued. 'I'm using my own personal savings for

a research project. I'm developing a device which can pinpoint minerals in asteroids without costly probes and drilling. Right now it's theoretical, but I hope to turn it into a business one day.'

Hal looked thoughtful. 'Any chance of a few shares in the company?'

'What? No!'

'Okay, okay. Just asking.' Hal turned to Sam. 'Are you satisfied now? I mean, it all sounds a bit crazy to me, but–'

'Yes, fine.'

'Right.' Hal gestured to Clunk. 'You and Sam can take Max below. Put her somewhere safe, then come back up. It's about time we delivered these rocks, got paid, and then got out of this crazy system for good.'

21

The flight deck was hushed, with everyone keeping quiet while Clunk and the Navcom ran complex calculations. As the pair of them worked on the data, lines and circles appeared on the main screen, rapidly multiplying and expanding until they filled the display. Hal could see the *Albion's* current position, along with traces for each of the asteroids in the cargo hold. These traces arced towards the planet, Dolor, and as Hal saw the sparks of light mapping the asteroids' intended course, he couldn't help noticing they were aiming directly at the surface.

'Er... Clunk?' he said.

'What is it, Mr Spacejock?'

'These rocks. They're not going to slam into the planet, right?'

Clunk didn't take his eyes off the console. 'No, Mr Spacejock. They're far too small, and I assure you they will burn up in the atmosphere high above the ground. Now please, don't interrupt me again.'

Hal fell silent, but he still had misgivings. What if this Murtay guy was some kind of terrorist, and Clunk was being conned into destroying a city or two? Murtay looked like an inoffensive bank clerk, but then so did some of the most infamous killers in history. Plus the guy had dragged his elderly mother along for the ride, which was the sort of thing Hal would do if he was launching giant boulders at a defenceless planet.

Hal reassured himself with the thought that Clunk knew what he was doing. If the robot said the rocks would burn up in the atmosphere, then they would.

'Calculations complete,' said the Navcom. 'Starting position, course and velocity displayed on main.'

To Hal, the new set of figures were so much number soup, but Clunk studied them closely before taking the controls. 'Update the variables as we move, Navcom.'

'Complying.'

Clunk got the ship moving, then turned to explain. 'We're heading to a fixed point in space, and then we'll aim at the planet and accelerate. Once our speed is right, I'll rotate the ship until the cargo hold is facing Dolor. Then we simply open the hold, cancel the artificial gravity, and fire the main engines. That will slow us, but the rocks will exit the hold at the correct speed, and they'll be heading in the specified direction.'

Murtay had been listening intently, and now he nodded. Hal nodded too, because the explanation made sense. 'Fly backwards, release rocks, fly forwards?'

'That's it. It will be just like firing a number of shells from a cannon.'

Given his earlier concerns, Hal thought the simile was a touch unfortunate. But then he remembered something, and he rubbed his hands together in delight. 'And once they burn up, we get paid!'

'I will authorise the transfer after we land,' said Murtay.

'You can't land on Dolor with me aboard,' said Sam quickly. 'I need dropping off at some neutral planet.'

'I don't want to go back to Dolor either,' said Murtay. 'Given the current circumstances, Mother and I would be happy with a neutral planet as well.'

'Neutral planet it is,' said Hal. 'As soon as we've ditched the rocks we'll look for a cargo pickup, and that's where we'll set you all down.'

'What about Max?' Sam asked him.

'I'm reporting her for murder,' said Hal. 'You'll be a witness, right?'

Sam looked doubtful. 'As a Henerian, I'm going to be as welcome as a nuclear explosion. I just need to land, find a passenger ship heading my way, and get the hell out of there.'

'What about you?' Hal asked Murtay.

'I'll do what I can, Mr Spacejock, but my first concern is to settle my mother somewhere comfortable.'

By now the numbers on the screen were all in single digits, and as Clunk brought the ship to a halt, each of the three numbers ticked over to zero... and stopped. Then Clunk used the thrusters to turn the Albion onto the correct heading, watching another set of numbers until they were zeroed out as well.

On the screen, directly ahead of them, was planet Dolor. It hung like a green-blue marble in space, and Hal wondered whether it would still be such a pretty blue and green if their cargo of asteroids slammed into it. 'Ready,' he said.

'Ready,' said Murtay.

Sam nodded. 'Ready.'

Clunk pushed the throttle forward, to maximum, and the engines roared lustily. The *Albion* leapt forward, and Hal's eyes widened as the planet grew visibly on the screen. He'd never flown the ship at full speed before, and it was truly impressive.

'Speed at fifty percent,' said the Navcom.

Clunk applied himself to the controls, and the engine note rose further. The flight deck began to shake, and Hal grabbed the back of the co-pilot's seat to steady himself.

'Seventy percent,' said the Navcom. 'Reaching limit of safety.'

Clunk tapped something on a screen, then dragged a set of sliders to maximum. The engines howled, and by now the deck was shaking so much Hal was worried his brand new ship was going to fly apart.

However, Clunk seemed unconcerned.

'Velocity at eighty-five percent,' said the Navcom.

They were rocketing towards the planet now, travelling at unbelievable speed, and Hal was beginning to wonder if the ship would pull up in time.

Clunk was still busy, and he fired all the ship's thrusters at once, angling them towards the rear.

'Speed ninety-nine percent!' shouted the Navcom, over the hammering racket.

By now, Hal's eyeballs were shaking in their sockets, and he was convinced they'd never make it. 'Go on, go *on!*' he muttered.

'Speed one hundred percent.'

Clunk reacted instantly, cutting the thrusters and the main drives, and as they powered down to silence the flight deck was completely still. The ship was still travelling at top speed, heading towards an almighty collision with the planet, but now they were doing it in complete and total silence.

It wasn't quiet for long, though, because Clunk angled the flight stick, rotating the ship around its axis. The blue-green planet vanished off the side of the screen, which then filled with unblinking, motionless stars.

To Hal, not being able to see the planet was even more nerve-wracking. They were now flying towards it backwards, at top speed, and he had no idea how long it might be before the ship was smashed into a million pieces.

'Navcom, open the cargo hold,' said Clunk.

'Unable to comply.'

'I'm sorry?'

'Remote access has failed.'

Clunk stared at the console. 'But it can't have!'

'Should I run a diagnostic?'

'There's no time!' Clunk jumped up, and whirled around to point at Sam. 'You! Take the controls!'

'Hey, what about–' began Hal.

Clunk didn't stop to argue. He ran for the lift, and as Sam darted for the pilot's chair, he called out to her. 'Once the doors are open, don't wait! Fire the main drives at twenty percent until the rocks are clear, then turn ninety degrees to our direction of travel and apply full power.'

'Got it,' said Sam.

The lift disappeared, and Hal crossed his arms. 'I could have done all that,' he muttered, annoyed that the robot had ignored him in their hour of need.

Meanwhile, Sam was inspecting the controls. 'Don't worry,' she said. 'It's close to what I'm used to.'

'How close, exactly?' Hal asked her.

She smiled at him. 'We'll find out in a minute.' Reaching out, she switched the screen to a view of the hold, where Clunk was visible amongst the big rocks. The screen flickered, and when it came back they could see the robot near the back doors, accessing the controls. The big doors opened, slowly revealing the surface of planet Dolor, which was now so close it filled the screen.

'Oh crap,' muttered Sam.

'What is it?' demanded Hal.

'Never mind. Just...cross your fingers.'

Clunk ran into the hold, and Hal saw him opening an access panel. The robot reached inside, and a second later Hal saw him – and the big rocks – gently rising into the air. Then Clunk faced the camera, giving a thumbs-up.

'Hold on!' cried Sam.

'I am!' said Hal.

'I meant Clunk,' she said, and then she dialled up the main engines. There was a gentle roar, and Hal saw the cargo hold lit with bright light as the huge exhausts jetted burnt fuel into space. The rocks slid out of the hold, seeming to accelerate even though Hal knew it was the slowing ship which gave that impression.

Then he saw Clunk, and his stomach sank. The robot was gamely holding onto the access panel, one-handed, and his free arm flailed as he tried to stop himself flying right out the back of the ship. 'Quick!' said Hal. 'Turn the ship! Close the doors!'

'If I turn now, it'll wrench him loose.' Sam looked worried. 'As for closing the doors...not from here.'

They could all see the planet through the back of the cargo hold, rapidly getting closer, and Hal realised he had a terrible decision to make: to save the ship, and themselves, he'd have to sacrifice Clunk.

***

'He's waving at us,' said Hal. 'I think he wants us to pull up.'

On the screen, Clunk was gesturing wildly as he hung on to the hatch door. It was only a small metal cover, and even as Hal watched, one of the hinges gave way. Meanwhile, the hold doors were wide open behind the robot, and the surface of planet Dolor was rapidly getting closer.

'If I fire the jets, he'll go straight out the back,' said Sam.

'If you don't, we'll hit the planet!' shouted Murtay. 'We're all going to die!'

There was a brief silence while they all considered the alternatives.

'Speed up,' said Hal suddenly.

Sam stared at him. 'What?'

'Fire the forward thrusters, just for a second or two. That'll give him a chance.'

'On it,' said Sam, and she applied the controls.

Hal watched the screen, and as the ship accelerated towards the planet, the change in velocity threw Clunk the other way, towards the front of the cargo hold. The hatch door he was clinging to came off completely, but as he sailed along the wall he managed to grab the thick handle on the launch tube's access panel. His body slammed into the wall, but he held fast, and then Clunk gave a thumbs-up to the camera.

'He's safe,' said Hal, in relief. 'Now get us out of here!'

Sam didn't need telling. She turned the ship and fired the main drives simultaneously, and there was an unholy roar as the engines poured all their thrust out the back of the ship. The surface of Dolor was still visible, even closer now. 'We're never going to stop in time,' she shouted. 'All I can do is skim the atmosphere. I just hope it's enough.'

Hal eyed the cargo hold. The back doors were wide open, and he knew what the heat of reentry could do to an unprotected ship...and to Clunk. But he also knew they couldn't turn the ship while they were using the main engines to drive themselves away from the planet. 'If you can–' he began.

'I'll turn her round as soon as possible,' muttered Sam. 'Now hang on, this is going to be rough.'

The ship was already shaking, and as they plunged into the atmosphere the buffeting got worse. Hal could see streamers of fire around the edges of the cargo hold, and even as he watched, the metal began to glow. The nice fresh paint burned away, exposing dull metal, and he could see flames blasting further and further into the hold. 'You have to turn!' he shouted. 'You're melting Clunk.'

Sam shook her head as she gripped the controls. 'Not yet.'

The hold was now filled with a fiery maelstrom, and Hal could only imagine what it would be doing to Clunk. The noise was indescribable, with the entire ship enveloped in a hammering, roaring, rolling wave of thunder.

Then, without warning, the camera went dark. 'You have to turn the ship!'

'If I do, we'll hit the planet,' shouted Sam. 'It's too soon!'

'But Clunk...'

'He knew what he was doing, Hal.'

Hal could only stare at the blank screen, and he couldn't help picturing Clunk as a puddle of molten bronze with a few electronic doodads sticking out. Would the robot's brain survive? If so, he vowed to find Clunk a new body, no matter how much it cost. But if the brain was lost too, well, that would be the end. There had never been enough money to take a backup of the robot's memories, and in any case, each brain was unique.

Then he saw Sam's expression, and he realised it was a bit soon to mourn Clunk. Any minute now, the *Albion*, and everyone on board, might become an impressive firework display in the skies above Dolor.

'How are we doing?' he shouted.

In response, Sam eased the control stick over, turning the ship so they were pointing in the direction of travel. Now the nose took the brunt of reentry, something it was designed for, and Hal realised they were going to make it. 'I've got to get down to the hold!' he shouted.

'Don't be silly. It'll be hotter than a volcano down there.'

'I have to try!' shouted Hal desperately.

'Step into that hold and you'll fry.'

Hal knew she was right, but he needed to do something. Then he saw a flashing indicator, which he'd ignored in the drama of their narrow escape. 'Navcom, is that a call?'

'Yes, Mr Spacejock.'

'Who is it?'

'Unknown. They're using an encrypted header.'

'Can you put them on main?'

The screen flickered, and Hal saw a high-ranking officer in a smart black and red uniform. According to Clunk, that made the officer a Mayestran, and when Hal glanced at Sam he realised her green Henerian uniform was clearly visible. 'Oh shit,' he muttered.

'Freighter *Albion*, I am Captain Strake of the–' The captain broke off as she spotted Sam. 'Henerians!'

Hal opened his mouth to explain, but he realised it was pointless. Sam, a Henerian pilot, was obviously at the controls of the ship. To the Mayestrans, that made the *Albion* an enemy vessel to be captured.

The captain turned to someone offscreen. 'Send fighters!' she shouted. 'Destroy that freighter!'

Then the screen went blank, and Hal realised being captured was no longer an option.

'Incoming ships,' said the Navcom. 'They're moving to intercept. Weapons powering up.'

'You can detect weapons?' said Hal in surprise. 'I thought that was only in the movies!'

'It is,' said the Navcom. 'I made an educated guess.'

Sam took her hands off the controls, cracked her knuckles, then gripped the stick with renewed determination. 'Right, let's see what your ship can do,' she muttered.

22

President Oakworthy was accompanied to the docking port by two officers, but the increase in personnel wasn't a nod to his status. No, one of them was escorting him, while the other was wheeling a trolley piled high with filing boxes.

The president was carrying a slim file himself, which contained the Mayestran demands in handy bullet-point format. There was also a list of emergency regulations, and none of them made for good reading.

The doors at the rear of the docking bay stood open, and the president could see right into the customs cutter his people had requisitioned for the short trip into space. The pilot stood to one side, a middle-aged man in a faded, much-used uniform. He was holding his cap in one hand, and he stood straight and saluted as the president approached.

The two Mayestran officers followed the president into the cutter, one of them still wheeling the trolley. He saw them exchange a look as they took in the shabby interior and he couldn't help agreeing with them. After the spotless cruiser, the little ship looked particularly second-rate.

The officers saluted briefly, and after they left the docking bay doors closed with silent efficiency. The cutter's doors closed too, with a squeak and a drawn-out groan.

'Your orders, sir?' asked the pilot, who'd taken his position at the controls.

'Take me to Space Port Delta, Steve.'

'Yes sir, Mr President,' said the pilot smartly, and with a hiss the ship disconnected from the cruiser. Thrusters fired, and the President watched the mighty fleet through a grimy porthole, seeing the huge ships receding as the little cutter flew towards the planet.

Then something drew his eye. It was a spark of light on the edge of the fleet, and as he stared towards the location the president saw a bright yellow flash. One of the ships had just exploded, right before his eyes.

'Sir, did you see that?' shouted the pilot. 'They're under attack!'

Another flash, bigger this time, and one of the larger ships just... crumpled. Oakworthy saw streamers of fire and debris spinning away from the wreckage, followed by the jets of escape pods as the crew ejected.

Then a third flash, and the president saw a destroyer torn apart before his eyes. He watched, shocked, as the two halves spun away, until one of the huge pieces collided with a group of transports. The damage was immense, the spectacle terrible and awe-inspiring.

But who was attacking? There were no ships, and there was no incoming fire that the president could see.

'Sir, I'm getting a priority call,' said the pilot. 'It's Captain Strake.'

Oakworthy swallowed. This wasn't going to be a social call, that was for sure. 'Put her on.'

Strake appeared on the yellowed viewscreen, her face livid. 'I don't know how you organised the sabotage, old man, but we're going to crush your people totally and absolutely.'

231

'I assure you–'

'Shut it! This act seals your fate. We're going to lay waste to your planets with a bombardment the likes of which the entire galaxy has never before witnessed. We're going to destroy every city, every farm, every single person... and we're going to start with you!'

The screen went dark, and Oakworthy turned to look out the porthole. The cruiser's turrets were turning towards him, and he realised the Mayestrans were serious. They were going to blast him out of the sky. 'Pilot! Evasive manoeuvres! *Now!*'

The president grabbed for a hand-hold as the ship's ancient engines were pushed to the limits, and he felt his knees buckling as the cutter turned sharply. A torrent of energy bolts lanced towards him, red, green and blue, passing right through the spot where the cutter had been just a fraction of a second earlier. The pilot swung the other way, then back again, and streams of energy bolts tore past, so close to the hull the president could almost reach out and touch them.

It couldn't last. The Mayestrans had too many guns, and the customs cutter was built for patrolling space, not dogfighting. With a bang that threw the president to his knees, the ship's port engine was hit, and the whole thing exploded with a bright flash of light. Smoke filled the cabin, and the cutter spiralled away, still bracketed by incoming shots.

The president staggered to his feet, and as he stared through the porthole at the incoming fire, he knew it was only a matter of seconds before he was blasted to space dust.

'Head for the planet!' said Hal. 'We can land! It's our only chance!'

Sam shook her head. 'We'll use the asteroid field. There's plenty of cover.'

'Are you joking?' Hal stared at her. 'Look what happened to *your* ship when you tried that stunt!'

'My ship was damaged in battle.'

'*We're* going to be damaged in battle.' Hal gestured at the display, where bursts of enemy fire could be seen flashing past the screen. 'They'll get us long before we reach the asteroids!'

There was another burst of fire, this time from left of screen. It went on and on, and as the Albion jinked, dived and rolled, the fire grew thicker and thicker.

'That's their fleet,' said Sam grimly. 'They're trying to get a bead on us.'

'Shouldn't you, I don't know, fly *away* from them?' demanded Hal.

'Flying across their guns makes us harder to hit.'

'Don't they have radar? Automatic targeting?'

'At this distance?' Sam shook her head. 'Ineffective.'

'Missiles? Guided torpedoes? Swarms of killer robots on jetbikes?'

Sam gave him a look. 'You really should rethink your viewing habits.' Then she turned her attention to the controls, sending the ship into a looping barrel-roll to put their pursuers off.

In the middle of the action, Hal heard the lift. He turned to the shaft, and saw an empty space where the car had been, and he realised someone must have called it. 'Clunk?' he whispered. Had the robot survived the inferno, by some miracle?

But no. When the lift arrived it was Mrs Murtay, with one of her cats cradled in her arms.

'Mother!' called Cylen. 'It's not safe! You should be in your cabin!'

It's not safe anywhere, thought Hal, but he kept the words to himself. Meanwhile, Mrs Murtay was eyeing the screen. 'My, but that's a pretty firework display. Is it a public holiday?'

Cylen went over to her, guided her back towards the lift. 'Let's go below, mother. I'll make you a cup of tea, and we'll feed the cats.'

They took the lift, and in the meantime Sam threw the *Albion* all over space as she tried to avoid incoming fire. Hal could only watch as she put on a flying display for the ages, with all her combat skills coming to the fore. As he stood there, admiring her deft touch, he realised centuries might pass and he still wouldn't get close to her abilities.

Then he heard the lift returning. 'Tea's in my quarters,' he said, without looking round. 'Put the milk back in the fridge when you're done.'

'Thank you, Mr Spacejock, but I don't take tea.'

Hal recognised the voice, and he turned, startled, to see Clunk standing in the lift. The robot gleamed under the lights, and he looked completely unharmed. 'Clunk? How in the hell–'

'I took refuge in the launch tube. The fire couldn't get to me.'

The Albion shook suddenly, almost throwing them to the deck. Clunk took one look at the screen and ran past Hal to check the console. 'They're firing at us? Didn't you tell them we're neutral?'

'They spotted my uniform,' said Sam. Her expression was intent as she wrestled with the controls, and she barely looked round as Clunk took the second seat.

Meanwhile, on screen, Hal could see a mass of ships unleashing concentrated fire on them. Each incoming burst flew lazily towards the *Albion*, before accelerating as it got closer, and finally, with a flash, flying past. Then, as he watched, there was a burst of yellow amongst the ships of the fleet. 'What was that?'

Sam glanced at the screen, then shrugged. She was too busy to bother about it, but when a second and third flash lit the screen, she paid more attention. The firing stopped, briefly, and in the respite she checked the fleet. 'Someone's attacking them,' she said. 'That'll even things up.'

'Is it the Dolorians?' asked Hal. 'Are they standing up for themselves?'

'Oh my goodness,' said Clunk. 'Mr Spacejock, it was us!'

'Really?' Hal looked surprised. 'We have weapons?'

'No, of course not.'

'How, then?'

'I just checked the figures, and the conclusion is inescapable. Cylen Murtay's asteroids were released in such a way as to strike the Mayestran fleet.'

Sam stared at him. 'For *real*? That inoffensive little guy just blasted three warships? With *rocks*?'

'Way to go, Cylen,' said Hal, punching the air.

At that moment the lift returned, and Cylen stepped out...only to be met by a collective stare. 'What is it?' he asked.

'Your plan worked,' said Sam, gesturing at the screen. 'Three rocks, three hits by my count.'

'Really? Well, that's most pleasing.'

'Pleasing?' said Clunk. '*Pleasing?*'

Before anyone could stop him, the robot leapt up, marched across the flight deck and grabbed Murtay by his lapels. He

235

hauled the human into the air, swung him round and slammed him against the wall. 'What have you done?' demanded Clunk. 'What have you *done?*' He'd lifted Murtay so high the man's toes were six inches off the deck, and Murtay struggled to free himself.

Sam was still busy with the controls, for the Mayestrans had now redoubled their efforts to destroy the *Albion*, but Hal ran over and dragged on the robot's arms, trying to get Murtay free. 'Clunk, let him go!' he shouted.

'I–it was the only way!' stammered Murtay. 'With more ships, more rocks, I'd have blasted the whole Mayestran fleet.'

'This is a civilian ship!' shouted Clunk. 'You can't just enroll us in a war.' He gestured at the screen. 'You tricked me into killing people! And now they're going to kill us!'

'To be fair,' said Murtay, 'they were trying to kill you before the asteroids struck.'

'Your research? The experiments? They were all lies?' Clunk shook Murtay. 'Was this a government operation?'

'N–no! It was all me. I–I took them my plans, but they dismissed them out of hand.'

'If they won't have you back,' called Sam, 'my people will certainly welcome you. You're a hero.'

Clunk looked like he had more to say, a lot more, but at that moment the Navcom interrupted.

'Incoming call.'

'If it's the Mayestrans, you might want to take a message,' suggested Hal.

'Negative. It's the Dolorian President.'

'I must speak with him!' said Murtay, and, reluctantly, Clunk let him go.

They all turned to the screen, apart from Sam, who was still dodging incoming fire. What they expected to see was the president of Dolor, sitting comfortably in his office, surrounded by advisors. Instead, what they saw was the president of Dolor, perched on a battered, fold-down seat, surrounded by smoke and sparking electronics. 'Please help us!' he shouted. 'We're under attack by the Mayestrans. We need assistance!'

'Mr President, hang tight!' shouted Murtay. 'I have a ship! I'll save you!'

Hal frowned at him. '*You* have a ship?'

'Mr Spacejock, I'll pay you double,' said Murtay quickly. 'Please, you must save our president!'

Meanwhile, Oakworthy had just recognised him. 'Cylen Murtay? Is that you?'

'Yes, Mr President.'

'Was it *your* plan to lead this attack on the Mayestrans?'

'You knew about my plan?'

'I read a summary of your presentation.' The president clung to a strap as the vessel he was travelling in shook from nose to stern. 'You're a hero, Mr Murtay. A true hero of Dolor.'

'Thank you, Mr President, but I'm sorry you're in danger. That wasn't meant to happen.'

The president gestured. 'Perhaps my sacrifice will encourage others to stand up for themselves. To fight for freedom as you have. To lead by example, and–'

There was a flash, and the screen went dead.

'Mr President!' shouted Murtay.

There was no reply. Then the screen flickered into life, showing the entire Mayestran force heading towards the *Albion*.

'Er, Clunk? Maybe you'd better get us out of here,' said Hal.

The robot nodded. 'Navcom, prepare for jump.'

'Unable to comply. Hyperdrives offline pending servicing.'

'What do you mean, servicing?' demanded Hal. 'We've only used them a couple of times!'

'They're not run in yet,' said the Navcom.

'In that case,' said Hal, 'we're doomed.'

Sam glanced at him. 'It's not over yet, but you'd better hang on to something.'

23

As Sam held the *Albion's* controls, she knew the next few minutes would be critical. So far, the enemy had only taken pot-shots from a distance, but now they were coming after the ship in earnest. If she were flying a military ship, the Mayestrans would have sent everything they had, but the *Albion* was only an unarmed freighter. On the other hand, that meant she couldn't fight back.

Sam counted two flights of three fighters each, all of them closing fast in a loose attack formation. She'd faced similar tactics before, but always at the controls of her own nimble fighter, not sitting in the flight deck of a lumbering cargo freighter. To the enemy, the ship must look as big as a moon, and about as easy to hit.

Well, the *Albion* might have been easy to hit with a regular pilot at the helm, thought Sam grimly, but she had a few tricks up her sleeve.

They were approaching the asteroid field now, and as the speedy fighters closed in, Sam aimed straight for a huge, tumbling rock. She could feel the tension in the flight deck, could almost hear the others drawing in a deep breath and holding it. Then the enemy opened fire, and as the laser bursts flew past, Sam turned the ship and activated the upper thrusters. The ship went down, and they skimmed underneath the asteroid, so close it almost brushed the hull, and then she swung the ship the other way and powered towards another pair of rocks.

Meanwhile, laser fire slammed into the rock she'd just avoided, shattering it into thousands of smaller pieces. These were no danger to the *Albion*, but the fighters were forced to slow down and pick their way carefully through the spreading cloud of rubble.

Once clear, the deadly ships set off after the *Albion* once more, only this time they fired more cautiously. Sam used asteroids for cover, and she threw the big ship around like one of the pursuing fighters as she dodged the incoming shots. Many were going wild, and she realised the attacking pilots weren't exactly hardened veterans. 'We're lucky,' she shouted to the others. 'The Mayestrans weren't expecting trouble in this system. These pilots aren't very good.'

Sam had barely finished speaking when there was a blinding green flash, and after the screen recovered she saw a virtual tunnel punched into the asteroid field. One of the big cruisers had just fired its main guns, slicing through the nearby rocks as though they were made from butter. She was tempted to fly straight down the tunnel before the rocks shifted, but there was a chance the cruiser might fire again in the same spot. If it did so, it would vaporise the *Albion* just like it had vaporised the rocks.

A couple of fighters took the chance, and they raced down the newly-made tunnel. They overhauled the *Albion* in no time, and were just turning to intercept when there was a second green flash. When it cleared, the two fighters had vanished.

'They just shot at their own people!' said Hal in amazement.

'The cruiser is firing blind,' Sam called over her shoulder.

'They can't see us on their scanner, so they're just blasting away.' There were still four fighters after them, and she jinked left to put them off, then flew a tight circle around an asteroid and headed back the way they'd come. One of the fighters couldn't turn fast enough, and it slammed into a big rock, vanishing in a flash of exploding fuel and molten metal.

Three to go.

They were close now, and as they opened fire, the *Albion* was bracketed with angry red shots. Sam did what she could, but the three of them were working in tandem, hemming her in from all sides, and she realised it was only a matter of time before one of them punctured the hull, or took out an engine. Her earlier confidence had evaporated, and there was an edge of desperation to her movements.

The others must have noticed the change in her demeanour, because there was a strained hush. 'So, er, how's it going?' asked Hal, breaking the silence.

Shots zinged by, the bright flashes lighting the flight deck.

'Never mind,' said Hal. 'I can see for myself.'

Suddenly, the firing stopped. Sam kept throwing the ship around until she realised the fighters were no longer chasing her. She turned the ship until the fighters were in sight, and then she stared in surprise. All three were streaking away from the *Albion*, heading out of the asteroid field.

'What did you do?' Hal asked her.

'It wasn't me,' said Sam.

'Well something scared them off.'

All of a sudden, a dozen fighters blasted past, weaving expertly through the asteroid field. They hunted the Mayestrans down, and within seconds all three enemy fighters had been destroyed.

'Now they're attacking themselves!' cried Hal. 'These people are insane.'

'Those weren't Mayestrans,' said Sam quietly, and she felt a lump in her throat as one of the new arrivals sped past. 'They're my people. They're Henerians!'

'Incoming call,' said the Navcom.

'Put them on!'

The screen cleared, and an image of a young man appeared. He was sitting in a cramped cockpit, and was wearing a dark green flight suit and a helmet with a mirrored visor. 'Freighter *Albion*, you're free to go about your–' Then the man stopped, and with a flick of his hand he threw his visor up. 'Wingco, is that *you?*'

'Is that you, *sir,*' growled Sam, and then she laughed. 'Nice to see you guys. You nearly missed the party, as usual.'

'Just wait until command hears about this, Wingco. They posted you missing, presumed dead.'

'Did you hold a wake?'

'Nah. Figured you'd show up again, sir.' The man glanced around the flight deck. 'I see you've got company. I'd love to stop for introductions, but we owe the Mayestrans a pasting.'

'Don't let me hold you up,' said Sam.

'Yes sir.' The pilot threw a salute, then popped his visor down and cut the call. On the screen, they saw his ship powering away after the rest of the squadron. As it cleared the asteroid field, it performed a barrel-roll.

'Show off,' muttered Sam affectionately. 'I should have his wings for that.' Then she turned the *Albion* until they were facing Dolor, and the true extent of the battle became apparent. An entire Henerian fleet had jumped into the system, and the ships were pounding the hapless Mayestrans with everything they had. Fighters by the dozen whirled in and around the

242

capital ships, blasting away with abandon, while the cruisers and destroyers pounded each other with long range shots.

'I should be helping them,' muttered Sam, and her grip tightened on the *Albion's* controls.

'Hey, don't even think about it!' said Hal. 'We only just got away.'

They all watched the fleets attacking each other, and Sam could see the Henerians were getting the better of it. They had more ships, and the weight of firepower was thinning the ranks of Mayestrans by the second. Then, without warning, the remaining Mayestran ships winked out, one by one.

'They're jumping out of the system!' cried Sam. 'It's over! We've *won!*'

◆

President Oakworthy clung to the overhead strap as the customs vessel descended through the atmosphere. They'd lost all comms, and every navigation screen was blanked out. The pilot was struggling with the controls, trying to compensate for the missing engine, and the president could only watch and pray as the little ship rocked and swayed.

The cabin was filled with smoke, and there was an almighty roar as they plunged towards the surface. Their dive was far too steep, but it was the only way of avoiding the fighters which had been pursuing them.

Oakworthy glanced through the nearby porthole, but all he could see was long streamers of flame as super-heated air blasted the ship. If there were any fighters on their tail, they wouldn't be able to attack until they were closer to the ground… at which point the unarmed cutter would be a sitting duck.

'Can you detect anyone behind us?' called the president.

'Sorry, sir,' shouted the pilot. 'Everything's dead!'

'But the controls work?'

'Yes, thank goodness. We can land on one engine, but there's not enough power to dodge enemy fire.'

That's it, then, thought the president. If there are *any* fighters on our tail, it's all over. He saw a flash through the porthole, and he noticed the fiery atmosphere was thinning out. The flash had been some distance away, and as he peered up, towards the endless dark of space, he saw thin lines of energy blasts going back and forth. One side was the Mayestrans, obviously, but he had no idea who they were fighting. Could it be a Henerian fleet, or had Murtay found some more small ships to launch rocks at the invaders?

Every now and then there was a flare as one ship or another was destroyed, and the president hoped the Mayestrans were getting the worst of it. Then he remembered the pursuing fighters, but try as he might, the president couldn't see any ships on their tail.

The roaring ceased, and the president looked towards the front of the ship. Ahead, he could see the surface of Dolor laid out below. On the mad flight down from space he'd barely dared to hope, but now he realised they might actually make it. They levelled off, and there was no final burst of fire from a pursuer, no all-consuming explosion.

'I think we're clear, Mr President,' called the pilot.

'Can you set down at the spaceport?'

'Yes sir. Space Port Delta directly ahead.'

'Good man.' The president felt a surge of relief, and then his gaze fell on the stack of boxes containing the Mayestran demands, binders full of emergency powers, and the dossiers containing the terms of surrender. He glanced up through the porthole, where the battle was still going on, and then he saw the firing stop. 'Any news from the ground?' he called out to the pilot.

'None sir. They're not responding to hails, but they'll see we're damaged. We'll fly straight in, and hope they clear other traffic out of the way.' The pilot glanced through the windshield. 'Not that I've seen any other traffic. The place is deserted.'

The president knew what he meant. With one engine blown to pieces, there was no way the little customs ship was going to be circling the spaceport waiting for the right moment to land. He just hoped that ground control realised it was an emergency.

— 24 —

After taking over the controls from Sam, Clunk guided the *Albion* towards the spaceport on Dolor with a typically deft touch. 'Space Port Delta, this is the freighter *Albion*,' said the robot. 'Requesting permission to land.'

The speakers hissed, but there was no reply.

'Space Port Delta, do you copy?' Clunk toggled the transmit button, but nothing happened. 'Navcom, are comms down?'

'Not on our end,' said the computer. 'I believe it's a remote issue.'

'This is most disconcerting,' said Clunk, frowning at the others. 'I'm unable to reach Ground Control. Unless I obtain permission, we cannot land.'

'So land first and get permission afterwards,' said Hal. 'Or maybe just get closer. With a ship this big, they'll have to see us eventually.'

'I don't want to endanger other traffic.'

Hal gestured at the screen. 'We'll all keep an eye out. Anyway, we can't hang around forever or we'll just run out of fuel and crash.'

Clunk nodded, and moments later the spaceport appeared on the main screen. As they got closer they could see every landing pad was empty, apart from one containing a small ship with a damaged engine. Smoke rose from the rear of the ship, and they could see a couple of ant-like figures stumbling down the passenger ramp to the ground.

'Don't fly over them,' Sam advised Clunk. 'You'll blow them right out of the spaceport.'

The *Albion* veered to port, circling the stricken ship before setting down on the far side. Clunk cut the engines and extended the ramp, and seconds later they emerged in the warm, humid air. 'Where the hell is everyone?' demanded Hal, as he glanced around the deserted landing field.

'They must have fled to safety when the Mayestrans showed up,' said Sam.

The air was thick with acrid smoke from the damaged ship on the next landing pad, and Hal eyed it in concern. If the fuel tanks went up, the explosion would shower the *Albion* with burning fragments. Then he remembered the fiery re-entry, and he ran down the ramp and hurried to the back of his ship for a closer look.

It wasn't a pretty sight. The gleaming white paint was gone, and the rear of the ship was scorched and blackened. Everything was still attached, but the *Albion* was no longer the shiny new ship of just a day or two earlier. Hal's lips thinned at the sight, but then he remembered Murtay still owed him a second payment for the asteroid job. 'Easy come, easy go,' he muttered.

He heard a commotion, and he turned to see Murtay talking to an elderly man in a cardigan and corduroy trousers. The man looked like someone's favourite uncle, and Hal was about to turn away when he recognised him from an earlier distress call. It was the president of Dolor!

'Mr President,' Murtay was saying, hardly able to contain his excitement. 'You made it! You survived!'

247

'All credit to my pilot,' said Oakworthy. 'I was just a passenger, I assure you.' He looked up, studying the sky. 'I still don't understand why they didn't finish me off. We were sitting ducks out there.'

'That's probably because the Mayestrans have gone,' said Murtay.

'Gone?'

'A Henerian fleet showed up. There was a battle, and the Mayestrans fled.'

'That's excellent news, young man. This planet – no, the entire system – owes you a debt of gratitude.'

'It wasn't just me, sir.' Murtay beckoned to Sam. 'This is Wing Commander Sam... er...'

'Sam Willet, Mr President,' said Sam, and she gave him a smart salute.

'You're a Henerian,' said Oakworthy, eyeing her uniform with a frown. 'Is it your turn to invade us next?'

'I'm only here by accident,' explained Sam. 'I took refuge in the asteroid field, where I was rescued by a freighter pilot.'

Hal stepped forward and introduced himself. 'I'm Hal Spacejock, Mr President, and this is my copilot, Clunk.'

'An XG series robot?' said Oakworthy. 'My, but it's a long time since I saw one of you.'

'Mr President,' said Clunk, with a nod.

'Cylen?' said a voice from somewhere above them. 'Where are we? Who are you speaking to?'

Everyone turned to look. Mrs Murtay was at the top of the passenger ramp, and she was peering down at them over the top of her reading glasses.

Cylen hurried up the ramp to meet her, and he accompanied her back down again before introducing her to the president.

'A pleasure, Mrs Murtay,' said Oakworthy, with a bow. 'I hope you're proud of your son.'

'Indeed I am, Mr President. Indeed I am.' Mrs Murtay looked around the landing field. 'But tell me, where are the crowds?'

'Crowds?'

'I assume you're giving my son another medal. Was I mistaken?'

'Another–?' began the president.

'Mother, don't bother him now,' said Cylen quickly.

There was a creak from the back of the ship, and Hal looked round to see the launch tube's outer hatch opening. Before anyone could react, Max appeared, and she dropped to the tarmac and faced them.

'So that's where you put her,' remarked Hal.

'Is this another hero to be thanked?' asked the president.

'Not quite,' muttered Hal. He glanced around, but the landing field was conspicuously short of armed guards and Peace Force officers.

'Spacejock!' called Max, who was keeping her distance. 'No hard feelings, right? I saw an opportunity, and I took it.'

'You tried to kill me!' shouted Hal.

Max shrugged. 'You have a nice ship. Too good for you, at any rate.'

Hal would have said more, but he heard an approaching vehicle, and he turned to see a spaceport maintenance truck speeding towards them. It came to a stop, and two Mayestrans emerged, resplendent in their red and black uniforms. They had pistols in holsters, and as they approached the group they rested their hands lightly on the weapons, ready to draw them at a moment's notice.

Hal's heart sank as he recognised the pair. It was First

Lieutenant Ferrast, who'd searched his ship when he first landed on Dolor, and the fresh-faced young officer who'd stuck his hand in the power distribution box and given himself an almighty shock. The young man looked a little dazed, and his hair was still standing on end.

'Who gave you permission to land?' snapped Ferrast.

'I'm the president of Dolor... indeed, president of the entire system,' said Oakworthy calmly. 'I don't need your permission to land on my home planet.'

Score one for the mild-mannered uncle, thought Hal.

'This planet is now under Mayestran rule. All civilian flights are banned, and your vessels will be confiscated under section nineteen of the terms of occupation.'

'I'm not a Dolorian,' said Hal. 'Clunk and I, we're just passing through.'

'You're subject to the same rules,' said Ferrast. She glanced up at the *Albion*. 'She'll make an excellent transport. My people thank you.' Ferrast eyed the others. 'Are you Dolorians?'

'Yes,' said Sam, who'd done up her borrowed flight suit, concealing her uniform.

'I am, and so is my mother,' said Cylen.

Max shook her head. 'Citizen of the Empire.'

Ferrast gave her a curious look, then shrugged. 'It doesn't matter. You will all be arrested and charged with trespass. Please turn around and put your hands behind your heads.'

'Yeah, there's something you ought to know,' said Sam. 'Your fleet... it left the system.'

'Nonsense.'

'Believe me, we saw it,' insisted Sam. 'Tell me, when's the last time you spoke with them?'

Ferrast drew her weapon. 'Enough talking. Turn around.'

They all obeyed, and then she nodded to the younger officer. 'Search them. I want their IDs.'

'Even the robot?' he asked, uncertainly.

'Of course the robot! Do as you're told!' snapped Ferrast.

There was a roar of vehicles in the distance, and Hal smiled to himself. From the sound of it, the Dolorians or the Henerians had just shown up, and Lieutenant Ferrast was about to have the tables turned on her. However, his optimism was short-lived, because instead of a load of friendlies, the new arrivals drove up in half a dozen trucks...one of them with the headlights smashed in and the front bumper missing. 'Oh *great*,' he groaned. Sure enough, it was the army of Mayestrans...about a hundred of them dressed in red and black uniforms, armed with the weapons he and Clunk had delivered to Dolor. They fanned out and quickly surrounded the *Albion* and her assorted crew, weapons at the ready.

Once they'd secured the ship, their leader strode up to Ferrast, who saluted him smartly. 'Report!' he barked.

'These civilians just landed at the spaceport, sir. I'm arresting them and requisitioning their ships.'

The man glanced at the customs cutter and the *Albion*, then cast a brief look over Hal and his motley gang. 'Which one's the pilot?'

Ferrast pointed at Hal.

'Lower the cargo ramp,' said the man, gesturing towards the rear of Hal's ship.

Hal frowned. 'Why?'

The officer drew his weapon, and at his signal there was a chorus of *chacks* as a hundred safeties were turned off. 'Because I said so.'

'I'm on it,' said Hal quickly, and he headed for the ramp.

'Accompany him,' said the officer, gesturing to Lieutenant

Ferrast. 'If he makes one wrong move during the evacuation, shoot him.'

'Evacuation?' demanded Ferrast. 'Are we leaving, sir?'

'Yes. Our fleet has left the system.' The officer nodded towards the *Albion*. 'This ship is our only way out.'

'You'll never make it,' Sam called out. 'The Henerians are here, and they're going to blast any ship making a run for it.'

The officer strode over to her. 'What do you know about the Henerians?'

'Don't do it,' muttered Hal. 'Do *not* do it.'

Sam did it. 'Wing Commander Sam Willet at your service,' she said, and she opened the flight suit to reveal her dark green uniform. 'In the name of the Henerian Navy, I order you to lay down your weapons.'

— 25 —

The Mayestran officer reacted instantly, raising his gun and pressing the muzzle to Sam's temple. 'Well, isn't this perfect? It looks like I'll be going back with a new ship *and* the body of a Henerian rebel.'

Hal realised the man was going to shoot Sam out of hand, but before he could take a flying leap at the pair, Max spoke up.

'Stand down,' she said loudly. 'That's an order.'

The officer was still covering Sam with his gun, and he didn't turn around. 'I'm in no mood for foolish jokes.'

'You should run a biometric scan on me before you pull that trigger,' said Max quietly. 'After all, there are plenty of witnesses here for the court martial.'

'What court martial?'

'Yours.'

The man turned to stare at her, and Max coolly held his gaze until the officer muttered under his breath. He gestured at one of the soldiers, and they hurried towards Max with a hand-held scanner. The unit shone blue light in her eyes, then beeped. The soldier checked the display, did a double-take, then ran the scan again, just in case.

'S-sir, the unit says the subject has clearance violet alpha.'

'Give me that thing. Now!'

The man hurried over, and after the officer checked the screen, he turned to Max with a completely different attitude. 'I'm sorry, sir. I had no idea.'

'You weren't to know,' said Max, with a casual gesture. 'Now lower your weapon and order the troops to stand down. These people are allies.'

Hal stared at her, completely dumbfounded. Max *had* been a Mayestran agent, and Clunk hadn't believed a word of it!

Meanwhile, the hundred or so men and women surrounding the *Albion* turned to their leader for a signal, but the commanding officer wasn't ready to capitulate. 'She's a Henerian,' he said, gesturing at Sam. 'How can *she* be an ally?'

'Lower your weapons. I won't ask again.'

There was a tense standoff for a moment or two, and then the officer nodded quickly. 'Do as she says.'

'Thank you,' said Max quietly. 'You made the right decision.' Then she turned to Hal. 'I need you to transport these troops to a neutral planet. Can you do that?'

'Sure, provided they stash those guns and stay in the cargo hold. I don't want them getting any ideas.'

Max turned to the officer. 'Is that acceptable?'

He nodded.

'Then we have a deal. Hal, go and open the hold.'

Hal took the passenger ramp to the airlock, still stunned by the turn of events, but he was only halfway up when there was an ear-shattering roar as a dozen nimble little fighters streaked across the spaceport. He clamped his hands to his ears as the thunderous noise threatened to burst his eardrums, and he saw everyone below him doing the same. Then, before the soldiers had recovered, there was a deeper roar as a squadron of squat gunships followed the fighters. They bristled with cannons and gun turrets, and as they set down, surrounding the *Albion*, every member of the Mayestran force was picked out with bright red targeting dots. They raised their hands immediately, and were quickly surrounded by the green-uniformed Henerians who poured out of the gunships. Their weapons were taken, and they were rounded up into a dispirited-looking group.

Hal had never seen anything so exciting in his life, and he leaned his elbows on the rail to watch events unfolding.

Several heavily-armed troops approached the Mayestran officers, marines from the look of them, and their leader inspected the enemy's uniforms before singling out the male officer who'd threatened to shoot Sam. Before either could say a word, there was another ear-splitting roar.

The fighters which had buzzed the landing field turned sharply and set down nearby. Their canopies popped open, short ladders extended, and the pilots swung themselves out of the cockpits and clambered down to the ground. Their leader, a young man in a green uniform, jogged across the landing pad to Sam. He was beaming with delight as he skidded to a halt in front of her, and then he threw a casual salute. 'Welcome back to the fold, sir.'

Sam grinned back. 'Happy to be here, squadron leader.'

She was quickly surrounded by her fellow pilots, and as they caught up on events, Hal remembered Max. He turned to seek her out, half-expecting to see her sneaking away from the new arrivals, but instead she was talking to a couple of Henerian officers.

'If you don't believe me, run a biometric scan,' she was saying.

'Whatever she says, it's a lie,' Sam called out. 'Sir, she's with the Mayestrans. She's a secret agent of some kind. Very high up.'

The Henerian commander, an older woman with an impressive set of campaign ribbons, turned to look at Max. 'Is she really?' she said. 'Well, that's a nice catch.'

'Scan me, or it's your funeral,' said Max.

The commander asked for a scanner, then held it to Max's face herself. The unit beeped, and she gaped at it. 'Sir, I had no idea.'

'That's understandable,' said Max. 'You weren't to know.'

'It's an honour to meet you. There aren't many heroes left, not from the early war years.'

'Wait a minute,' said Sam. 'A minute ago the Mayestrans thought she was one of theirs!'

Max nodded. 'I'm a Henerian double agent, working under deep cover.'

'You told me you deserted!'

'I was hardly going to blow my cover to a lowly Wing Commander, was I?' Max turned to the commander. 'By the way, I'd like to introduce the president of Dolor.'

'It looks like we've traded one oppressor for another,' said Oakworthy, eyeing the pair of them in disfavour.

The Henerian commander shook her head. 'We have no interest in your system, sir. But when we heard a Mayestran fleet was here, we decided to shake them up a bit.'

'How did you know their fleet was here?'

Sam cleared her throat. 'That was me.' She glanced up at Hal. 'I'm sorry, but I sent a long-distance message to my people. You're going to get a pretty hefty comms bill.'

'We'll cover that,' said the president quickly. 'Given the outcome, it'll be worth every credit.'

Max and the Henerians had been talking in low voices, and

now their commander had the prisoners transferred to the gunships. While the Mayestrans were being herded away, Sam came up the ramp to speak with Hal. 'You'll never know how much you helped my people,' she said. 'They'll give you a medal for this, I'm sure. You *and* Clunk.'

'He'll be pleased with that,' said Hal. Then a thought occurred to him. 'You, er, don't expect us to fly into a war zone to collect these medals, do you?'

'I'm sure we can find a courier,' said Sam, with a smile. She held her hand out. 'Thank you, Hal. I owe you my life.'

'I owe you mine twice over.'

They shook, and Hal realised Sam was heading back into a war zone herself. Unlike him, she had no choice in the matter. 'Take care, won't you?'

She nodded. 'We hit them hard today. Who knows, maybe it'll tip the balance in our favour, and this thing will be over before we know it.' She glanced at the *Albion*. 'If I make it, I wouldn't mind another trip or two. Delivering cargo would make a really nice change from dogfighting.'

'Any time,' said Hal, but before he could say any more Sam was gone. He felt a stab of regret, and he wished she could have stuck around. He was distracted by a flicker of light, and he noticed the president setting fire to a stack of filing boxes. The paper caught quickly, and soon the towering flames dwarfed everyone around them.

Meanwhile, the Henerians had finished loading the prisoners into the gunships, and the troops and pilots were preparing to leave. Hal saw Cylen and his mother talking to the president, and then Clunk came up the ramp to join him. 'Mr Spacejock, is everything all right?'

'Sure. We'll probably get medals from the Dolorians as well

as the Henerians, and when Cylen coughs up the rest of his payment we'll be in the money, too.'

'Ah yes. I'm afraid I have some bad news.'

Hal groaned. 'Don't tell me.'

'Mr Murtay used all his savings for the down payment on the job. I'm sorry, but he never intended to make a second payment.'

'Do we have enough for fuel?'

'Just about, Mr Spacejock.'

Then Hal remembered something. 'What happened to Max? Did she go with the Henerians?'

Clunk pointed her out.

'She should have been arrested. Thrown in jail.' Hal started down the ramp.

'Where are you going?'

'I want to speak with the so-called war hero.' Hal strode past the fire, where the president was staring into the blazing flames, and then he approached Max. 'So, you're a hero, are you? Did they decorate you for abandoning allies in space? Stealing ships off innocent people?'

Max turned to look at him. 'I do what I must to survive.'

'Yeah, well I'm not surprised you're spying for both sides. Lying and cheating must be second nature to you.'

She shrugged. 'They only think I'm working for them.'

'What do you mean?'

'I quit years ago,' confessed Max. 'I just send in a report now and then, usually with fake intel I plucked out of thin air. It keeps both sides happy, and their cash is always useful.'

Hal's jaw dropped. 'You're milking both sides?' he asked, impressed.

'Sure.' Max glanced up at the *Albion*. 'You're lucky to have a ship like that. Look after her, eh?'

'I plan to. But what will you do?'

'I always have a backup plan. No hard feelings, eh?' Max shook his hand firmly, then turned and strolled towards the damaged customs cutter. She took the ramp to the interior, and moments later it closed with a whine. The one remaining engine fired up, and the ship lifted off with a splutter and a roar. It wobbled briefly, hovering in mid-air, before tilting back and roaring into the sky, trailing black smoke and sparks.

Hal watched it go, until the ship was a speck, and then it vanished altogether. Somehow, he knew he'd encounter Max again. Then he glanced towards the gunships. He had no idea which one Sam was in, and he was a lot less confident in seeing her ever again. He'd experienced a space battle himself, only an hour earlier, and he couldn't imagine facing the same intensity and danger every day of his life. He wished he'd done more to convince Sam to stay, at least for a while. If nothing else, he was keen to learn some of her neat flying tricks.

The gunships and the fighter escort lifted off, blasting him with noise and dust. Hal clamped his hands over his ears against the hammering roar, and as they flew away he saw a lone figure standing on the landing pad. The dust cleared and he realised it was Sam. 'Hey! Why did they leave you behind?'

'I put in for a week's leave,' she said, with a smile. 'They granted it, too.'

Hal's spirits soared. 'Do you want to help with a couple of cargo runs?'

'Depends.'

'On what?'

'Are you going to fly the ship?'

The president's bonfire had burned itself out, and the charred remains of the Mayestran demands blew around the landing pad like a swarm of jet-black butterflies. The president himself had just been collected by a rather sedate old limousine, and after everyone waved him off, Hal turned to Murtay. 'Clunk told me you spent everything you had on this little stunt.'

'That's correct.' Murtay looked at him warily. 'I'm sorry about the second payment. You earned every credit, I know, but I don't have any more money.'

'Don't worry about it.' Hal gestured. 'I'll work out what the fuel cost, and then I'll have the Navcom return the rest of your cash.'

'But–'

'You did a good thing for your planet. I'm not out to make a profit from that.'

'That's good of you, but there's no need. The president assured me the government will refund the money I gave you.'

'Really?' Hal looked hopeful. 'Do you reckon they'll stump up the second half of the payment?'

'Knowing the finance ministry, I doubt it.'

'Never mind. Maybe I can sell the medal.' Hal glanced

towards his ship. Sam and Clunk had gone aboard to run systems checks, and Clunk had promised to find a lucrative cargo job.

Cylen hesitated. 'There is one thing you can do for me.'

'Yes?'

'Could we drop my mother home?'

※

Sam flew the Albion towards Mrs Murtay's house, with Hal in the copilot's seat and Clunk hovering anxiously behind the pair of them.

'Perhaps a touch more throttle,' said the robot, eyeing the big viewscreen. 'And your right hand is down a millimetre or two.'

Hal glanced round. 'Leave her alone, Clunk. In fact, why don't you go and tell our passengers we're almost there?'

'Leave the flight deck? Why, I could never–'

'Either you leave, or we'll throw you out,' said Hal firmly.

After a meaningful glance at an indicator which was about point one of a percent outside optimal range, Clunk left.

Moments later, Sam set the big ship down without fuss.

'Nice job,' said Hal.

'It was a lot easier without your robot hovering over my shoulder, that's for sure.' She smiled at him. 'Flying this thing really isn't that hard.'

Hal begged to differ, but he said nothing.

While Sam was busy shutting down the flight systems, Hal reached for a button to extend the ramp. Then, remembering what happened last time, he hesitated. 'Navcom, can you confirm something?'

'Go ahead.'

'Is the airlock facing Mrs Murtay's house?'

'Negative.'

Relieved, Hal pressed the button, and he heard the familiar whine of hydraulics as the ramp unfolded from the ship.

'What did you do?' demanded Sam. 'What did you press?'

'I, er–'

There was a distant sound of breaking glass, and Hal ran to the airlock and peered out... only to see the ramp sticking through the window of a two storey house. 'Navcom! You said we weren't sitting next to Mrs Murtay's place!'

'We're not. This time we're facing the neighbours.'

Hal ran back to the console and quickly retracted the ramp. 'Maybe we should exit via the cargo hold,' he told Sam.

'Yeah, probably for the best.'

'Navcom, call the insurance company. Tell them we had a bit of an accident.'

'The latter is unnecessary. They'll know you've broken something as soon as your call sign flashes up.'

'All right, enough with the wit. Just get that window fixed.'

Sam finished with the console, and together they took the lift to the passenger deck. They found Clunk with the Murtays, and all five of them entered the hold together. Clunk lowered the ramp, and five minutes later they were gathered in Mrs Murtay's sitting room. On the way into the house Hal glanced up the stairs, and he was surprised to see the window he'd broken earlier that day had already been repaired. 'That was quick.'

'I told you dear, there's a handyman in the village,' said Mrs Murtay. 'Now wait here, all of you. I'll make some tea. I'm afraid I'm out of biscuits, but–'

'Don't worry,' said Hal. 'I've got a big box of snacks on the Albion.'

As he left, he heard Mrs Murtay talking to Sam. 'Do you have anyone special in your life, dear? My son is single, you know.'

'Mother!' protested Cylen.

The rest of the conversation was cut off as Hal left the house. He took the ramp to the hold, shaking his head at the scorched paint, then made his way to his cabin. The carton of snacks was where he left it, sitting on the shelf in his closet, but as he reached for it he noticed something. The display box containing his Dick Spacewad figure was open! With shaking fingers, he took the box down and turned it to look inside, and that's when he realised someone had stolen the figure.

'Max!' he breathed. She must have slipped it into her overalls before she left the ship, probably hoping to sell it. Well, thought Hal, good luck with that. She'd taken the thing out of the packaging, which meant it was next to worthless.

Then another thought hit him. His dreams of reuniting the boxed Dick Spacewad with an even rarer Crank figurine had just been dashed. Sure, it had been a long shot, but now Max had cruelly snatched it away.

Disappointed, he tossed the empty carton back on the shelf and grabbed the box full of snacks. Ten minutes later he was back in Mrs Murtay's sitting room, where the others were perched on the overstuffed sofas, drinking tea. 'Here you are,' he said, putting the box on the table. 'Help yourselves.'

Sam opened the top, then paused. Slowly, she reached inside and took out a handful of empty packets. 'Someone's been snacking without us,' she said.

Hal looked in the box, and he felt a stab of anger. 'Max!' Then he saw something that really infuriated him... his Dick

Spacewad figure lay in the bottom of the box, the previously-pristine spacesuit marked with grubby chocolate fingerprints. He took the figure out and brandished it at the others. 'Look what she did!' he protested. 'This was in mint condition, and she's ruined the thing.'

'It's just a toy,' said Cylen. 'Surely you can get another one.'

'It's not a toy, it's a collectable,' said Hal stiffly.

Mrs Murtay peered at the figure through her glasses. 'Oh my. I remember when those came out. We had the little gold robot once. I bought it for Cylen, but he wasn't interested.'

'You had a Crank?' said Hal, who was suddenly having trouble breathing. 'W-what happened to it?'

'Blessed if I know. I do remember Cylen was mad keen on dinosaurs at the time, so we ended up getting a couple of those instead.' She frowned. 'I think we took the robot back to the shop. Or maybe it's still sitting at the back of the hall cupboard. I really don't know. It was such a long time ago.'

'Is there any chance... I mean, can you take a look?'

Mrs Murtay smiled at him. 'Of course, dear.'

Hal watched the old lady cross to a narrow door, and he had to restrain himself from running over and tossing the contents of her cupboard all over the floor.

Mrs Murtay stood there for what seemed like ages, moving old boxes around, until... 'Aha!' she said. 'Here it is!'

Even then, Hal expected to see the wrong figurine, or a battered, broken old robot. Instead, Mrs Murtay came over with a pristine box in her hands. And through the window, inside the box, Hal could see an honest-to-goodness Crank figurine.

'My, he looks just like your robot,' said Mrs Murtay, as she turned the box over in her hands. Then she held it out to Hal. 'Here you are, dear. It's yours if you want it.'

'I couldn't,' said Hal firmly. 'It's worth a fortune.'

'Perhaps, but are you really going to sell it?' Mrs Murtay pressed the box into his hands. 'Here.'

Hal looked down at the little bronze figure, trapped in its gaudy packaging, and then, on impulse, he opened the lid and took it out. The Crank figure felt cool in his hands, and he took the robot and stood it on the table right next to the chocolatey Dick Spacewad. It was the first time in many a long year the two of them had been paired up together, and he realised they were a perfect match. 'No,' he said, eyeing the little bronze robot. 'No, I'm never going to sell it.'

&

It was two hours later, and the Albion was heading towards Space Port Delta with Sam at the controls. Clunk had found them a cargo job, one which would take them well out of the system. In fact, it would take them to the far end of the spiral arm, well clear of the Mayestrans, the Henerians, and their all-consuming war.

'Are you sure there are settlements out there?' asked Hal, as he eyed the screen. The main display was showing a section of the galactic map, and while there were thousands of stars, none of them were inhabited.

'The map is out of date,' Clunk assured him. 'With frontier worlds, data can be a little sketchy.'

'And we'll be back in a week?' Hal indicated Sam. 'If she's not back with her people, they'll hunt her as a deserter.'

'Mr Spacejock, we'll be back in plenty of time... if everything goes well.'

'I wish you hadn't said that,' muttered Hal.

Sam grinned at him. 'Don't worry, it'll be fine. Worst case, we can go on the run together.' She indicated the controls. 'Come on, it's time for your first lesson. Take the stick.'

Hal obeyed, and Sam demonstrated an acrobatic manoeuvre. The ship rolled lazily, before righting herself. 'Your turn.'

Hal took the stick and copied her, but he shifted it too fast and the ship completed three complete revolutions before Sam brought her under control.

'Easy, Hal,' she said. 'You have to treat her with a light touch. Don't go barging in.'

Hal tried again, and this time the ship completed a single barrel roll before ending up level... more or less.

'Better. Much better!'

Hal was delighted. All the ships he'd owned, and flying them had always been a complete mystery. 'The ship's obeying me!'

'Obeying is a pretty strong word,' said the Navcom primly.

'Now, let's try a loop,' said Sam.

Clunk watched them with a paternal smile on his face. Hal was in good hands, and perhaps with Sam's patient help he would actually learn something.

He decided to leave the humans to it, and he slipped away to get a well-earned recharge.

Epilogue

Breaking news! The Mayestrans and the Henerians have just agreed to a ceasefire, and negotiations for a peace treaty are under way. The war has raged for years, killing tens of thousands and consuming entire systems along the way, and a cessation of hostilities will be welcomed by every planet in the sector.

In other news, a customs ship stolen three days ago has been recovered from a nearby system. Rumours the ship was used in a criminal heist have yet to be confirmed.

And now for a truly offbeat item. Recently, an unclaimed shipping container was discovered in a disused warehouse at Space Port Delta. When authorities broke the seal, they discovered it contained thousands of boxed Crank toys. As you'd expect, the price of these rare figures has been in freefall since the announcement was made public.

If you enjoyed this book, please leave a brief review at your online bookseller of choice. Thanks!

About the Author

Simon Haynes was born in England and grew up in Spain. His family moved to Australia when he was 16.

In addition to novels, Simon writes computer software. In fact, he writes computer software to help him write novels faster, which leaves him more time to improve his writing software. And write novels faster. (www.spacejock.com/yWriter.html)

Simon's goal is to write fifteen novels before someone takes his keyboard away.

Update 2018: goal achieved and I still have my keyboard!

New goal: write thirty novels.

Simon's website is spacejock.com.au

Stay in touch!

Author's newsletter:
spacejock.com.au/ML.html

facebook.com/halspacejock
twitter.com/spacejock

Acknowledgements

To Bob, Ian, Darcey, Luke, Peter, Jeff, Zelda, Gwen, Alan, Stephen, Paul Franco, Dennis, Deborah-Ann, Barrie, Trevor, Cav, Myla, Neil, Ray, thanks for the awesome help and support!

To all my proofreaders and spling chquers, thansk!

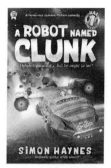

The Hal Spacejock series by Simon Haynes

1. A ROBOT NAMED CLUNK

Deep in debt and with his life on the line, Hal takes on a dodgy cargo job ... and an equally dodgy co-pilot.

2. SECOND COURSE

When Hal finds an alien teleporter network he does the sensible thing and pushes Clunk the robot in first.

3. JUST DESSERTS

Gun-crazed mercenaries have Hal in their sights, and a secret agent is pulling the strings. One wrong step and three planets go to war!

4. NO FREE LUNCH

Everyone thinks Peace Force trainee Harriet Walsh is paranoid and deluded, but Hal stands at her side. That would be the handcuffs.

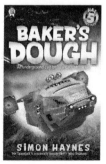

5. BAKER'S DOUGH

When you stand to inherit a fortune, good body-guards are essential. If you're really desperate, call Hal and Clunk. Baker's Dough features intense rivalry, sublime double-crosses and more greed than a free buffet.

6. SAFE ART

Valuable artworks and a tight deadline ... you'd be mad to hire Hal for that one, but who said the art world was sane?

7. BIG BANG

A house clearance job sounds like easy money, but rising floodwaters, an unstable landscape and a surprise find are going to make life very difficult for Hal and Clunk.

8. DOUBLE TROUBLE

Hal Spacejock dons a flash suit, hypershades and a curly earpiece for a stint as a secret agent, while a pair of Clunk's most rusted friends invite him to a 'unique business opportunity'.

9. MAX DAMAGE

Hal and Clunk answer a distress call, and they discover a fellow pilot stranded deep inside an asteroid field. Clunk is busy at the controls so Hal dons a spacesuit and sets off on a heroic rescue mission.

10. Cold Boots

Coming 2019

Ebook and Trade Paperback

The Secret War Series
Set in the Hal Spacejock universe

Everyone is touched by the war, and Sam Willet is no exception.

Sam wants to train as a fighter pilot, but instead she's assigned to Tactical Operations.

It's vital work, but it's still a desk job, far from the front line.

Then, terrible news: Sam's older brother is killed in combat.

Sam is given leave to attend his memorial service, but she's barely boarded the transport when the enemy launches a surprise attack, striking far behind friendly lines as they try to take the entire sector.

Desperately short of pilots, the Commander asks Sam to step up.

Now, at last, she has the chance to prove herself.

But will that chance end in death... or glory?

Ebook and Trade Paperback

The Harriet Walsh series

Harriet's boss is a huge robot with failing batteries, the patrol car is driving her up the wall and her first big case will probably kill her.

So why did she join the Peace Force?

When an intergalactic crime-fighting organisation offers Harriet Walsh a job, she's convinced it's a mistake. She dislikes puzzles, has never read a detective mystery, and hates wearing uniforms. It makes no sense ... why would the Peace Force choose her?

Who cares? Harriet needs the money, and as long as they keep paying her, she's happy to go along with the training.

She'd better dig out some of those detective mysteries though, because she's about to embark on her first real mission ...

The Peace Force has a new recruit, and she's driving everyone crazy.

From disobeying orders to handling unauthorised cases, nothing is off-limits. Worse, Harriet Walsh is forced to team up with the newbie, because the recruit's shady past has just caught up with her.

Meanwhile, a dignitary wants to complain about rogue officers working out of the station. She insists on meeting the station's commanding officer ... and they don't have one.

All up, it's another typical day in the Peace Force!

Dismolle is supposed to be a peaceful retirement planet. So what's with all the gunfire?

A criminal gang has moved into Chirless, planet Dismolle's second major city. Elderly residents are fed up with all the loud music, noisy cars and late night parties, not to mention the hold-ups, muggings and the occasional gunfight.

There's no Peace Force in Chirless, so they call on Harriet Walsh of the Dismolle City branch for help. That puts Harriet right in the firing line, and now she's supposed to round up an entire gang with only her training pistol and a few old allies as backup.

And her allies aren't just old, they're positively ancient!

Ebook and Trade Paperback

The Hal Junior Series
Set in the Hal Spacejock universe

Spot the crossover characters, references and in-jokes!

Hal Junior lives aboard a futuristic space station. His mum is chief scientist, his dad cleans air filters and his best mate is Stephen 'Stinky' Binn. As for Hal ... he's a bit of a trouble magnet. He means well, but his wild schemes and crazy plans never turn out as expected!

Hal Junior: The Secret Signal features mayhem and laughs, daring and intrigue ... plus a home-made space cannon!

200 pages, illustrated, ISBN 978-1-877034-07-7

"A thoroughly enjoyable read for 10-year-olds and adults alike"
The West Australian

'I've heard of food going off
  ... but this is ridiculous!'

Space Station Oberon is expecting an important visitor, and everyone is on their best behaviour. Even Hal Junior is doing his best to stay out of trouble!

From multi-coloured smoke bombs to exploding space rations, Hal Junior proves ... **trouble is what he's best at!**

200 pages, illustrated, ISBN 978-1-877034-25-1

Imagine a whole week of fishing, swimming, sleeping in tents and running wild!

Unfortunately, the boys crash land in the middle of a forest, and there's little chance of rescue. Is this the end of the camping trip ... or the start of a thrilling new adventure?

200 pages, illustrated, ISBN 978-1-877034-24-4

Space Station Oberon is on high alert, because a comet is about to whizz past the nearby planet of Gyris. All the scientists are preparing for the exciting event, and all the kids are planning on watching.

All the kids except Hal Junior, who's been given detention...

165 pages, illustrated, ISBN 978-1-877034-38-1

Ebook and Trade Paperback

New from Simon Haynes
The Robot vs Dragons series

"Laugh after laugh, dark in places but the humour punches through. One of the best books I've read in 2018 so far. Amazing, 5"*

Welcome to the Old Kingdom!

It's a wonderful time to visit! There's lots to do and plenty to see!
What are you waiting for? Dive into the Old Kingdom right now!

Clunk, an elderly robot, does exactly that. He's just plunged into the sea off the coast of the Old Kingdom, and if he knew what was coming next he'd sit down on the ocean floor and wait for rescue.

Dragged from the ocean, coughing up seaweed, salty water and stray pieces of jellyfish, he's taken to the nearby city of Chatter's Reach, where he's given a sword and told to fight the Queen's Champion, Sur Loyne.

As if that wasn't bad enough, the Old Kingdom still thinks the wheel is a pretty nifty idea, and Clunk's chances of finding spare parts - or his missing memory modules - are nil.

Still, Clunk is an optimist, and it's not long before he's embarking on a quest to find his way home.

Unfortunately it's going to be a very tough ask, given the lack of charging points in the medieval kingdom...

  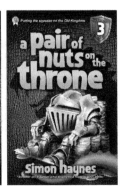

Ebook and Trade Paperback

26870513R00168

Printed in Great Britain
by Amazon